INFERNAL DARK

BRIGHT WICKED 3

EVERLY FROST

Frost, Everly
Infernal Dark

Cover design by Claire Holt with Luminescence Covers
www.luminescencecovers.com

Illustration by fantasybookdesign.com

For information on reproducing sections of this book or sales of this book,
go to
www.EverlyFrost.com
everlyfrost@gmail.com

DISCOVER THE EVER REALMS

Seven series set in the same world.

Suggested Reading Order:

Bright Wicked
Storm Princess
Assassin's Magic
Soul Bitten Shifter
Supernatural Legacy
Dark Magic Shifters
Kingdom of Betrayal

For everyone who dares to hope.

CHAPTER 1

I claw a path through the dirt in the center of the arena.

Blood and dust coat my fingers, my torn armor, and even my white hair. Cyrian's dark magic courses through me, raking at my insides like daggers.

The weight of agony forces me closer to the ground until I'm dragging myself through the dust.

I won't stop until I reach Nathaniel's side.

He lies a few paces away, his body laid out where Hagan left him.

Even in death, Nathaniel's powerful figure fills my senses, his arms corded with muscles, his broad shoulders and strong thighs demanding my focus.

Every part of him—his body and his absent soul—calls to me as if he were still alive.

His eyes are closed, his chest is still, and the pool of blood beneath him continues to grow, a steady increase that grips my heart more painfully than Cyrian's magic. Strands of

Nathaniel's walnut brown hair are plastered to his jaw, sweat and blood making them cling to his full lips.

A single delicate line of blood cuts through the sand between him and me, the path I now travel.

My only goal is to drag myself close enough to draw his hair away from his face, to straighten the strands.

It's a hopeless, helpless goal. But it's all I have.

The onlookers up in the stands shout and scream at me. Now that the fight is over, Cyrian's hunters are forcing the humans to leave the arena at knifepoint. Many of them cry Nathaniel's name. Others scream at Hagan, calling him a monster, but many more—so many more—scream for my blood.

"Hurt her!"

"Make her pay!"

Their vengeful shouts strike through me. I am the fae who brought about Nathaniel's death. For what I suspect might be the first time, the humans scream their support for Cyrian.

Nathaniel was their hope. The true heir to the human throne. The rightful Fell King.

It's my fault he's dead.

Two days ago, I invoked the Law of Champions. I bound Nathaniel to fight me to the death at the end of the third day. I invoked the Law by mistake—a challenge spoken out of anger and fear.

The outcome of the fight will determine the fate of both lands. If I win, my queen will rule over both Bright and Fell. If Cyrian's champion wins, Cyrian will rule.

Yesterday, Cyrian invoked the Three Chances to replace Nathaniel as his champion. For Cyrian to succeed, Nathaniel had to die by dawn today.

The sky is growing brighter by the second. Within minutes,

the sun's first rays will shine through the haze that covers Fell country.

Once that happens, Hagan will replace Nathaniel as Cyrian's champion, and I will be bound to fight Hagan before dawn tomorrow.

Four paces away, Hagan hasn't left the spot where he retreated after he killed Nathaniel. He is the only other human with the strength to truly challenge Nathaniel. Hagan's broad chest is inked with runes that are visible through the rips in his shirt. Two thick scars twist and intersect across his stomach, perceptible beneath the tattered edges of his clothing.

His expression is blank, his shoulders hunched, his lips drawn and pale. The braid of his black hair is matted with blood where it sits close to his scalp. The usually sharp intelligence in his tawny brown eyes is dull, his gaze hollow.

He pushed Nathaniel out of the way of an attacking wolf during the fight, shoving Nathaniel into one of the deadly spikes that jut from the walls of the arena.

As much as I want to hate Hagan, I don't believe he was trying to kill Nathaniel in that moment.

Cyrian paces beside me as I crawl through the dust, his jubilant laughter crushing me as badly as his magic.

I draw on a trickle of my starlight power to help ease the pain he's causing me.

Now that the sun is rising, my power is finite. I have to be careful how much I use because once it's gone, I'll have nothing left until sunset.

Towering over me, Cyrian's dark light flickers around his torso and arms. It plays across his black hair, highlighting the colorful runes that run all of the way from his right shoulder to the silver wristband he wears.

His dark brown eyes glitter with triumph.

"Where are you going, Aura?" Cyrian laughs, kicking sand into my face.

I manage to close my eyes before the dirt hits me, coughing and tipping my face away, my eyes streaming as I continue to crawl along my painful path.

"Nathaniel's dead," Cyrian snarls. "There's nothing you can do now."

I'm not strong enough to stop Cyrian from hurting me. He warned me that I'm no match for his limitless dark magic. I didn't believe him at first, but I do now.

Drawing on another trickle of my power to give me strength, I drag myself the final agonizing distance to Nathaniel's side.

Cyrian doesn't try to stop me as I lower myself to Nathaniel's chest, curl my fingers around his hand, and press my forehead to his.

I'm breathing heavily, nearly passing out. It took everything I had to make it back to him. I'm lucky that the Law of Champions stops Cyrian from killing me.

If not, I'd be dead now.

Nathaniel's palm and face are warm against mine, giving me the illusion that he's still alive. The space between us glows just like it always did when we touched.

I gasp air into my chest, trying to stay lucid, trying to contain my screams.

There was nothing I could do to save him. The Three Chances stopped me from using my power to influence the outcome of the fight between Hagan and Nathaniel.

When the Vanem Dragon flew to Fell country to bind Nathaniel and Hagan to their fight, he warned both me and Cyrian that fae magic and dark magic couldn't be used to interfere with the fight.

Until dawn breaks, neither of us can touch Hagan or Nathaniel with our magic.

Despite that, I tried. After he was impaled, I pressed my hands over Nathaniel's heart and flooded his chest with my power in an attempt to cauterize his wounds and stop the bleeding.

Desperate to save his life, I dared the Three Chances to repel or even kill me. It didn't do any good. My magic glowed, but Nathaniel's breathing stopped.

Releasing his hand now, my arm shakes as I press my palm against his cheek. My hand comes away coated in gray dust. My power leaks between us despite my every effort to contain it.

I'm shivering and in pain but determined to straighten his hair despite the blood and dust on his face.

Now that I'm touching him again, my control is breaking.

Everything inside me is breaking. My mind, my body, even the cavity inside my chest where Nathaniel's death tore my heart apart.

Where is your heart?

I shake my head violently, trying to displace the question Cyrian whispered to me during the fight. He looked at me as if I'd suddenly been a mystery to him. The intrigue in his eyes filled me with fear.

I didn't have an answer for him because his question didn't make sense.

All I know is that I spent the last day as Nathaniel's shield, protecting him from wolves, hunters—even Cyrian's torture— but in the end, I couldn't shield him from death.

Before I can finish my task, Cyrian bends over me, wraps his fingers into my hair, and yanks my head away from Nathaniel's.

My arms whip out, refusing to let go of Nathaniel's shoulders even when the pain Cyrian's dark magic causes me reaches the point where I can no longer function.

My thoughts are simple, reduced to a single, overwhelming instinct: *Don't let go.*

Cyrian's breath is hot against my ear as he kneels and curves over me, still gripping my hair.

"Hold on to him while you can, Aura," he whispers. "The moment the sun rises, I will use my magic to tear Nathaniel's body apart. I might leave you with his hand, but that is all."

My whimpers turn into a scream—loud now that the arena is nearly empty. "Get away from him!"

Out of control, my power blasts between us, cold starlight sizzling through both of my arms—one outstretched to push Cyrian away, the other pressed against Nathaniel's chest.

Cyrian jolts away from me.

The wash of dark magic surrounding his body protects him from the burning impact of my starlight—and I'm lucky it does. Until the final fight, I can't hurt a human. The punishment for breaking that rule is my instant death.

Even so, Cyrian releases my hair so suddenly that my head whips to the side.

I end up facing Nathaniel, watching helplessly as the power I released flows through his chest, bright streaks like lightning—a blast strong enough to stop his heart if it were still beating.

A sob rises inside me, but before I can release it, Cyrian backhands me so hard that my head knocks into Nathaniel's. The impact cracks between us, a spark of starlight igniting across our faces.

The flash is so bright, it's as if our bodies are flint.

Tears of pain stream down my cheeks. I grip Nathaniel's shoulders, trying to stop the world from spinning as I drag in another scream.

My cry chokes in my throat as I inhale the scent of his skin. Powerful burned caramel, so warm I'm sure I'm the one who burned him.

Cyrian grabs me again, but his hands barely brush my shoulders before Hagan barrels into him with a roar. "Let her grieve!"

Shocked, I stare up at Hagan as he grips Cyrian's chest, pushes him off-balance, and flings him into the dirt.

Hagan was never my friend. He and Nathaniel trained side by side as boys, called each other brothers, but that had been before Cyrian took control of Hagan and the other hunters and turned them into his killers.

Cyrian hits the ground on his backside, his face filling with rage. "That was a mistake, Hagan."

Quickly jumping to his feet, Cyrian brushes himself off, closing the gap so that the two men stand face to face. Cyrian was once a champion, a warrior. His physical skills have given way to his reliance on magic, but he is still stronger than the average human.

Hagan gives a slow shrug as he stands his ground. He glances at the sky. "I'm guessing I have another ten minutes before your dark magic can touch me again. After that, it's up to you what you do to me. You should consider the outcome if you hurt your champion before the final fight."

Dark light fills Cyrian's eyes. He grits his teeth. "You will regret defying me."

Hagan returns Cyrian's stare. He shakes his head, a slow and certain side-to-side motion. "My family's dead. Christiana's safe. I have no honor left, no reputation to tarnish. There's no way for you to hurt me other than to torture and kill me."

"Everyone has a breaking point."

Hagan points to the scar that cuts across his stomach. "You already found mine and used it to your advantage. Nathaniel is dead. So is my half-brother. You have no leverage over me now."

Cyrian takes a step back, his sharp eyes raking across Hagan's defiant face before landing on me. Cyrian's hand flies out, dark light spears the air into my chest, and pain shrieks through me again.

In response, Hagan's fist flies out, catching Cyrian across the chin, but Cyrian continues to pour darkness into me even when Hagan hits him again.

My magic was already simmering at the surface, leaking between Nathaniel and me. It bursts around me, a glowing shield. I can't afford to use this much of it, but I can't seem to stop it.

I close my eyes as the pain eases the more I focus on my starlight and its source deep within my chest, far within the reaches of my mind. That vast, silent place where nothing exists except my light.

Dropping my head to Nathaniel's chest, I drag in the scent of his skin again as my fingers curl into his torn shirt, pressing against his chest.

His *warm* chest.

I pull back to study him.

He shouldn't be this warm. He shouldn't seem this alive.

Pressing my ear to his heart, I listen… waiting… hoping… for a beat. Hoping I was wrong when I saw his breathing stop. When he became completely still.

I don't hear anything. No breath sounds. No bright heart thudding in his chest.

Tears slip down my cheeks as I open my eyes. I'm conscious of Hagan lifting Cyrian off his feet and throwing him across the arena so hard that Cyrian bounces and rolls. The hunters haven't returned, but they'll be back soon. Hagan may be their leader, but it won't take Cyrian long to order the hunters to restrain him.

"Nathaniel," I whisper, pressing my cheek to his. "Where are you?"

Running my fingers through his hair, I'm shocked to see his

skin flush when I press my hand against his jaw.

His heart may not be beating, but somehow, impossibly…

He's alive.

There's no other explanation for his warmth and the reaction of his body to mine—the glow between us, his scent, his immense presence filling my senses…

Acting quickly, I rip at the hole in his shirt where the spike broke through. The wound sits above his heart, through his shoulder.

I stare in shock at the skin around the exit point.

It's partially cauterized. Blood oozes from the cut but only at a trickle.

My head begins to shake as I try to understand *how*. The only explanation is that I did it.

It might have been when I first pressed my hands to Nathaniel's chest before Hagan pushed me away and told me he had to end Nathaniel's life. Or it could have been when my anger soared through me just now and I screamed at Cyrian to get away from Nathaniel.

None of that should be possible.

My fae magic shouldn't be able to touch him…

Reaching around his chest, I struggle to turn him onto his side to check the entry wound in his back.

The weight of his torso and muscles and the blood coating his chest make my task difficult. Quickly repositioning myself and drawing my legs under me, I use my knees as a wedge beneath his back so that I can slowly lift him.

With a final heave, I finally succeed in getting his left arm to drop across his chest so that gravity pulls him far enough onto his stomach that I can pull up his shirt and study the wound on this side.

It's also cauterized.

I don't understand how my magic worked, but if I did this—

if I somehow minimized the flow of blood—then I can finish the job.

Leaning across him, I slip my right hand over his back and my left hand across his chest, covering the entry and exit points of the wound.

I have to be careful.

Yesterday, Nathaniel described my power as having many facets—the capacity to destroy as well as the power to heal. I'd eased the pain in his bruised ribs by warming his torso with my starlight.

Now I need the sharp edge of my power—the fiery element. Too much will destroy whatever life clings within him. Too little won't work.

Drawing on the well of power inside me, conscious of the limited amount I have left, I allow starlight to flow from my chest down my arms.

I don't temper it, don't soften it, allowing it to remain sharp and prickly. A burning cold.

Pinpoints of starlight widen beneath my palms as I block out Hagan's and Cyrian's shouting only a few paces away from me.

I hold on to my power for another second before I release it.

Light flashes on both sides of Nathaniel's chest.

Rapidly shutting off my power, I check his back first, then his front. Both sides of the wound are completely cauterized.

I haven't healed him. His internal injuries are still catastrophic, but I've stopped him from losing any more blood.

Now I need him to breathe again. And then I need to get him to a healer. I don't know how I'm going to do that, but I tell myself to face one problem at a time.

Lowering him onto his back, I fit my lips to his.

Exhaling, I breathe into his mouth, the same way he breathed into mine after we visited the burn site where I killed my parents. It feels like a lifetime ago that Nathaniel brought the breath back into my chest.

At the same time as I breathe into his mouth, I press my fingertips against his temples, allowing my hands to warm with my power, but this time, I draw only on the calming power that I used to ease his bruised ribs yesterday.

I need to ease his mind, keep him asleep so that he doesn't feel the pain of his wound or wake up in shock.

I need to keep him alive for as long as it takes to get him to a healer.

Taking another deep breath, I exhale into his mouth again, making sure to seal my lips completely against his, sensing the air pass into his body.

I repeat this process three more times, but nothing changes and my breathing becomes desperate.

Panic threatens to overwhelm me. For all I know, the spike nicked his heart and it will never beat again.

"No!" I reject my fear, shouting it out, refusing to give in to it.

Forming a fist, I thump his chest, wishing I could reach beneath his skin and force his heart to beat again.

My power flows out from the impact point, lighting up his ribs. Tears drip from my cheeks onto his.

I breathe into his mouth again before I thump his torso once more, my power streaking across his body.

"Nathaniel" I scream at him. "Wake up!"

My fist crashes against his chest, a spark ignites between us, and starlight flashes back at me, rebounding so brightly that I fall back onto my hands.

I gasp before I force myself to become quiet. Force myself to listen.

A soft whisper reaches me.

The gentlest breath.

Scrambling back through the dust, I lean over Nathaniel, desperately seeking the rise and fall of his chest.

Just as I press my ear to his heart, rough hands grab me and drag me backward through the sand.

Cyrian shakes me so hard, it feels like my teeth rattle. "What are you doing?"

I glare up at him in defiance, but he's already turning to Hagan, who bends at Nathaniel's side.

Hagan presses his hand to Nathaniel's heart.

His voice is a low, shocked whisper. "Nathaniel is breathing."

Cyrian whirls back to me. "That's impossible! Your fae magic can't touch him. Not until dawn!"

Dropping me into the dirt, Cyrian storms back to Hagan. "Finish him before the sun rises!"

Hagan tips his head back as he considers the sky. Then his eyes meet mine. He has seconds to kill Nathaniel before the Three Chances expire. If he doesn't, he won't replace Nathaniel as Cyrian's champion. If he isn't Cyrian's champion...

Hagan is a dead man.

The sharp intelligence returns to Hagan's eyes as his gaze settles on my cheeks, following the tear tracks from my eyes down the scrubbed-out ink of Nathaniel's family name.

The harsh lines of Hagan's expression soften. "No."

"What did you say?" Dark light grows around Cyrian's hands in the form of spikes, his razor-sharp anger manifesting along his arms. "You will kill Nathaniel! *Now!*"

Hagan rises to his full height. He's bruised, bloody. Beaten. "I won't kill for you again."

"Then you're breathing your last air," Cyrian snarls between gritted teeth.

Hagan nods. Slowly. With certainty. He shocks me even more when he points at me. "Aura Lucidia, be sure to tell Nathaniel that I repaid my debt twice over."

As he speaks, the sky brightens.

I can't see the sun because of the haze, but the darkness lifts so suddenly that I can imagine its rays finally rising across the horizon.

It's dawn and Nathaniel is alive.

The Three Chances are over.

Nathaniel is still Cyrian's champion.

The third day has begun.

CHAPTER 2

I rise to my feet, overcoming my fatigue as a new sense of purpose fills me. Healing Nathaniel is now my only goal.

Cyrian whirls toward me, his face pale.

His champion lies unconscious in the crimson sand. If Nathaniel dies, Cyrian will lose his throne to Imatra.

The runes along Cyrian's arm are suddenly dull and his eyes appear hollow.

It occurs to me that he's used up a lot of his dark magic—just as I've used up most of my starlight. He draws his power from the hearts of living humans, leeching their life force so that the Ebon Rot sets in, an illness that slowly disfigures the humans until their bodies succumb and they pass away before they reach the age of forty.

Cyrian was at his strongest surrounded by a stadium of humans, tapping into their life energy, but the arena is empty now.

He directs his rage into a stream of dark magic that sizzles around his torso.

I'm certain he intends to immobilize me with pain like he did before, but I shout before he can release the torturous darkness into me.

"If Nathaniel dies, you'll lose everything! Let us leave, Cyrian," I cry. "You can't kill me or you'll forfeit your life. You can't allow Nathaniel to die now or Imatra will win. I've proven that I will do everything I can to keep Nathaniel alive. I'm the only one keeping you on the throne."

Cyrian freezes. His magic sputters and vanishes while his hands clench. He roars in anger, a stream of profanities so loud, I can't distinguish the sounds.

I flinch but force myself to allow his anger to wash over me. There are only two ways to heal Nathaniel. Either I fly him all of the way to the mountains in Bright where my adoptive father, Crispin, lives, or I take Nathaniel west within Fell country to Mathilda.

Of the two, Mathilda is closer.

I consider for a moment whether or not Cyrian could use his dark magic to heal Nathaniel—because that's what Mathilda will have to use—but I don't trust him. He could heal Nathaniel well enough to fight but implant some sort of curse in him at the same time.

Mathilda may have been angry at Nathaniel yesterday when he brought me to Null, but she was also incredibly protective. Even if she hates me, I can trust that she will do everything in her power to heal him. I just have to hope that I can keep him alive until we reach her.

Backing away from Cyrian, I raise my fingers to my lips and give two short, sharp whistles.

My hands are covered in dirt and blood, leaving the taste of death in my mouth, but I don't hesitate.

I pray to the stars that my thunderbird, Treble, is still flying above the haze, watching over me. If he is, his keen hearing will pick up my call.

Continuing to pace toward Nathaniel, I locate myself between him and the King. Inadvertently, this also means I'm acting as a shield between Cyrian and Hagan, who stands on the other side of Nathaniel.

I whistle for Treble again, my nerves setting in as I wonder whether he flew back to Bright after all.

Concealing my anxiety, I angle toward Hagan. "When my thunderbird arrives, you will help me lift Nathaniel onto my bird's back."

He nods. It's in his interest to help me. As long as he remains close to Nathaniel, Cyrian won't risk attacking him. It will be a different matter when we leave, though.

Just as I lift my fingertips to my lips for a third desperate time, lightning crackles across the haze above us, lighting up Treble's silhouette in brilliant blue-gray streaks.

Glowing and rippling with electricity, he plummets straight toward us before he spreads his wings and cracks them to slow his descent. The thunder created by his wings explodes around us, loud enough to thud through my hearing, but it's a welcome beat.

As the wind from Treble's wings gusts across us, my thunderbird casts a dangerous glare at Cyrian. The flickers of Treble's lightning cut through the darkness swirling around the King, forcing Cyrian to backstep farther away from us.

I don't have time for relief. Movement at the far end of the arena indicates that the hunters are returning. The last time they saw Treble, they tried to shoot him from the air.

I need to move quickly.

Hagan is already kneeling beside Nathaniel, carefully hooking his arms around Nathaniel's torso and lifting him. He glances at me with a gruff command. "Help me keep his head steady!"

I race to Hagan's side, supporting the back of Nathaniel's head as Hagan draws Nathaniel carefully upward. While he strains under Nathaniel's weight, he uses the strength in his thighs to rise as he pulls Nathaniel over his shoulder.

It's a much more careful and labored maneuver than the way Hagan barreled into me yesterday and threw me over his shoulder. I guess it helped that I was already standing up. Also that I'm much smaller than Nathaniel.

Making sure Nathaniel's head doesn't drop back during the process, I remain conscious of the oncoming hunters.

Snake—the hunter with a long scar meandering down his arm—and the other men flood through the gate at the end of the arena. They shout in anger as they draw their bows and arrows.

"Don't kill the bird!" Cyrian bellows, skirting around Treble and backing toward his men. "Hold your attack!"

Treble cracks his wings as Hagan and I approach, giving Hagan a warning glare.

Now that Nathaniel rests safely over Hagan's shoulder, I hurry toward my thunderbird, willing him to listen to me. "This human is not my friend, but I need his help. Please give him your wing."

I nearly cry when Treble shows me how much he trusts me, immediately extending his wing so that Hagan can climb up onto his back.

Hagan only stares at the extended wing. "What is this?"

"You have to walk up his wing bone. Like this." I hurry to demonstrate, running up Treble's wing, while Hagan takes a hesitant step. Just like Nathaniel the first time he rode Treble, Hagan casts Treble concerned glances. "I'm a lot heavier than you—especially carrying Nathaniel."

"His bones are as strong as metal," I say, holding out my hand to Hagan to urge him toward me. "Trust me."

His gaze flashes to me, suddenly sharp. "Trust you? I will never trust my enemy."

"Then don't trust me as a fae," I snap. "Trust me as Nathaniel's wife."

Despite the scathing glare he casts at my face, he takes another step, continuing up Treble's wing. "You deliberately scrubbed Nathaniel's name from your face before the ink wore off. Only Nathaniel can decide if you are still his wife."

My stomach falls and my hand lowers.

When Nathaniel first drew the symbol representing his family name on my face yesterday morning, I didn't know that he was offering me his love and his loyalty.

After I gave him permission to paint his name on my face in golden lacquer, I accepted everything the symbol meant—that we would love and protect each other.

Then I found out who he really is—the true heir to the Fell throne. I'd scoured at the mark on my face with dirt, wanting to put as much emotional distance between us as possible.

I'd scrubbed my skin raw to remove the ink in an effort to make it clear to Nathaniel that he couldn't jeopardize his safety for me.

"I told you yesterday," I say, my voice bleak. "I will do whatever it takes to keep Nathaniel alive."

Hagan scowls at me. "I don't understand your motives."

"You don't need to understand me. Only believe that I'm not lying to you."

Hagan's glare deepens. He will never trust me. No matter what I do or say.

Taking the final step onto Treble's glowing back, he turns and slides carefully downward so that Nathaniel is facing forward. Positioning Nathaniel there requires Hagan to carefully maneuver himself into a sitting position at the same time, even though he's facing Treble's tail.

I glance at the hunters who are approaching with stealth, their weapons ready as they creep toward us. They may not be attacking, but they're preparing to kill Hagan the moment he leaves Treble's back.

My eyes widen as I realize that I could slip onto Treble's back right now and we could fly away, all three of us.

I have no reason to save Hagan other than instinct, but I hear Nathaniel's voice in my mind, telling me not to rethink, to trust my feelings.

I slide into position so that Nathaniel's back rests against my front, quickly positioning his head against my shoulder. His heavy weight settles against me, nearly crushing my chest, but I wrap one arm around his waist and refuse to let go.

I wasn't sure if Treble could hold all three of us, but he's already proving capable, unflinching as our weight settles on his back.

Reaching around Nathaniel, I grab Hagan's arm before he can begin the awkward task of extricating himself from his current position.

"Come with us," I say, gripping his bicep as hard as I can. It's difficult, given that my hand barely reaches around half of his upper arm.

The moment I speak, I regret it.

Dark stars, what am I thinking?

Hagan has made his hatred of me clear. I was the fae who killed Nathaniel's mother, Paloma Exalted, at the border years ago. Hagan considered her his mother too—she raised him, trained him, gave him a home and a purpose. Even though Paloma came to the border to end the agony the Ebon Rot was causing her, I was the one who struck her down, burying her in the muddy earth within the Misty Gallows.

I was the one who ended the human's beloved Queen.

The astonishment in Hagan's eyes now tells me he thinks I've lost my senses.

"I'm a dead man," he says. "I'm prepared to take my last breaths."

I refuse to let go, gripping harder as he tries to shake me off. "I'll need help when we land," I say. "I can't move Nathaniel on my own."

It's not completely true. The last time Nathaniel was mortally wounded, I managed to drag him off Treble's back, but carrying him farther than that on my own will be very difficult. I don't have the power of a Frost fae to control the wind that could carry him easily. My twilight power has many facets, but lifting things isn't one of them.

Hagan shakes his head—already saying *no*—but I allow anger to flood through me. "If you want to meet your death once Nathaniel's safe, then feel free. But until then, you *will* help me."

His eyes widen at my anger, then narrow. Finally, a perplexed crease grows on his forehead. "I don't—"

"We're wasting time," I snap. "Decide whether to help me or not. If not, then get off my bird."

A dangerous smile settles on his lips. The light of intelligence in his eyes grows even brighter. "I will help you. *Then* I will die."

I'm already regretting my actions as I lean forward, crying to my thunderbird, "Treble! Fly!"

I won't tell Treble where we need to go until we're in the air. I can't chance Cyrian following us.

Treble cracks his wings, a single powerful sweep carrying us up into the air.

I grip with my thighs and wrap both of my arms around Nathaniel to keep him securely positioned. He's heavy and it's difficult, but I've held him in place on Treble's back before. I wasn't so fatigued then as I am now, but I tell myself that I can do it again.

Hagan lurches with the sudden movement, his knees knocking into Nathaniel's before his reflexes kick in—the muscles in his arms and legs visibly tensing as he adjusts his balance. He's not in the most comfortable position, facing backward, squished between Treble's wing joints and Nathaniel's unconscious form.

Below us, Cyrian raises his hand in Hagan's direction, preparing to let loose the dark light he controls, but Treble is already banking to the left. Once again, I become a shield between Cyrian and Hagan.

As Treble rises into the haze, seeking concealment in its murky depths, I take one last look at the arena below us.

Cyrian's arm drops to his side. The hunters watch us leave, their faces upturned while their weapons lower.

The patch of bloody sand where Nathaniel lay becomes smaller as we rise. Finally, it's nothing more than a crimson bloom far below us.

As the haze envelops us, I face forward again, finding myself the focus of Hagan's attention.

I may have left one danger behind, but I've brought another threat with me.

CHAPTER 3

I meet Hagan's eyes across the small gap between us.

Now that we've entered the haze, the air is murky and cold, visibility obscured, but I can see the dangerous glint in his eyes all the same.

I'm not too concerned since he isn't carrying any weapons now, while I still have my hidden sword and dagger.

Leaning to the side, I call past him again. "Treble, take us west. Look for a patch of overgrown plants and vines that are as black as night and as red as blood. We need to fly west of the Bitter Patch into Mathilda's territory."

Without taking his eyes off me, Hagan repositions his grip on Treble, his hands settling across the top of Treble's wing joints on either side.

He inclines his head sharply at Nathaniel, raising his voice over the rushing wind. "You're destined to kill Nathaniel, yet you've saved him many times. Why?"

Inwardly, I sigh. I guess it was too much to hope that he wouldn't demand answers while he has my undivided attention.

I snap back. "Why did you push Nathaniel out of the wolf's path?"

Hagan takes a sharp breath as if he's preparing for an equally sharp response, but he slowly exhales instead.

His shoulders hunch. "All I had to do was keep Nathaniel fighting until dawn. No matter how tired we got, as long as we kept fighting, we would both get what we wanted."

My lips part slowly with shock as I register the meaning behind his statement. He'd bargained for control over Christiana and then he'd set her free.

I speak slowly, testing my thoughts. "You wanted Christiana's freedom. Volunteering to challenge Nathaniel was the only way to free her."

Hagan gives a single nod. "She despises me, but she's all I've got left that's worth fighting for."

I narrow my eyes at him. "What about the fight between you and Nathaniel?"

He shrugs, his voice so quiet that I almost don't hear him over the wind. "Nathaniel and I used to spar against each other all of the time. We could fight for hours and neither of us would win." He looks up again. "Nathaniel would have remembered that."

"You really intended to keep fighting until dawn."

"As long as Nathaniel was alive at dawn, he would remain Cyrian's champion," Hagan says. "Then I could walk away knowing Christiana was safe."

I search Hagan's face, wondering how much of his story I can take as truth.

Sudden pain overwhelms me.

My voice holds my accusation. "You may claim your motives weren't malicious, but when Nathaniel was dying, you chose to finish it."

Hagan's jaw clenches. "I pushed him out of the wolf's path.

Everyone saw me do it. If we'd kept fighting, I could have made it look like I'd done it to protect myself. Once Nathaniel fell, I had no choice but to follow through."

I shake my head in disagreement. "But—"

"No!" he bellows. He leans forward, his eyebrows drawn down. "If Nathaniel bled out slowly until after dawn and *then* died, your queen would rule Fell country by default. Cyrian may be brutal, but he needs us. Your queen will eradicate the human race as soon as she has the chance."

I can't control my rage. "I would have saved him!"

Hagan jolts back as far as he can without upsetting his seat on Treble's back, surprise flooding his expression at my vehemence.

He starts to speak, but I shout him down. "The minute dawn arrived—the first instant that I thought I could use my power—I would have saved Nathaniel. The same way I did just now. He was never going to die. He will *not* die!"

I take a deep, shuddering breath, trying to calm my emotions. Starlight leaks through my armor again and I can't afford to lose any more of it.

Hagan is equally angry as he glares back at me. "Why would I believe you?"

We're right back to where we started. He's demanding to know why I want to save Nathaniel when I'm supposed to kill him—when Nathaniel's life means my death.

It's the most important question I'll ever need to answer and it's being asked of me by a man who, for all intents and purposes, is one of my most dangerous enemies.

"Because I don't belong to Imatra," I whisper.

Yesterday, Nathaniel gave me the message that his dying father asked him to deliver to me. He promised his father he would find me—the girl with hair the color of bone—and tell me I didn't belong to the fae.

I didn't understand it yesterday—still don't understand it—but since then, I've seen how the humans live. I've seen their country, their hollow eyes, and felt Nathaniel's determination to free them, his unbending certainty about his path.

My loyalties can't belong to the fae anymore—or even to the humans.

I have to be loyal to myself.

I have to be true to the only outcome that can possibly bring peace to both Bright and Fell: Nathaniel has to rule.

Hagan leans forward again, but this time, he moves slowly and carefully, his head tilted, his lips pursed in a questioning line. "What did you say?"

I raise my voice so he can hear me over the wind. "I don't belong to them! I betrayed my queen when I crossed the border. If it weren't for the Law of Champions, she would have hunted me down and killed me, the same way Cyrian wishes he could kill Nathaniel. Neither of us is fighting for our monarchs. We're fighting..."

Pressing my lips together, I squeeze my eyes shut, desperate to stop giving away so much of my heart to this hunter. "*I'm* fighting for Nathaniel. That's my only purpose now." I grit my teeth. "As long as you believe that, then you don't need to know anything else about me."

Hagan leans back, a deep crease forming on his forehead. "You can't expect me to believe that you'll welcome your own death—"

"Yes," I say, cutting him short. "That's exactly what you need to believe."

Before he can object, Treble rises above the haze, breaking through it into the clear sky beyond. The sun's rays are soft with the new day's light, the air crisp and clean.

Hagan throws an arm across his eyes with a pained shout. "Fuck, that's bright!"

Sunlight has never been my friend, but even so, I welcome the clean air and the sense of space. The land below the haze in Fell feels so closed in.

Assuming Hagan lived his whole life beneath the vapor, he may have never seen or felt the full effect of the sun before. He squints, removing his arm a little. His eyes grow wide before he shuts them again.

His question is gruff. "Is that what the sky looks like?"

Around us, the soft azure blue air extends as far as we can see in every direction. It's a beautiful, clear day. Only a few pristine clouds float higher above us.

"You've never seen the sky before?" I ask.

From what I've seen of Fell country so far, he would have had to step right up to the border to see clear sky. That would have been suicide, given the Border Guards' ferocity. My brother, Evander, is never cruel, but he's always vigilant about cutting down any Fell creature—any human—who steps out of the Misty Gallows.

Hagan's response is a growled curse. I guess his pride is hurting now that he's weakened by the light around us.

"I've never traveled farther north than the Misty Gallows," he says. "I've heard that there is clear sky above the Spire. Along the southern coast, too, but I've never been to either of those places. Is it always this bright?"

My voice softens. "When you're ready, take a look. It's worth seeing. If you look hard enough, you might even be able to see some of the stars before the sun dominates the sky. Just don't look directly at the sun itself."

I inhale a calming breath, holding tightly to Nathaniel as we fly in silence for the next few minutes.

It takes Hagan several tries before he can remove his arm from his eyes and study the sky.

His gaze runs carefully from one side to the other, following the edges of the haze that forms a strange sort of misty horizon around us.

His lips part as he inhales more deeply than before, his chest filling before he coughs.

I watch him carefully as he inhales again. His pupils are increasingly small pinpricks in the bright light, abnormally unfocused.

I jolt toward him in alarm when he sways in his seat. "Hagan!"

His only answer is another cough.

The air must be affecting him. When Cyrian was trying to bribe his hunters to volunteer to challenge Nathaniel, he promised them the life of a champion—access to real sunlight, fresh air, and fresh food.

Nathaniel spent much of his life above the haze in the castle. He had the chance to adapt to the environments both above and below the vapor, which would have allowed him to adjust much more quickly to Bright's environment.

Not so for Hagan, who said he's never seen the sky before. He must have regularly visited the throne room where I first met Cyrian, but while it's located high enough to allow weak sunlight through, it's still well within the haze.

"Don't breathe too deeply," I warn Hagan sharply. "You're used to breathing polluted air. You'll get dizzy—"

His expression turns blank a moment before he tips to the side.

"No!" My right hand darts out to grab his shirt, desperate to keep him upright.

A fall from this height means certain death.

I grapple to support Nathaniel with my left arm while I tug fiercely at Hagan's shirt. The material is already torn. I nearly rip it off Hagan's chest as I yank him toward me.

His head drops onto Nathaniel's shoulder with a heavy thud.

Hagan's eyes are closed and his arms are slack, folded up awkwardly against Nathaniel's chest.

Dark stars! I'm using every muscle in my fatigued body to keep both men on the bird's back. It would be hard enough with regular-sized men, but both Nathaniel and Hagan are heavy with muscle, taller than average.

I won't be able to sustain my hold on both of them for longer than a minute. Maybe not even that long.

If Hagan falls, he could drag Nathaniel off with him.

"Treble," I scream, tears of fright falling down my cheeks. "Take us down. Quickly!"

To my relief, Treble has already sensed the disturbance on his back. He angles downward, but not too sharply or Hagan will slip right over his head and take Nathaniel—and me—with him.

Treble plunges through the haze.

My heart lurches into my throat to see the Bitter Patch directly ahead.

I need to travel farther west to find Mathilda's home, but I can't hold on to Hagan for that long.

I have to land, revive Hagan, and then leave him behind so I can proceed on my own. I thought I could ask for his help with moving Nathaniel when we landed, but I'll have to count on Mathilda's magic instead…

Just as Treble soars toward the wheat field on the eastern side of the Bitter Patch, a whooshing sound meets my ears and my senses prickle.

Heightened alarm shoots through me a second before a silver projectile whistles past my left side.

It glints and gleams, a deadly crossbow bolt. Its path is so accurate that it grazes my thigh. If it weren't for my armor, it would have sliced through my muscles.

My breath halts before I scream. "Treble! Evade!"

Treble banks left. He's agile and adept at evasion in the air, but he carries three people on his back, two of whom are unconscious. Sudden movements are incredibly dangerous right now.

A volley of bolts flies around us, dangerously close to cutting us down.

I try to locate their source, dismayed to find they're coming from the direction of the Bitter Patch.

If Nathaniel's people are shooting at us, it must be because they consider Treble a threat—a thunderbird is a fae weapon. We're too high for them to see that Nathaniel rides on his back.

But if Christiana came back here after Hagan freed her, then —*surely*—she should recognize Treble from last night. She knows that Treble is my bird.

Nathaniel warned me that every human would want to tear me apart if they found out who I am. Christiana made it clear last night that she doesn't trust me.

I just hope she has warned Nathaniel's people that anyone who kills me will also die.

As Treble tilts, banking quickly to the right, I make out the row of human warriors cleverly camouflaged in their beige clothing within the wheat field that stretches across the distance up to the border of the Bitter Patch.

There are at least twenty of them, positioned close to the edge of the crimson and black plants, as hidden as they can be among the stalks of wheat while maintaining their proximity to the protection of the Patch.

Nathaniel trained them well. Their aim is sure and true despite Treble's evasive maneuvers.

Another three bolts sail past Treble's wing, nearly piercing his neck.

My heart thuds a wild beat inside me as I try to find a way through this.

We can't rise above the haze because I won't be able to hold on to Hagan that long.

We can't land, either, because then the trainees will have a clear shot, which they could take before they realize they're shooting at Nathaniel.

There's only one way we'll survive this.

It will only make them hate me more, but I have no choice.

CHAPTER 4

"*T*reble!" I scream. "Rise and drop!"

Treble knows the maneuver I'm talking about. He and I have trained in every possible aerial tactic since I chose him to be my thunderbird.

With a thunderous crack of his wings, he sweeps us upward for a sharp beat before he abruptly changes direction and drops into a dive.

Gravity shifts around us.

My stomach drops with sickening speed.

For a moment, all three of us catch air, lifting off Treble's back, suspended in space.

I only have a moment to act while we're weightless.

My left arm flies out from Nathaniel's waist, releasing him.

At the same time, I call my power, digging into the far recesses of the vast, empty space inside me to harness its explosive force. Starlight rushes across my chest, hot and angry, screaming through my outstretched arm and into my hand.

It takes me a split second to aim for the empty patch of field just ahead of where we need to land.

A massive bolt of starlight shoots from my fingers, spreading wide like the rays of the sun. It explodes across the ground in front of the humans—far enough away from them that they won't be hurt. Close enough to make them dive for cover.

I've bought us precious seconds to allow us to land, but now I need to regain control of Nathaniel's and Hagan's unconscious bodies.

My right hand never released Hagan. I yank him toward me at the same time my left arm wraps around Nathaniel again, clamping tightly and pulling him against me just as gravity kicks back in.

Screaming with effort, I cling to both of them as Treble descends at full speed, a sharp incline.

The drop is too sharp.

Hagan's weight falls toward Treble's neck. My hand clamps tighter around his shirt, but the pressure is more than my body can take.

I scream as the muscles in my right arm tear and my shoulder dislocates.

Treble drops to the ground. He digs in his talons, flattening his body, landing as quickly as he can.

As we pull to a stop, my fingers are somehow still gripped around Hagan's shirt, held shut even though I can't feel my hand.

The jolt as Treble lands causes Hagan to slide all of the way off Treble's back, Hagan's weight carrying him so far that the part of his shirt I grip rips in my hands, tearing up to the seam until it finally stops.

In a flash, Treble extends his wing beneath Hagan's falling body to halt Hagan's downward trajectory. Hagan ends up with his feet resting against Treble's neck while his torso lies across Treble's wing.

The problem is that Treble's feathers are smooth. Only my

hold on Hagan's shirt keeps him from sliding all of the way off. A fall from this distance could break his bones—even his neck.

Nathaniel has slipped in the other direction—toward my left. I'm keeping him upright with my drawn-up leg partially hooked around his hip, my knee bent beside his torso, my boot now planted on Treble's back.

Treble quickly extends his wing on the left as well, ready in case I need him.

"Cease fire!" I scream at the humans, my chest heaving. "I have Nathaniel."

The field smolders ahead of us, the scent of burned wheat filling the air as Nathaniel's people step out from their hiding places, their weapons aimed squarely at us.

Ten of them break away from the others, running toward me. Their crossbows are raised and ready to fire as they drop to the smoldering ground with military precision and take aim.

One of them is Esther, her blonde hair flying and her lithe form agile as she runs and takes up an offensive position on my left, nearest to Nathaniel.

"Esther!" I shriek, unable to keep the pain from my voice. "Help Nathaniel."

Her eyes widen and her crossbow lowers before it jolts back up into position, resuming her steady aim at me.

She shouts back toward the Bitter Patch, "She has Nathaniel!"

I recognize Christiana's mahogany armor as she darts from the darkness of the Bitter Patch and races toward Treble.

She notches an arrow to her bow—a seamless and expert move—as she runs. Sliding to a neat stop beside Esther, she takes perfect aim at my face.

Her finger twitches on the bow as if she's about to release it.

It would be a perfect shot through my right eye.

As I sight down the weapon to her face, I'm shocked to see

that she still wears Hagan's mark, drawn in blood on her cheek. I was sure she would have washed it off by now. Her chestnut brown hair is pulled back off her face. The bruise Cyrian gave her yesterday darkens the skin across her cheekbone.

She falters as her gaze passes from me to Nathaniel's unconscious body.

"Nathaniel!" The fear in her voice when she cries his name strikes through me.

"Take him," I plead, my left arm shaking violently around his chest. I know Christiana doesn't trust me, but I don't understand why she hasn't reached for her brother already. "Take Nathaniel. *Please*."

She starts to rise before she reasserts her offensive position, anchoring herself back to the ground.

Her wild gaze flickers between me and her brother, but her aim remains steady despite the stormy emotions filling her face.

Esther is equally pale beside her. "Is it a trap?"

Christiana shakes her head. "I don't know! He could be hurt —dying. But we can't trust her. She's already betrayed us."

Betrayed them? The last time I saw Christiana, she was running into the dark after Hagan made her leave. After that, Hagan and Nathaniel fought, and then I brought them both here.

I don't know why she would say I've betrayed them.

"Where's Mathilda?" Christiana asks Esther. "I need her power. Only she can see the truth."

"She should be on her way," Esther says. "She was making sure it's safe inside."

Safe inside... Between their comment about betrayal and making things safe, I can only assume that something happened inside the Bitter Patch—an event that has made Christiana distrust me even more than she already did.

"I'm not here to hurt you," I cry.

Whimpers escape my lips. My right arm feels like it's completely separated from my body.

I recognize Geordie—the man with a mop of blond hair—crouched in position among the trainees on my right. He can see Hagan, but I don't think Christiana or Esther can. Treble stands too high and Hagan's lying completely on Treble's right wing now.

Probably all Esther and Christiana can see is my outstretched arm but not whom I'm holding.

Like Esther, Geordie lowers his weapon for a second, but he lifts it again when Christiana shouts, "Keep up your guard! She's already betrayed Nathaniel. We can't trust her until Mathilda says it's safe."

To me, she says, "I'm sorry, Aura. I can't risk my people's lives."

Agony is making logical thought difficult. "You're risking *Nathaniel's* life! Christiana, you have to believe me—"

"No!" she shouts. "I can't believe a word you say. You could have deliberately knocked him out. You could have spelled him. All of this could be a trap! You know our location. Your queen has already attacked us. The minute we lower our guard, you'll kill us."

"I don't... have the power... to spell him..." Like other humans, Christiana doesn't understand how fae magic works, that my power is limited to my control over starlight. Dark magic can be used to control someone's actions—like Cyrian used to subdue Christiana yesterday—but fae magic can't. "I don't know anything about an attack."

I beg Christiana to believe me, but the line of her lips remains determined. "Mathilda will tell us the truth," she repeats.

Deep down, I understand her distrust. I know she would do anything for her brother, but if she truly believes I've betrayed his people, then she has to think of every human here. They're Nathaniel's family. He loves all of them like brothers and sisters.

She has an awful choice in front of her.

I wouldn't believe me, either.

My head lowers, pain and exhaustion taking its toll, before I wrench myself upright again, determined not to reveal the true extent of my current physical weakness.

Treble turns his head toward Christiana. His eyes are filled with rage on my behalf, but he knows better than to try to get in her way. She'll let her arrow loose at the slightest provocation.

She continues to point her weapon directly at my right eye.

I guess she's considering whether or not to take the shot.

It might be her only chance to kill me. I'm completely vulnerable, holding Nathaniel with my left arm and Hagan with my right. I won't be able to get my hands up in time to defend myself—assuming I'm prepared to drop both men.

Despair fills me—a slow, cold darkness growing inside my chest.

The Law of Champions is clear: Any human who spills a drop of my blood or kills me will be killed instantly.

If she's willing to kill herself to end me, then there's nothing I can do or say to convince her this isn't some kind of trap. Using my starlight to create the opportunity for us to land certainly wouldn't have helped her view of the situation.

She will never trust me. No matter what Mathilda says.

My only ally is Nathaniel, and he's unable to speak.

I drag air in and out of my chest. Each breath is harsh with pain and emptiness. I count each one, not sure if I'll make it to the next.

"Do it," I snarl at her, no longer able to see beyond my pain and despair. "Kill me! Just make sure someone catches Nathaniel before he falls."

She jolts. Her voice rises to a scream. "Mathilda! *I need you now!*"

My vision blurs, but I make out the ripple in the middle of the wheat field as a patch of wheat crumbles into dust.

The air in front of me flickers.

Mathilda appears a few paces behind Christiana. The witch's hair is as loose and wild as it was yesterday morning. Her fire-colored pelt sits around her shoulders, billowing in the rush of her movement. Today she's wearing a low cut, faded violet dress that hugs her voluptuous figure.

Mathilda's piercing green eyes are wide as she takes in the scene: Treble, Christiana, the trainees, and finally me and Nathaniel.

She moves with speed. As she crosses the distance between us, her hand shoots out toward Christiana, a flash of dark light spearing across the air.

Christiana shouts and jumps back when the dark magic hits her arrow, burning it instantly to ash that wafts away in the rushing breeze of Mathilda's arrival.

Despite Christiana's alarm, Mathilda continues to storm toward her.

"Christiana Exalted," she rages. "Have you lost your senses? Without Nathaniel, you're the only true heir to the throne. You must not kill yourself!"

Christiana stares back at Mathilda, her eyes wide with shock. "The fae have already struck at the heart of our home. Aura could be here to finish the job. I have to defend my people!"

Mathilda grabs Christiana's arm, peering deep into her eyes. "Has fear taken priority over your brother's life? What about your own life?"

Christiana's face crumples. "We could have lost everyone this morning. I won't take any more risks."

Mathilda's expression softens, but she whirls to me, her gaze quickly taking in the way I'm holding on to Nathaniel and his precarious position on Treble's back.

His black clothing and his position pressed up against my chest hide the worst of the blood, but her gaze seeks the rip in the front of his shirt where the spike protruded.

"He's dying," Mathilda cries, clutching her heart. "His bright heart is barely glowing. Every second we waste takes Nathaniel closer to death."

She swings back to Christiana. "A few glitter bulbs are nothing! If Nathaniel dies, Imatra will control our land."

Glitter bulbs? I sway on Treble's back. My left arm has turned numb. Mathilda said something about glitter bulbs, but I'm too unfocused to make sense of it.

"What about Aura?" Christiana asks. "Is she here to kill us? You have to look into her heart and tell me. Until I know for sure, I have to treat her as a threat."

Dark light builds under Mathilda's feet, lifting her up so that she rises to eye height with me, floating in the air between Treble and Christiana.

When we first met yesterday morning, Mathilda tried to kill me. She called me a weapon, the murderer of a thousand human warriors. She thought Nathaniel should have ended me, not brought me to Fell country.

Her attitude toward me shifted when she tried to look into my heart—she closed off and refused to say what she'd seen.

Now, she considers me with just as much distrust, but behind her expression is another emotion I can't make out through the haze of my pain.

I can only assume it's fear. There's no doubt in my mind that Mathilda still believes Nathaniel should have killed me.

"I can't do that, Christiana," she says, a gleam in her luminescent green eyes. "Aura's heart is hidden from me."

Christiana's jaw clenches. "Then I have no choice. Aura Lucidia is our enemy until Nathaniel can tell us otherwise. Now, please, Mathilda, take him from her."

Mathilda lifts her arms toward me. Her voice is gentle now, coaxing me to believe her. "It's okay, Aura. You can let Nathaniel go. I've got him."

"Hagan too," I say, uncertain whether Mathilda will agree to heal the hunter. *"Please.* He needs a second chance."

Christiana startles, lowering her weapon when she hears Hagan's name. I guess she really can't see him from the ground.

"I can't hold on to him," I say to Mathilda. "My shoulder's dislocated."

"Ah. I sensed your pain." A wave of dark light flows across Mathilda's face, casting her features into shadow. "I can take both men, but I'm afraid you will need to walk on your own. I will have to drain the environment too much to constrain you to Christiana's satisfaction while I carry them both."

"I'll follow you. I won't fight," I whisper, struggling to hold my head up. "You need to heal Nathaniel first. Then Hagan."

"You're in pain too," Mathilda says, her gaze narrowing in an assessing look.

I meet her eyes. "You said I would be."

She told me that Nathaniel would hurt me more than she ever could, that whatever remained of my heart would be torn apart before the beginning of the third day.

Nathaniel's near-death destroyed me.

Even now, my chest feels empty, a painful void. Until he's healed, my heart won't be healed, either.

Mathilda gives me a cold nod. At the same time, her magic washes around my left side, icy fingers of power tugging my left arm open and prying Nathaniel from my grip.

I shudder to feel her dark magic against my skin, the same

sensation as Cyrian's magic even if Mathilda isn't causing me pain.

I struggle to release Nathaniel into her hold. Not only because of the darkness in her eyes. I've forced my arm to clamp so tightly around him that I have trouble straightening my limb.

Letting Nathaniel go makes me feel powerless again.

Whether he lives or dies is no longer within my control.

Now it's all up to Mathilda, a dark witch who wants me dead.

CHAPTER 5

*N*athaniel's unconscious body tips and straightens until he lies parallel with the ground.

Finally relaxing, I allow my left arm to slide to my side, a dead weight.

I sense the rush of blood into my hand, but it's a distant pain, my muscles too stretched to feel much of anything.

On my other side, Hagan's weight also lifts, his torn shirt fully exposing his scar. His chest rises and falls evenly, his breathing more regular than Nathaniel's.

As his unconscious body rises up beside Treble, Christiana takes a step back.

Last night, Hagan forced her to marry him so that he could take control of her fate, for the sole purpose of freeing her. She fought him every step of the way, even when he told her to leave.

Now, she presses her lips together in a hard line, but she doesn't fight Mathilda as the witch slowly guides both men ahead of her and begins the careful walk back to the Bitter

Patch. The plant life around Mathilda's feet dies with every step she takes as she drains the environment to fuel her magic.

Carefully testing the range of movement of my right arm, I draw it slowly up to my chest, nursing it.

My dislocated shoulder bone protrudes at a nasty angle and the pain refuses to ease.

Treble turns his head to see me, his brilliant eyes casting rapid glances across my face and torso.

He bounces his head at me while making a low keening sound. I want to reassure him, but I can't lie and tell him I'm okay.

I also can't get off his back until I'm sure he won't be fired upon.

"Get everyone back inside the Bitter Patch," Mathilda says to Christiana as she passes her. "Quickly now. Cyrian will soon sense the magical disturbance here. I won't be able to mask our presence out here for long. We'll be safe inside."

"Lower your weapons," Christiana calls to the trainees still standing guard around us. "Do everything Mathilda tells you to do. Esther and Geordie, you remain with me. We will escort Aura Lucidia inside."

The trainees quickly disengage their crossbows, pulling the bolts off them and slipping the projectiles into pouches attached to belts around their waists. They each carry at least twenty bolts, enough to take down many thunderbirds if shot accurately.

As soon as the trainees turn their backs, I hoist my right foot over to the left, managing to extend both of my legs along Treble's outstretched wing so I can slide to the ground.

I stumble awkwardly before I reach the bottom and fall the remaining distance onto my backside with a quiet thud.

It's hard to care about my pride right now.

Treble quickly drops his belly to the ground and folds his wing around me to hide me in a protective cocoon for a moment. He turns his head into the gap at the edge of his wing, keening at me again.

"You have to fly," I whisper. "Ascend above the haze, where you'll be safe. Don't show yourself unless I whistle for you. They don't trust me, Treble. They will kill you if they have the chance."

My heart already hurts for him. My people tried to burn him out of the sky. Now the humans will target him too. All because he's loyal to me.

I lean against his side, unable to raise my hands to stroke his feathers as he nudges me gently.

"You can't stay with me," I say. "The situation here is too volatile. I can't lose you, Treble. You're my only friend."

Treble's glare tells me he would rather risk death than leave me on my own, but the sharp light in his eyes fades. He nudges me again, soft and gentle this time. He appears resigned now.

I close my eyes, a small part of my heart healing because of his friendship. "Go now. Be safe."

A savage tug pulls me to my feet. It's the same tug that left me with a bruised nose two days ago. Nathaniel must be on the verge of traveling too far away from me.

Treble immediately opens his wing and I stumble away from him, coming face to face with Esther and Geordie, who both hold their crossbows ready. Christiana stands between them. She has put away her bow, but it's not far from her reach, along with the dagger at her waist.

"You lied to us about who you are," Esther says, the cold light of betrayal in her eyes hurting my heart.

Esther was betrayed by her sister, Ethel, and left for dead. Nathaniel rescued her and brought her here. Nathaniel told me that Esther finds it difficult to trust people. She's also very protective of the trainees.

When Christiana returned here last night, she would have told everyone who I really am, including that the Law of Champions has been invoked.

"You're Aura Lucidia," Esther says. "Our mortal enemy. Only Nathaniel can explain what you're really doing here. Until then, we can't believe anything you say."

Nathaniel asked me to come to Null with him. He wanted me to meet his people, to fight with them. But he warned me that they would try to kill me if they found out who I am.

Esther may be wrong about my motivations, but she's correct that I deliberately deceived her. When I chose to reveal my identity to save Nathaniel's life yesterday, I knew the consequences.

I draw myself upright, trying to mask the screaming pain in my right arm. I won't get any sympathy from the humans and I need to reassert my defenses. "The Law of Champions forces me to go where Nathaniel goes. I need to follow him now or Mathilda won't be able to move him any farther."

Christiana steps right up to me. "My brother is the least vengeful, most forgiving person I know. He believes there is good in nearly everyone." Her voice lowers to a quiet threat. "Do not confuse me with him. I have none of his virtues. I will do whatever it takes to protect my brother and my people from you."

She spins on her heel. "Bring Aura Lucidia inside."

Esther and Geordie incline their weapons sharply toward the Bitter Patch. I don't need any prompting. My entire body tugs fiercely in Nathaniel's direction. Mathilda won't be able to take him into the Bitter Patch without me.

I force myself to move as fast as I can, nursing my injured right arm with my wounded left arm. Neither limb is entirely functional. Sharp pain jars through me with every step. I spent the last few hours at Cyrian's mercy. My ability to compartmentalize the pain now is stretched to its breaking point.

I can't stop the tears falling down my cheeks, a necessary release. It might make me look weak, but I have to deal with the pain somehow.

Focusing on my exhalations and inhalations, on the rush of air in and out of my mouth, I block out the threat of the crossbows held by Geordie and Esther, who keep pace with me on either side.

Mathilda waves us forward as we approach. All of the trainees have disappeared into the Bitter Patch ahead of her.

Nathaniel and Hagan float, waiting, in front of the wash of crimson and black foliage. My heart lurches, knowing that I'm holding up Nathaniel's healing.

I race forward, pushing myself as fast I can go. I'd run if I could.

As soon as I reach Nathaniel's side, Mathilda uses her magic to pull aside the vines covering the opening into the tunnel through the Bitter Patch.

Nathaniel appears calm. He could be sleeping except for his shallow breathing. His expression hasn't changed since I used my power to ease his mind, his face free from pain, even though he's deathly pale.

I hurry behind them as Mathilda maneuvers both men through the opening. They won't fit side by side. She floats Hagan ahead of her while Nathaniel follows. It's a small mercy that I can follow right behind him as he proceeds through the tunnel of vines and bushes.

Yesterday, he dyed my hair in the tunnel on the other side of the Bitter Patch. He planted kisses on my neck and cheeks, and I fell asleep because of his touch, a rare moment of peace.

Esther follows close behind me with Christiana behind her and Geordie taking up the rear.

"Aura," Mathilda calls back, turning slightly. "Will you tell us what happened in the fight between Hagan and Nathaniel?"

I open my mouth to answer, but Christiana interrupts me. "We can't trust her version of events."

Mathilda presses her lips together. "Very well. If you won't believe her, then we will wait to hear it from Nathaniel himself."

We travel silently for the next ten minutes. The pace is grueling—it would be nothing if I weren't injured, but every step hurts.

I watch Nathaniel's chest carefully, checking for signs that his condition is deteriorating, but he appears stable. Hagan remains unconscious, although the color is returning to his cheeks.

Finally, we exit the protective boundary of the Bitter Patch into Null itself.

I sense the spell lift from my tongue—the protective magic that stops anyone speaking about what happens here—finally able to think clearly about this place and the people who live inside its walls.

The other trainees have already taken up positions to form a wide guard around us, keeping their eyes on me, even if their weapons are lowered.

I recognize many of their faces, but I don't see Emily or the other teens among them. It appears that only the older trainees have come out to guard me.

Mathilda calls ahead of us. "Hurry! I will take Nathaniel and Hagan to the food hall. I can treat them there."

"What about Nathaniel's hut?" I ask, not expecting her to answer me, but she half-turns again.

"See for yourself," Mathilda says, pointing.

Nathaniel's hut is set slightly back and apart from the others, closest to the eastern side of Null. As we pass it, I inhale the scent of cedarwood and follow Mathilda's pointed finger toward the porch.

I miss a step.

A sea of glitter bulbs fills the space between the top step and the door.

CHAPTER 6

*E*ach glitter bulb is no bigger than my closed fist, but there are so many of them that they gleam and sparkle like a deadly ocean.

My voice is strangled as I ask, "What is this?"

"Don't pretend you don't know!" Christiana snaps, suddenly a picture of rage beside me. "They floated into Null this morning. All of them landed right there on Nathaniel's porch. A clever assassination plan. The only way your queen would know where to send them is if you told her about us. If Nathaniel had been inside his hut, he would have been killed."

"You brought terror into the heart of Null," Esther says with an angry stare. "We evacuated everyone to the other side of the village."

Mathilda casts me a quick glance. "I've placed a protective barrier around Nathaniel's hut to stop anyone going near it, but it will take a miracle to contain the explosive power of that many bulbs if they're triggered."

I shake my head in shock.

Until yesterday, I'd never seen or heard of glitter bulbs separating from the field.

Imatra created the glitter field during the final battle between the fae and the humans—the battle during which I annihilated the human army. The glitter field is meant to be a defense mechanism along the border.

Every stem of glitter grass carries a deadly bulb at the top. If disturbed by a living creature, the bulbs explode, cutting to shreds anything within its wide blast radius.

Last night, when the Vanem Dragon flew to Fell country to bind Nathaniel and Hagan to their fight, he also brought news that parts of the glitter field had become airborne.

The Dragon said that several glitter bulbs had drifted into Bright and exploded there. Luckily, nobody was hurt, but it prompted Imatra to gather her guards and prepare for an attack, believing that Cyrian's dark magic was at play.

Several bulbs also drifted into Fell country and exploded in the Misty Gallows.

Now there are possibly a hundred of them, gathered like a humblebee swarm on Nathaniel's porch, some of them piled precariously high on top of others.

All it would take is a living presence to disturb them and they will explode with enough force to cut through every person and building around them.

They would cut down the humans like a scythe through wheat.

Nathaniel's people will never believe that I had nothing to do with this.

In my deepest heart, I'm worried that I caused it somehow.

The Vanem Dragon said that the first bulbs lifted off the field at the same time a glowing mold moth landed on top of it. I don't know for sure, but I suspect it was the same moth that consumed the dust that remained on my hand after I stopped breathing at the burn site where I killed my parents.

"You sent the glitter bulbs here," Geordie says, speaking up for the first time, his accusation striking my heart as hard as Esther's declaration did. "This is the only place we've ever felt safe. We don't anymore."

I have no reply. I don't even know if I can defuse the glitter bulbs. I've walked into the glitter field before and not been hurt, but I'm not sure what that many separated glitter bulbs will do if I step near them.

Mathilda's expression remains shuttered as she hurries us along. When we reach the dining hall, she quickly orders the nearest trainees to shift the closest two tables so that they rest perpendicular to the door. She lays Nathaniel and Hagan down on them so that their feet are closest to the open door.

I move to follow her, but Christiana's arm shoots out like a barrier, thumping into my stomach.

"You will stay out here," she says. "Where we can see you." She spins to Geordie. "Get the pole."

He quickly disappears into the nearest building. I catch sight of tools inside it—shovels and fencing materials—before the door closes behind him.

Returning my attention to Nathaniel, I stand my ground as Mathilda's dark light flashes.

Pain strikes through me as patches of grass on the courtyard ahead of me shrivel and die. I'm worried about the extent to which she'll have to drain our surroundings to heal him.

Anxiety builds inside me as she works. I can't see what she's doing or whether Nathaniel is responding to her power, whether or not he's healing.

Geordie returns, holding a metal pole a little more than half his height that has a spike at the end of it and a hole through the center. He's also carrying a large hammer, a coil of rope, and a short metal chain with large links at each end.

I eye all four items, my wariness increasing when he hammers the pole into the ground, his muscles bunching with every strike, until it stands securely and doesn't move when he leans on it.

As soon as he threads the chain through the hole, wrapping it securely around the pole before attaching one end of the rope to one of the links, I take a step back.

I bump right into Christiana.

"I'm sorry, Aura," she says. "This is going to hurt, but we can't take any chances."

Geordie reaches for me, his expression hardening. "Hands behind your back," he orders me.

He's going to tie me to the pole, but I can barely move my right arm, let alone extend it behind me. "No. My shoulder—"

"Give me your hands!"

I'm still nursing my right arm across my chest. I'm already at breaking point. Any increase in pain will be the final straw.

My voice rises to a scream. "No!"

"Luciana Elect!" I recognize Maggie as she runs from the nearby building that houses the kitchen. She's Null's oldest resident. Her light brown hair is tied back in a single, long braid that thumps against her back as she runs.

Esther grabs Maggie before she can reach me. "That's not Aura's real name."

Maggie yanks herself out of Esther's hold. "What are you doing to her?"

Yesterday when I first met Maggie, she was hunched, aged, and sick with the Ebon Rot, but she was trying to hide it. I healed her. Now, she stands tall and strong, her hair glossy and her cheeks full of life.

"This woman saved my life," she cries. "She isn't like the

other fae. Nathaniel trusts her. He loves her. Anyone can see that."

Christiana reaches for her. "It's not enough, Maggie. It's my responsibility now to protect you—"

Maggie steps up to her. "You choose to ignore the truth because the truth makes you afraid. She is not our enemy."

A deep, pained crease forms on Christiana's forehead. "Until Nathaniel revives, we don't know what she is."

Maggie gestures at the pole and then me. "Aura's in pain. She needs our help. Not to be tied up like an animal. She isn't going to hurt us—"

"Didn't you hear me? I can't take that risk!" Christiana grips Maggie's shoulders as the older woman stares at her, wide-eyed. "Until Nathaniel wakes up, it's my duty to protect everyone. Including you. Even if I have to be a monster to do it."

Christiana is unyielding as she gestures to several trainees at the side. "Go back to Emily and the others, Maggie. We'll call you when it's safe."

Maggie whirls as the trainees grab hold of her. "No! I won't go. You can't do this to her!"

She struggles and kicks, but she isn't trained in combat and the more she tries to slip their hold, the harder they pull, forcing her back around the building and out of sight until her shouts fade.

I turn right into Esther's fist.

The impact cracks across my temple, dropping me to the ground. Geordie catches me before I can hit the earth, yanking my arms behind my back at the same time.

I land on my knees.

My right shoulder pops.

Excruciating pain shoots through my chest and the world shifts, tilting in a sickening drop.

My scream fills the air and the ground moves beneath me as Geordie drags me back toward the pole.

Sickening agony burns through me so fast that I dry-wretch into the dust. If my stomach weren't empty, its contents would be all over the ground.

As soon as he draws me to a stop, Geordie loops the rope around my wrists and secures the rope to the chain.

The chain through the pole means that I can't attempt to fray the rope to free myself. It also means I'll have to lift the pole from the ground if I want to escape—an impossible task while my shoulder is dislocated.

In the blurry distance, Hagan's feet suddenly shift. His big body rolls off the table and he lands at a crouch, shaking his head as if he's trying to clear it.

Mathilda shouts for him to stay down, but he doesn't appear to listen to her, rising groggily to his feet before he stumbles halfway down the stairs at the front of the hall.

"What are you doing to Aura?" he bellows, swaying on the spot, his gaze unsteady. He presses his hand to his head. "I heard her scream."

His knees buckle as he tries to take another step. Reaching out to steady himself, he crashes against the railing, still shouting, "Christiana! Leave Aura... the fuck... alone..."

His eyes roll back and he drops where he stands.

Christiana is frozen, her eyes wide, but she quickly whirls back to me, bending to glare into my streaming eyes.

"What did you do to my husband?"

Gasping for air, I meet Christiana's angry gaze. Last night, when Cyrian used his dark magic to swing me up into the air, she winced, as if she still had some empathy left for me.

Now, her expression is completely hard.

The edges of my vision blur and darkness threatens to overcome me.

Inside the hall, Mathilda's magic flares again, an inky black flash that spreads across my vision, widening and swallowing everything I see.

The silhouettes of the people standing guard around me warp and shift, indistinguishable from the dark light.

I don't see humans anymore.

When I finally black out, all I see are shadows.

CHAPTER 7

$\mathcal{I}$ can't breathe. The world explodes around me, white light rippling in every direction, filling the sky as I lie on the burning ground.

I'm facing upward.

I know I'm dreaming. The same dream I had yesterday in the greenhouse.

But I have an impossible choice: I can continue to dream about my past or wake up to the pain that waits for me in the present.

I choose to dream.

Embers float across the sky above me, glowing pieces of ash and hurtling shards of wood that resemble tiny suns circling my location.

The sun is my enemy. A fiery force that chases my power away every morning, but it can't stop my energy emerging every night at dusk.

A raging fire burns behind me, its heat and light so intense that the crackling sounds drown out the footsteps of the woman who runs toward me.

I still can't see her face.

Her features are concealed by a cloak of dark light that prevents me from seeing through it. Her silhouette glows crimson, but now I think the glow is from the fire raging behind me and the fiery embers flickering across the space above our heads.

She drops to her knees beside me, her dagger raised, its blade the only clear object in my vision. It is wickedly curved, a hunting knife.

The man darts across the space behind her, dodging the falling debris, swinging his own blade across the air, aimed precisely at her neck.

Unlike the woman's face, his face is clear to me now. His features are drawn, dangerous, the anger in his brown eyes relentless. An older version of Nathaniel, but with lighter hair.

His armor and blade are pristine, not a drop of blood on them, only ash falling around him, clinging to the sweat dripping down the side of his face.

Golden light pours from his blade as he swings it.

If the vision above me wasn't so horrifying, it would be beautiful. The man's golden light crashes into the woman's crimson silhouette and all of it is backlit with the brightest white skyscape. Three forces raging against each other.

The woman screams and ducks just in time.

She wrenches the dagger from my chest, drops to the side, and balances on her dagger hand. Her free hand flies upward, a streak of burning firelight pouring from her palm.

She is fae.

Yesterday, I guessed she was Imatra, but now I'm sure of it. She is the queen I trusted, who betrayed me.

Blood drips down her arm from her powerful fingers as Solstice fae power pours from her hand.

She was clutching a small, gleaming object, but she loses hold of it as soon as she opens her palm to protect herself.

The object drops to the space beside my head, glinting at the corner of my eye.

It's a curved piece of stone, barely bigger than my fingertip and covered in blood. Its glowing surface is tinted scarlet like Imatra's hair.

Nathaniel's father retracts his weapon with impressive speed and tilts its blade, bracing for the onslaught of her power.

I'm shocked when the stream of firelight hits the blade's surface and rebounds.

Imatra screams. Her power flashes, a sudden rush of wind sweeping the flames to the side before she would be burned by her own ricocheting magic.

Nathaniel's father shouts, a deep roar. "She's just a girl!"

"She's not a girl," Imatra screams, her usually serene voice harsh and full of rage. "She was never a girl!"

The dream flickers, the images vanish.

Suddenly, the world explodes around me again, the same bright, white light filling the sky, rippling across my vision.

The same spiraling embers float above my body, close enough to touch.

The dream begins again.

"Aura?"

Nathaniel's voice breaks through the exploding dark, pulling me away from the nightmare. His fingers brush my cheek, and his scent fills my head, dispelling the darkness.

He's alive.

My eyes open, but they're gritty. I can barely raise my

eyelids. I don't know how long I was asleep. It could be late morning now.

I make out Nathaniel's shape, kneeling in front of me before my head drops to my chest again.

My hands are still bound behind me, my legs folded beneath me. I barely feel his touch because my entire body is numb.

"Darkest star," he whispers.

He's still wearing his torn clothing, his hair matted and dirty, but his face is no longer beaten and bruised. His skin is perfectly smooth. Healed and clean.

Strands of his brown hair fall across his eyes, dark shadows building, the inky flecks in his gaze becoming darker still.

"Breathe for me, Aura." His voice is low and urgent, his fingertips seeking my lips, his forehead pressing to mine so that his face blurs in my vision.

His thumb presses gently to the curve at the top of my mouth before he presses a light kiss right across the top of it. *"Breathe."*

My lips part and air slips through.

He draws back as I cough.

I exhale dust into the air—charcoal gray dust from my mouth. The same dust that the moth consumed yesterday. The same dust that coated my body when I stopped breathing at the burn site.

My eyes brim with tears as oxygen fills my chest.

I didn't think I had any tears left, but they trickle down my cheeks.

"Are you alive?" I ask, afraid that I'm still dreaming—a cruel twist.

"I'm alive because of you." His lips draw into an unforgiving line. "I need to undo your bindings now."

Pure panic races through me, drowning any rational thought. My shoulder has already been forced out of joint and then wrenched around on top of that. I can't stand another move.

"No!" I scream, making him jolt. "Don't touch me!"

"Aura—"

Sobs tear out of me. "Please don't... Don't touch..." My head drops again. "You're alive. Everything will be okay now. Just let me go back to sleep."

His jaw tenses before he places both of his palms against my cheeks, lifting my face so I'm forced to meet his worried eyes. "Aura, you're in pain. I need to unbind you so I can help you."

I grit my teeth at him, a cold calm filling me. "I won't let you help me. If you make me healthy, I'll be strong enough to fight you. Leave me be, Nathaniel."

Turning my face away, I close my eyes and exhale before I sink into the waiting *nothing* again, the cold, empty dark where I don't need to breathe anymore. Where I can fall like a dead stone into icy water.

I'm only asleep for an instant before Nathaniel's frustrated roar jolts me awake again.

He lurches away from me, rising to his feet to pace back and forth across the dirt, wearing a track across the ground in front of me.

The path between the buildings used to be grassy, but every living plant in sight is crinkled and withered. Mathilda must have used up every shred of natural energy to heal him.

My vision is fuzzy, still gritty with dust, but I make out Mathilda, Christiana, and Esther standing behind Nathaniel, watching him pace. The other trainees have fanned out behind them.

I also make out Hagan. He stands apart from the others, an immense figure, a mirror to Nathaniel's strength. He's alert again, the sharp intelligence returned to his eyes. He isn't in chains and I don't know whether that's because Nathaniel ordered that he remain free or because nobody could subdue him. Either is possible.

He tried to stop them tying me up before he collapsed again.

Now, Hagan breaks his piercing study of me to glance at Nathaniel, but he doesn't attempt to speak.

Nathaniel pauses in front of me.

He doesn't reach for me, doesn't try to touch my injured arm, because he will never knowingly hurt me, but his voice rises to a violent roar as he turns to the others. "Who did this?"

His glare rakes across the humans as the silence stretches around us.

"Answer me!" he roars. *"Who. Fucking. Did this?"*

CHAPTER 8

*G*eordie steps forward from the row of trainees, his head down, his shoulders hunched, and his mop of golden hair falling across his face, but Christiana quickly steps in front of him.

"I ordered Aura to be restrained," she says. "But we didn't dislocate her shoulder."

"But you knew she was hurt when you tied her up and left her here for hours," Nathaniel says, an accusation.

Christiana tips her head back, her long braids sliding across her shoulders, her gaze flashing with defiance. "It's her sword arm. Like she said, it's better that she's wounded."

Nathaniel advances on Christiana, his voice a sharp demand. "Where is your honor, Christiana?"

She stands her ground, her armor dull in the gray light. "I've never been afraid to play dirty, Nathaniel."

Nathaniel turns his head so that I can see the careful glance he casts at Hagan. His voice lowers. "Be careful about getting into the dirt, Christiana. One day, you might find yourself desperate to wash it off."

She glares back at him. "I would tie her up again to protect our people. As many times as it takes."

Nathaniel's expression darkens, a snarl on his lips. "You didn't do it to protect anyone, Christiana. You acted out of revenge."

She inhales sharply at the accusation, but the flush rising to her cheeks betrays the truth in his claim. Sudden tears fill her eyes, but she bats them away. "She deserves to suffer for hurting our family."

Nathaniel takes an angry step toward his sister. "For ending our mother's pain? Or for keeping me alive?" he asks, his voice dangerously quiet. "Which 'hurt' are you talking about?"

The blood drains from Christiana's face. "For our mother... I would never wish harm on you."

Nathaniel shakes his head, a slow, angry movement.

He raises his voice to address the humans. "Aura Lucidia saved my life! She saved me when her people tried to burn me to death. She protected me from the wolves. She stepped between me and hunters' arrows. She took the lash of Cyrian's whip that would have killed me. She turned her back on her own people and came here. And why?"

He roars at them, his anger a violent storm. *"Because I asked her to."*

His teeth are gritted. "She did it for *me*. And this is how you repay her."

He turns back to his sister, his voice barely controlled. "Aura has the power to defeat Cyrian. We need her." He shakes his head, slow, full of rage. "But I won't ask her to fight for us now."

He points to Mathilda. "You will ease Aura's pain so I can unbind her."

Mathilda's wild hair swishes around her face, her luminescent eyes wide. "I told you, Nathaniel. I can't. I've already drained the environment—"

"Then take the energy you need from my heart," he says.

Mathilda gasps, jolting back so fast that she nearly loses her balance. "Never!"

My head snaps up at the same time. "No!"

As our shouts echo, Hagan steps forward with a quiet statement. "Take from my heart."

A hush falls over the humans.

Christiana stares at Hagan, her lips parted in surprise.

She steps toward him as if she's going to stop him, but before she can say anything, Hagan points to Geordie.

"That man said that when we arrived, Aura was holding on to me." His arm slowly lowers as he meets my eyes. "I remember tipping off the bird, but something stopped me from falling. You tore your arm to keep me alive. Didn't you, Aura?"

When I don't respond, Hagan strides toward me, only stopping when Nathaniel steps in his path.

"That's close enough," Nathaniel says.

The tension rises as the two men face each other.

"I'm the reason she's hurt. Let me help her," Hagan replies, appearing to choose his words carefully. "Take my life energy. Then I can die—"

"No," I shout. "You will not!"

Hagan blinks at me. He's a massive man who matches Nathaniel in strength, yet my shout seems to have stunned him.

Nathaniel, too, turns to me, but unlike the others, he doesn't appear surprised. A resigned expression settles onto his face.

"I didn't save your life to watch you throw it away, Hagan Sever," I snarl.

I turn my glare on Mathilda. "As for the witch, she will *not* come anywhere near me with her dark magic."

Nathaniel turns to kneel in front of me again, a challenging glint entering his eyes as his big body casts me into shadow. "Then will you let me unbind you?"

My gaze flickers to Mathilda. Then Hagan.

Christiana folds her arms, as if she's suddenly cold.

Icy anger rushes through me. "I'll do it myself."

I pull at my power, a harsh tug, tearing at what remains of my starlight now that it's nearing the middle of the day.

It's a painful wrench, like clawing at the bottom of an empty well, as if I'm trying to steal a drop of water from dusty earth.

My power flashes. The briefest burst.

I'm quickly exhausted, but a sickly burning scent fills the air as the rope catches on fire.

I lean forward over my knees as my hands separate behind my back. The chain clanks against the pole as the rope falls away, but I don't move any farther.

The humans take quick steps away from me, flickers of fear on their faces, but Nathaniel and Hagan are quiet.

I remain leaning forward, my right arm lying at an awkward angle across my back, my face raised to see them. Any further movement will invite more pain.

Nathaniel speaks quietly to Hagan. "Help me, please."

Hagan gives him a nod and kneels on my other side before Nathaniel runs his hand down my injured right arm. "Easy now, Aura. We'll keep your arm where it is."

Hagan gently presses my limb, keeping it in its current position against my back so that Nathaniel can lift me without hurting me.

Nathaniel presses my chest against his as he slowly rises and finally shifts his arms so that he can hold me without Hagan's help.

"I can take it from here," he says to Hagan.

Hagan gives a silent nod before he steps away.

Without another word, Nathaniel strides away from the humans. Across his shoulder, I can see Hagan remain where he is, his expression unreadable, while Christiana and Mathilda hurry after us.

"Wait, Nathaniel," Christiana calls, unwrapping her arms from her chest to follow us. "Where are you going?"

"To my hut."

"You can't! The glitter bulbs will kill you."

"Then you'd better not follow me," he says.

"Nathaniel!" she screams, digging in her heels as if she can somehow plant him to the spot. "Stop!"

When Nathaniel continues walking, she spins to Mathilda, crying, "You have to stop him."

Mathilda shakes her head, wide-eyed fear filling her expression. "There's nothing I can do. I can't access any more power inside Null. We brought this on ourselves."

The other humans run up behind them, watching us go. They're all shouting for Nathaniel to stop now. They won't only be afraid for him. If he sets off the bulbs, the explosions will cut through the entire camp.

Nathaniel continues walking, his steady footsteps carrying me away from them. He presses his cheek to the top of my head while I listen to his deep inhalations.

"Nathaniel!" Christiana screams again. "You have to forgive me."

"I don't have to do a fucking thing for you," he murmurs. "Not for any of you. Not anymore."

He doesn't turn back, even when Christiana buries her head in her hands, and Mathilda wraps her arm around Christiana's shoulders.

I've never heard Nathaniel speak like that. He's always held tightly to his convictions, his path. He's always operated according to an unbending code of love and loyalty.

I sense bitter anger in him now, the kind that could fester.

I want to reach for him, but I can't move.

He continues to stride toward the glittering bulbs, their deadly glass surfaces winking.

I can only just see them out of the corner of my eye and only if I crane my neck. I quickly return my head to his chest, afraid of upsetting his balance.

I protected him from the glitter field once, but I don't know why the bulbs are here, how they got here, or whether the protection I experienced before will keep us safe now.

The barrier of dark magic that Mathilda placed around the hut shrieks as Nathaniel barrels through it.

Directly in front of me, golden light glows across his chest, shining brightly through the rips in his shirt as he plows through the dark light as if it's nothing more than mist.

Again, I want to reach out and touch him, but I have no control. My breaths bounce against his chest. My heart pounds so hard, I can hardly hear his footsteps.

Without hesitation, Nathaniel strides up the porch steps, the impact of his boots on the wood striking through me.

He trusted me to keep him safe from the glitter field when we fell from the sky, but he's never taken a risk like this before.

I sense his simmering anger as he approaches the top step and recklessly strides onward.

Closing my eyes as he steps into the sea of bulbs, I brace for the explosion.

CHAPTER 9

Quiet whispers rise up around us like far-off voices calling our names.

I open my eyes as Nathaniel stops in the middle of the porch.

Light dances across his chest and face, reflected off the glassy surfaces of the glitter bulbs as they lift up and float in the air around us like gentle bubbles.

To my surprise, Nathaniel is watching me instead of our surroundings.

His expression has softened, the hard edges of his gritted jaw easing, his shoulders relaxing. "How many times will you save my life, Aura Lucidia?" he asks.

"As many as it takes," I say, exhaling my fear.

Releasing me from his gaze, he raises his head, his focus shifting to the glitter bulbs.

One of them drifts up to my eye level. Colors swirl inside it, shapes taking form only to quickly vanish, leaving misty shadows behind.

"I didn't bring them here," I say.

"I know you had nothing to do with this," he says. "We'll figure it out later. Right now, I need to get you inside."

Carefully and quietly, Nathaniel picks a path through the bulbs until he reaches his door and nudges it open with his boot. Some of the glitter bulbs spill inside the hut as he turns to enter sideways and carry me through the opening.

The silence behind us is thick. I can't see very far back now, but the humans are no longer shouting. They are quiet instead. Shocked, I guess, that nothing happened. No doubt relieved, too.

As Nathaniel nudges the door closed, a final bulb floats inside before the lock clicks and we're alone again.

Yesterday, he told me that Mathilda placed a spell on this hut at his request so that nobody could enter without his permission. Hopefully, the additional spell she placed around the hut this morning will keep the humans away from the porch. Even if Nathaniel walked unharmed through the bulbs, that doesn't mean anyone else can.

He carries me to one of the kitchen chairs, awkwardly dragging it out from the table with his boot before easing me onto it. He positions me so I'm sitting with my left arm to the chair's backrest. His mother's pelt is slung over the chair where I left it, a soft surface against which I can lean.

I sigh as I drop my head to the top of the backrest, feeling safe for the first time since we left this hut yesterday.

Nathaniel quickly pours a glass of water and raises it to my lips. I take it from him one-handed, managing to drink all of it before he passes me some dried fruit, followed by some day-old bread.

He tells me to chew slowly. He keeps refilling my glass until I've drunk as much as I need, and he also eats and drinks, promising as he swallows, "I'll make sure we get some proper food soon."

Finally, he kneels in front of me again, stroking the strands of my white hair from my face. My hair is coated in a film of sweat and dirt, the scent of death thick in my senses.

His hand pauses on my cheek. "I have to fix your arm now."

I squeeze my eyes closed for a moment. "I know."

"It won't hurt. I promise."

I give a short laugh. "You said you'd never lie to me."

"Do you think I'd start now?" He arcs his eyebrows at me in a challenging expression.

Shifting forward, he eases his palm around to the back of my neck. His thumb strokes the aching spot at the base of my neck, easing the sore muscle there.

Despite how much his touch soothes my pain, I'm wary, narrowing my eyes at him.

A small smile lifts his lips. The challenging light grows in his eyes. "Does this hurt?"

"No," I say, still guarded.

His thumb lowers, but only by an inch, slowly working down the side of my neck. "What about this?"

"You know it doesn't hurt," I grumble, my accusation only half-hearted.

The corner of Nathaniel's mouth twitches up. He slowly leans in and brushes a kiss across my lips, a tingling contact, before he rises from his seat.

My eyes fly open as he circles around behind me. I'm not sure what he intends to do and every part of me is suddenly on edge.

"Trust me," he whispers, dropping a kiss on the top of my head before he reaches for the clasps down the left side of my armor.

He's watched me either peel the armor off myself or do it up multiple times, so he knows how it works.

I relax when he doesn't touch my joint. Instead, he carefully opens the armor across my back, but only to expose my skin.

Easing my hair aside, he gently kneads the muscles down the left-hand side of my spine, easing down to my lower back and over to my right side, working his way slowly upward but remaining close to my spine.

Now that he's positioned behind me, I can't tell if I'm glowing at his touch.

His hands soothe the screaming muscles all of the way from the small of my back to the base of my neck. He doesn't deviate from that path, simply working his way back down. Then up again all of the way to the base of my neck.

I shiver when he drops a kiss on my bare skin beneath my left shoulder blade.

I hear the smile in his voice. "You couldn't scrub this one off."

His family name is painted across my left shoulder as well as across my heart.

I stiffen a little. "Hagan said I dishonored you."

The smile doesn't fade from his voice. "That's a human law. You're not human, remember?"

He's trying to ease my worry the same way he's easing my muscles, but it won't work. "He said it was up to you whether or not we're still married," I say.

Nathaniel trails kisses down my spine, seeming unfazed by the question in my voice. "Aura... *beautiful woman*... the choice will always be *yours*."

"Then we're still married." I relax again, leaning against the chair while his hands pass across my ribs, slowly easing across all of the muscles of my back, one hand finally kneading the spot beneath my right shoulder blade while his other hand slowly clasps my right hand where it rests against my side.

His thumb presses into my palm, easing across each of my fingers and moving on to my wrist.

Inch by careful inch, he works his way up my arm, along my forearm and then my bicep, firm enough that I can feel his touch beneath the sleeve of my armor. He works his other hand along the ridge at the top of my shoulder until his hands meet in the middle across my shoulder.

He promised me it wouldn't hurt.

It doesn't.

My right arm gently lowers away from my back, slowly shifting to my side into a more natural position.

"Easy, Aura," he whispers, planting kisses up the side of my exposed neck. "Not too fast or your muscles will tense up."

He shifts again—without taking his hands from my back—so that he's kneeling at my right side.

Gradually bending my arm at the elbow, he guides my arm forward the slightest distance while he continues to knead at the muscles across my shoulder, until I can rest my hand on the top of my right thigh.

"Nearly there," he whispers, shifting around to my front again.

Tears suddenly burn at the backs of my eyes, slipping down my cheeks before I can stop them. "I thought you were gone."

"Never." He smiles, leaning forward to continue massaging my shoulder as he takes my right hand and softly draws it forward and up.

At the same time, he leans across to brush another kiss across my lips. It's so much like the move he made against me when we first fought that it takes me back to our first encounter in the Misty Gallows. I drove my dagger toward his stomach. He pulled my dagger arm forward but past his torso so that I ended up plastered against him.

That was the first time I inhaled his body heat, his caramel scent.

I swallow a sob, unable to hide my vulnerability. "I thought you were really gone."

"I'm not going anywhere." He presses his cheek against mine, smudging the tears trickling down the side of my face. Then he turns so his lips nudge mine, a gentle reminder that he's right here, warm, alive, and determined to help me.

I'm covered in dust and blood. His clothing is still tattered and filthy, but his skin is clean. Even so, his kiss deepens as he continues to draw my arm up, placing my hand on his lowered shoulder.

His fingertips press along the sleeve of my armor until both of his hands rest across my injured shoulder.

I sense my shoulder shift and the tension in my arm finally eases. A quick glance tells me that the joint is no longer pressing unnaturally to the front, even if I can't see the swelling and bruising beneath my armor.

"There," Nathaniel whispers against my lips, the same way he spoke when he first wrote his name on my face.

He lowers my arm to my lap and then his fingertips rise from my body for the first time since he started massaging my back.

Gripping the base of his shirt, he peels the torn material off his body. The deadly wound in his torso is healed, but I gasp at its appearance.

A small, crescent-shaped scar now sits above his heart.

It's exactly the same as mine.

He gives me a wry smile. "We have the same scar."

I'm shocked as I study it. "Always a mirror. Why does this happen?"

I've asked this question before. Along with why I glow when

he touches me. The connections between us are far too strong to be caused by a Law I invoked only two days ago.

"We could chase answers. Or we could focus on the present," he says with a gentle smile that tells me what he's already told me: He doesn't know.

Returning his attention to his torn shirt, he considers its structure before he rips sections of it to extend its length. Then he carefully wraps the makeshift bandage around my forearm and neck, creating a sling.

"That will do until I can make you a better one," he says. "How does it feel?"

I allow the weight of my arm to settle into the base of the sling. "It's fine."

"Good. Go carefully from now on. No sudden movements."

I reach for him with my left arm before he can rise—an awkward movement on my part. "Nathaniel... When do we have to fight?"

He sinks back onto the chair opposite me, his expression suddenly drawn. "The Vanem Dragon will come for us when he chooses. He will take us to the border to fight there. Like last night, it will probably be around midnight."

"Then we only have twelve hours left. Possibly less."

My statement falls into a chasm between us. I press my lips together, trying to stop the tears. I'm tired of pushing away my paralyzing fear and grief about the path I have to walk. "I can't... This is not... How can we...?"

His big hand brushes my cheek. "Aura." He closes his eyes. Presses his forehead to mine. Exhales quietly. "These remaining hours are *ours*. Nobody else's. I want to spend them sharing everything with you that's good about my world. There are places in the Misty Gallows where the streams flow and the moss is like emeralds. I want you to see that not everything here is ugly."

I want to say 'yes' immediately, but reality presses in on me. "Cyrian still sits on your throne. You need to kill him before we fight."

Nathaniel nods, a slow acknowledgement against my forehead, but he says, "We nearly died trying to fight him, Aura. I had a path that I walked, and now I've reached its end. Cyrian's fate will be determined by the outcome of the battle between us. Until then, I don't want to think about him—or Imatra—or any other person except you."

"Okay," I whisper, hoping it will be that simple.

He pulls back with a serious smile. "Then let's start with a warm bath. We'll find a way for Maggie to smuggle us some food after that."

Capturing my free hand in his, he draws me to my feet and toward the bathroom, his footsteps slow and quiet.

He checks my position as he moves, as if we're running away together again.

I guess we are. Running away from the future, trying to stop each passing minute.

CHAPTER 10

$\mathcal{N}$athaniel draws me inside the bathroom, urging me to sit in the chair while he strides to the clawfoot bath that rests in the center of the room.

Reaching for the cast-iron water pump located at the back of it, he pumps the lever, but he only fills it half-full.

Then he returns to me, eases my arm out of the sling, and supports my limb while drawing my armor the rest of the way down my torso and then my legs.

Every move he makes is careful. Silent.

His fingers linger on my skin. My shoulder, my bicep, my wrist, my waist, extending each touch like it's the last.

Finally, my underwear lies on the floor, and I make my way to the bath. Sliding into it, I keep my arm pressed to my chest.

The bath is full enough for me to slip beneath the surface, immersing my hair for a moment, but it's shallow enough that I'm not forced to be completely submerged in the blood and dirt that wash off me.

Breaking the surface, I find Nathaniel kneeling beside the bath with a washcloth in hand. He sets about cleaning off all of the blood and dust that still coat my neck, face, hands—even my stomach where my skin was exposed.

He's careful around the scrapes across my stomach and pays particular attention to the scratches across my face—including the cut on my chin where Tanner's whip nicked me.

The water slowly turns red as Nathaniel's blood and my blood wash away from me.

"The wounds are clean," he murmurs. "I don't see any signs of infection, but we'll need to keep watch."

I burned the ends of my hair last night when I removed the black dye that had hidden my identity for part of the day, and he pauses as he draws the cloth across the strands. This time, he doesn't say anything.

He helps me out of the bath and wraps me in two towels—one around my body and another smaller one around my hair. After returning me to the chair, he drains the bath, refills it, turns his back to me to remove his clothes, and quickly disappears inside the bathtub.

Water splashes outside the tub as he slides beneath the surface.

The tug inside my chest is undeniable.

I need to be able to see him.

My feet move, taking me to the edge of the bath.

Nathaniel remains beneath the surface, his eyes closed, fists pressed against the inner sides of the bath to keep himself underwater. The liquid slowly turns red as the remainder of his blood washes off.

The surface breaks as he sits up, but he doesn't look at me, fixating on the opposite wall as water streams down his hair, face, and shoulders.

His eyes are red. "I made you a promise that I can't keep," he says.

I know the promise he's talking about: He swore to fight me

with all of his strength, to strike, hurt, and tear me apart. To treat me as his enemy.

"You won't be fighting me," I say, pushing my left arm free of the towel to reach across and rest my fingertips against his heart. "I will be tucked up in here. And in your memories. I will be the wife you once had, who no longer exists. The woman you fight will be the Fae Queen's champion. She will have no mercy and neither will you."

I inject the full force of my convictions into my speech. I need him to believe that I will fight him with all of my strength, that I will not give up.

He nods, but it's automatic. He has no choice but to agree. His movements are wooden as he rises from the water.

"I want to fight beside you, not against you," he says.

His statement tears at my heart.

When he steps from the bath, I close the gap between us, wrapping my free arm around his stiff torso, the towel hanging half off me, my hurt arm curled between us.

He slowly pulls the towel back up over my shoulders, but when I look up, his expression has softened. A faint smile touches his lips. "It's a shame we both need to eat right now."

I give him a sultry smile that seems to surprise him before I release him and shrug the towel right off my shoulders, allowing it to drop to the floor, leaving me naked. "It *is* a shame."

Turning, I reach for the folded-up beige training gear that I left on the seat in the corner of the bathroom yesterday. The rips in my armor are a liability and I don't want to put it on again now that it's covered in blood—even if the gore doesn't show against the black material. Luckily, Esther provided me with multiple pairs of clean underwear yesterday, so I pick some underpants and pull them on one-handed.

Staring, perplexed, at the top, I consider how I'll get my injured arm through the strap.

I sense Nathaniel come up behind me before he drops a kiss onto my bare shoulder, murmuring, "Let me help you with that."

When I turn back to him, he surprises me by tugging the underwear from my fingers and dropping it back to the chair. He's wearing a towel slung low over his hips, but it wouldn't take much to remove it.

He arches his eyebrow at me, a smile playing around his mouth.

I bite my lip before I take a step, rise up onto my tiptoes to meet his height, and plant a swift, brief kiss on his smiling mouth. His jaw is shadowed with growth and the bristles tingle against my lips.

With a tug as quick as the one with which he took the underwear from me, I loosen his towel.

His arms wrap around me and he lifts me, nudging soft kisses against my lips as he carries me from the room, making it to his bedroom in a few quick strides.

Glitter bulbs float up into the air, disturbed as we pass them, but they glide back to the floor again without any disasters.

I sense Nathaniel's restraint when he lays me on his bed, control in the way he makes sure my arm is resting at my side, bending it at the elbow so that my right hand rests on my stomach.

Planting tantalizing kisses along the back of my hand and my forearm, he follows the arch of my arm as far as my breasts before he kisses every inch of them, sending strikes of heat all of the way to my center.

I'm surprised when my skin reacts to his touch with the softest glow. I thought my power would be completely drained by now, but his nearness is too overwhelming, the promise of his body too much.

Heat rages through me by the time his lips crash against mine, hungry and demanding. Shivers rocket through me, rippling back and forth as his hands stroke down my sides, seeking the curve of my hips and my thighs.

I forget my injured arm, reaching for him before he takes hold of my wrist and presses my hand firmly back to my stomach, kissing the back of it again before his hand remains pressed over it, keeping me from hurting myself.

His kisses trail lower, down across my stomach and pelvis. When his mouth reaches my center, it's nearly more than I can take.

My breathing bursts out of control and my body is beyond ready. But the closer I come to complete release, the more my emotions spiral out of my control.

My heart hurts.

There isn't a part of my body and mind that isn't aching right now, screaming quietly. My future is as trapped as my right hand, clasped in Nathaniel's, forced to remain still, intertwined, when all I want is to break us both free from the rules, the magic, and the Law.

I flex my fingers beneath his palm, pushing upward before I slip his hold and tug on his arm, drawing him back to me.

The intensity in his eyes burns through me, cutting my heart as he hovers above me before he drops a soft kiss on my lips. "Aura? Do we need to stop?"

"No." I shake my head with a sob that I can't control. My emotions are a mess of heat and sadness, of physical need and emotional want. "I never want to stop."

Tilting my pelvis, I hook my legs around his hips, moaning out the intoxicating rush as he slides inside me.

He moves slowly, drawing out the joining so that every second of pleasure feels like it will last forever and release is a crash that will end it all.

Desperate to anchor myself in his body, I grip his shoulder with my good hand, my other resting on the bed as my body rocks against his. I would give anything for more time. Just one more day. Two. I need a lifetime with him.

I gasp. "Tell me a lie, Nathaniel. Just one."

He pauses mid-thrust, making my body ache even more, wanting and needing every part of him.

His jaw tenses, but a fierce determination enters his voice. "We will both be alive tomorrow."

I nod, choosing to believe that all of his rage and willpower can make it true. "We will."

I lose myself to the intensity of his touch, his lips, the heady strokes, the suddenly wild rhythm. I push back against the crash, holding on to every second of want and need until the intensity in his eyes and the way his hands stroke every sensitive inch of me, tip me over.

The crash feels like falling and never hitting the bottom, waves that promise a future I can't have.

Gathering me into his side, he holds me close, my head pressed to his chest.

His heart beats pound in my ears.

"We will both survive this," he says.

It is a beautiful lie.

CHAPTER 11

*W*hen we finally emerge from Nathaniel's room, we're dressed but beyond hungry.

Nathaniel wears a fresh set of black pants and a new short-sleeved shirt. He creates a sling for me out of a clean shirt and helps me put it on so it will be harder to accidentally use my sore arm.

I'm dressed in the human training gear that I'm sure will only invite their anger, since it will look like I'm trying to be one of them, but I have no other clothing options. I also have no choice but to put on the boots that are still coated in blood and dust, but Nathaniel cleans them for me first.

He surprises me when he pulls on a weapon harness, slipping a sword into the carry pouch across his back and also attaching three daggers.

He holds out a harness to me and helps me pull it on, clipping it beneath my sling before we retrieve the dagger and sword from my armor and he slips them into the harness for me —the sword at my back and the daggers where I can reach them with my left arm.

"Are you sure about this?" I ask him. "Me walking through Null carrying weapons like this could invite conflict."

"Our conflict already exists," he says. "I understand their anger, but I won't tolerate it."

My stomach growls loudly. I take hold of Nathaniel's hand to keep him safe from the glitter bulbs as he pulls me toward the door.

Shaking off his anger, he gives me a smile. "Let's go steal some food."

"What should we do about the bulbs?" I ask before we reach the door. "We can't leave them floating around outside."

"We could bring them inside," he suggests. "That way, they'll be contained."

"Okay." I laugh, picturing him chasing them across the porch. "But I'll be holding one of your hands to keep you safe, and I can't use my right arm. Will you be able to catch them all by yourself?"

He shrugs. "It will be like chasing bubbles." His free hand darts out in demonstration toward the nearest one, taking hold of it in a firm grip. "See? Easy as—"

A shock of light passes across his hand, shooting down his arm and across his chest so quickly that it bites my side where I'm pressed against him.

"Nathaniel!"

He freezes where he stands, his inhalation interrupted, his breath held as he stares at the bulb.

He exhales with a sharp question. "What is this?"

Inside the bulb, images swirl and shift.

The white light blazing across the bulb's surface clears, turning into steam that rises from a firehorse's nostrils. The animal's body is slick with sweat and fear. The saddle on its back is empty other than the gleaming halberd attached to the harness that rests around the horse's belly.

As its full body comes into view, the weight of a man drags across the moonlit ground beside it, his booted foot caught in the stirrups.

"This is the night my father died. Why is it showing me this?" Nathaniel grips the bulb so tightly that his fingers are becoming bloodless, so tightly, he might crush it.

Sliding my hand along his arm, I try to pry his fingers loose, worried about the destructive power inside the bulb.

More worried about the effect of the painful memory on him.

"Don't..." I whisper. "Don't watch it."

His father's body bumps across the stones leading up to the outer wall of the Fell castle, lit by the firelight flickering from lamps along the path.

A shout rises up from the battlements, so loud in the silence of the hut that I jolt.

Inside the bulb, the castle gate's large, iron spikes rise. A boy runs through the opening, darting to the man's side while the shouting continues above him. The boy has to be Nathaniel. I recognize his dark hair and eyes.

He's carrying a dagger that he uses to cut through the stirrups in one deft move before he drops to his father's side with a shout. "Where are you hurt?" His dark eyes are wild with fear. "Tell me!"

His father grabs Nathaniel's shoulders and draws him closer. The older man's voice is a bare rasp, fading with every breath. "Nathaniel... remember... when I die... it is up to you to keep the light."

Young Nathaniel's eyes widen. His shout breaks my heart. "No! You can't die!"

He struggles against his father's hold, but the older man grips him with bloody hands, his voice becoming stronger. An order that only a king can give. "Nathaniel! You will promise to carry out my final wishes."

Nathaniel's eyes fill with tears as he grabs his father's arms, but Nathaniel becomes still, no longer fighting. "Tell me what you ask. I will do it."

His father exhales slowly, his strength visibly failing. "Find the girl... with hair whiter than bone... Give this... back to her. Tell her... she doesn't belong to them."

"I don't understand. What girl? Why?"

"She has the power to turn the war. She has the power..."

Dark light washes across young Nathaniel's body, casting him into shadow. Mathilda appears behind him, her arms outstretched, her skirt swishing around her legs as if she just arrived in time to hear the king's last words.

"No! Tobias!" She bends to Nathaniel's father, but the older man's eyes are already vacant.

The tumult of sound inside the bulb stops and the image fades.

I stare at the glittering emptiness it leaves behind. "Nathaniel... I'm sorry."

His gaze is bleak. "That was the day our paths first crossed. Yours and mine."

Suddenly agitated, he turns to the other bulbs, his eyes narrowed as he snatches another orb out of the air.

There's a flash of color inside the bulb, another set of images, these ones disappearing so quickly that I can't catch them, but Nathaniel seems to recognize them immediately.

He grabs another bulb with the same effect, dropping it just as fast.

"All of these are painful memories," he says. "All of them are moments in time that brought me to you. The ripples of my life keeping me on the path to find you."

He releases the last bulb, dropping it to the floor as his gaze burns mine. "These bulbs aren't here because of you. They're here for *me*, to remind me what I need to do, to keep me on my path."

He steps away from the bulbs so that I can safely release his arm. The bulbs he touched are all piled in the corner of the room now, except for one, which has floated toward the table.

Cautiously, I reach for it, closing my fingers around it. Rather than bursting into images, the surface softens, transforming at my touch into a living daisy with pure white petals and a bright golden center.

I crush it slowly in my fist.

The day Nathaniel's father—Tobias—died was the day I woke up. Nathaniel's future was determined by his father's final words while my future was spent trying to understand my past.

Dropping the broken flower onto the table, I turn to press my hand against Nathaniel's heart, hoping to remind him that his heart is still beating, that he is not alone.

He's tense beside me. "I handed you the stone yesterday, but I was supposed to make sure you took it. My father told me to give it back to you."

Taking a deep breath, Nathaniel draws away from me, crosses to the mantelpiece, and returns with the small wooden box he showed me yesterday. I refused to touch it and we left it here when we went to find Christiana.

My response is sharp. "I don't want it."

He pauses, his arm half-outstretched toward me before he lowers it, the box gripped in his fist.

He studies my face. "I saw your fear of this stone yesterday, Aura. Why are you afraid of it?"

"I don't know," I whisper, taking a step back. I shake my head, trying to verbalize my feelings. "Because it feels like staring into an abyss. Like the *nothing* that I remember before I woke up for the first time at the burn site."

When I took Nathaniel to the burn site where my first memories began, I told him that I was born on that spot, a fully-formed seven-year-old girl. I remembered nothing from my life before I first woke up that night, but the *nothing* I remember is a vast, endless space. The same nothing that surrounds me when I sleep.

"I felt your nothing," Nathaniel says, surprising me. "This morning while I lay in the arena."

I shiver, trying to forget the way I tried to save him, only to watch him lie still. "You stopped breathing."

"Just like you stopped breathing at the burn site on our first day," he says, his gaze piercing mine. "And again when you were tied up this morning."

He takes a step toward me, the stone still gripped in his fist. "We've both stopped breathing, just like we both suffer the same wounds, but neither of us has died."

He wants to know *how*. I can see it in his eyes. Among all of the questions we already have, this might be the most confronting.

"How can any living creature stop breathing and remain alive?" he asks.

I take a step back. "I don't know how it's possible or why it happens."

"Maybe we'll never know." Nathaniel sidesteps to the table and places the box on it. "But I'm not afraid of this stone, and I don't think you should be, either. I'll show you why."

One by one, he removes his weapons from the harness resting around his torso and then the harness itself before he takes off his shirt, laying it neatly on the table beside his weapons.

"I told you yesterday that I've carried this stone with me every day since my father died," he says. "But I didn't tell you that I carried it next to my heart. It gave me strength when I didn't have any."

He opens the box.

The glittering, crescent-shaped fragment of stone glints at us. It's the same shape as both of our scars. The same shape as the jewel that Imatra dropped in my dream.

The moment I see it, an abyss opens up in front of me, as if the box is the gateway to a deep, frozen void, but Nathaniel picks up the stone without any hesitation.

He fits it to his thumb, showing me before he presses it across the location of his heart right below his new scar.

I gasp when the stone fits to his skin, molding itself to the curve of his chest as if it's part of his body. The rock conforms so completely that I can't even see its edges.

Light glows softly through his skin, a single ripple from the stone, the same golden light I saw shining from his chest when he defended me against the hunters yesterday. Then it vanishes and I can't see where the stone rests anymore. It's as if the rock has disappeared into his skin.

I cast glances from side to side, peering at the location of his scar. "It's *stone*. How does it do that?"

"It changes consistency when I touch it," he says, watching me carefully. "It turns from hard stone into soft material. It stuck to my hand the first time I held it. After that, I didn't want to lose it. It was the last piece of my father, so I kept it close. A memory. My promise to honor his final words."

He peels the stone from his chest, leaning forward, meeting my eyes, his own so dark that it scares me. "I promised him I would give it back to you. I think this stone is a piece of your life. Will you take it?"

My ears hum as he holds the rock out to me. The chasm inside me widens. The cold dark threatens to swallow me. It's an irrational fear. Nathaniel kept this tiny piece of rock safe all these years by carrying it next to his heart. It's the last connection with his father, but he's willing to give it to me—to complete his promise.

"Don't be afraid of your past," he murmurs, searching my eyes.

I step away from him. "I want you to keep it."

"Aura—"

"Just a bit longer. Please?"

A crease appears in his forehead. He looks perplexed by my request, but he nods before he positions the rock back on his chest. He pulls his shirt and weapons back on.

He holds out his hand to me with a smile that eases the tension between us. "Ready to hold my hand while I herd bubbles?"

I return his smile, taking his hand as we head to the door.

Outside, the path around Nathaniel's hut is quiet and empty. The village itself is also calm and still. In the distance, I make out the humans gathered in the courtyard, practicing their drills.

Directly in front of us on the porch, the glitter bulbs continue to spin gently and harmlessly in the air. They float toward us, bumping softly against Nathaniel's bare arms, the weapons on his chest, and even his face.

Each one contains light and dark, shapes that form and vanish, flashes of power and moments of emptiness.

He closes his eyes for a moment. If each bulb contains a painful memory for him, then his humor about herding them is forced. A bravery I wish he didn't feel he had to maintain in front of me.

He's careful at first, then impatient, as he pushes the bulbs inside his hut.

I bite my lip and hide my smile as he starts batting them inside, the tension in his shoulders easing and his smile becoming real, as if punching his painful memories is somehow cathartic.

He gives me a wonky laugh when he steps on one and nearly loses his balance. All the time, he continues to hold my left hand with his left hand, which means I'm facing the empty path while he attempts to pivot on the spot so he doesn't wrench me around.

One of the bulbs floats past my right hand where my fingers peek out of the sling. I poke my forefinger at it to push it along, surprised when colors flash across its surface.

For a second, a soft light dances through the bulb. A playful form, not quite humanoid or fae, skips across the surface, whispering softly. Darkness sprinkled with tiny lights surrounds the moving glow.

I stare at it in surprise, but the image quickly fades as Nathaniel plucks the bulb from the air in front of me.

Pushing it inside the hut, he gives me a victorious grin before he pulls the door closed.

"Food," he says. "I'm starving."

Just as we reach the bottom step, Mathilda appears on the path ahead of us, her violet dress swishing around her legs, her pelt flying as she races toward us.

"Nathaniel!"

He grips my hand tightly, a warning to stay where I am, as he positions himself slightly in front of me, his expression anything but welcoming. "What is it?"

Mathilda draws to a stop several paces away, smart enough not to invade Nathaniel's space.

Her quick gaze passes across my sling, my clothing, and my

loose hair before lingering on the still-healing cuts on my face—all of the bruises that must be visible now that the dirt and blood have washed off.

Then her focus flickers across the empty porch behind us.

She swallows visibly, as if she's trying to overcome her pride. "I need your help."

CHAPTER 12

$\mathcal{N}$athaniel gives Mathilda a dark look. "Helping you can wait. We need to eat."

He strides in the direction of the far path, aiming to steer a track around the witch while I follow closely. I'm comfortable letting him decide our actions right now.

Mathilda steps up to him. "Please. I'll have food brought to Christiana's hut. This can't wait."

Nathaniel is a wall of tension, the unforgiving line of his lips hardening so quickly that Mathilda steps away from him again.

When I first encountered her yesterday, she was angry and full of vengeance, calling me a fae weapon, insisting that I should be killed. When Nathaniel defended me with full force, she appeared shocked, as if he rarely went against her wishes. Now she looks uncertain, as if she's not sure where she stands.

"Christiana's hut?" His next questions are short and sharp. "Who needs help? You or her?"

Mathilda chews her lip nervously. "Both of us."

I squeeze Nathaniel's hand, urging him to look at me. I don't feel comfortable voicing my thoughts in front of Mathilda, but I don't want him to make decisions that alienate his people even more than he already has.

He reads my face as if he hears my thoughts, the hard edges of his expression softening, but his glare increases as he turns back to Mathilda. "We will come with you, but if you or anyone in this camp tries to hurt Aura, I will end you." He steps up to her as she backs away. "Even if I have to break my promise to my father to do it. At some point, it will be time to stop keeping the light."

She pales. "I broke your trust. I should have protected your wife."

"Yes, you should have."

She gives him a stiff nod of agreement before she turns on her heel.

Nathaniel murmurs to me as we stride after her. "Christiana's hut is closest to the training ground. She wanted it that way. She was always the first to start training each day and the last to stop." He sighs, some of the tension exhaling from his body. "Our mother's legacy was hard for her to live up to."

"If Christiana wasn't forced into this life, what would she have done?" I ask, suddenly wondering the same about myself. If I'd been given a true choice, would I have ended up right where I am?

Nathaniel contemplates my question before he responds. "When we were young, she loved spending time in the greenhouse," he says. "She liked to make things grow."

"Not a natural killer then," I say.

He nods. "She wasn't always so tough."

I squeeze his hand. "You have to forgive her, Nathaniel."

He shakes his head in disagreement. "When I was lying in the arena, not breathing but somehow alive... I heard my people —the people I was fighting for—shouting for your blood. They wanted Cyrian to hurt you."

He suddenly grips my arm, his touch firm and determined as he pulls me to a stop. "I heard your screams when my sister tied you to that pole. If I could have moved my body in that moment, she would not still be walking this earth."

The blood drains from my face at the raw anger in his voice.

"You don't mean that." I can't be the source of conflict between him and his sister. I unwittingly placed myself in that position when I ended their mother's life, but I won't accept that I have to remain a trigger between them. "Yesterday, you nearly died trying to free her. She's family, Nathaniel. You have to fight for her—"

"To what end?" he asks. "If I give my sister her freedom—if I give my people their freedom—what will they do with it? Will they continue to spill blood out of vengeance?"

"They won't," I say, not certain I'm speaking the truth or that I believe it.

All I can believe is what Nathaniel once said to me. "You told me that humans are capable of both darkness and light. I've seen both in them. Your people may have been screaming for my blood, but Hagan tried to stop Cyrian from hurting me. The man I least expected to defend me was willing to accept his death on my behalf. Darkness *can* turn to light." I will Nathaniel to believe me. "You can't give up on your sister or your people."

Nathaniel's palm brushes my cheek, a crease forming in his forehead. He doesn't reject or embrace my statement. The weight of his thoughts settles around me as he remains silent, taking my hand as we resume walking along the path.

Mathilda veers off the track ahead of us just as she promised, ducking into the kitchen and emerging swiftly with a small basket of freshly baked bread smothered in butter and slabs of cheese.

Nathaniel and I inhale the food as we walk and the basket is empty within minutes. It's just enough sustenance to take the edge off my hunger, but I'm dying for a hot meal.

Walking toward Christiana's hut means heading toward the courtyard, where the trainees are practicing their drills. They're dueling with partners now, so that many of them face in our direction.

Esther strides among them, shouting orders, her golden hair flowing past her shoulders.

Yesterday, I thought she was beautiful. I still do, but there is an edge of fear in her posture now that wasn't there before.

Her beige clothing hugs her curves as she moves along the back row closest to us, her voice raised as she addresses the trainees. "We need to be prepared for a future where our lives are ruled by fae. They may control magic, but they derive their power from their environment. It takes them a few seconds to build enough power to strike. Those are the seconds that you can use to kill them."

My stomach sinks as I listen to her instructing the trainees how to end my people. I understand why she's doing it. If Nathaniel dies in the final fight, then she needs to prepare the humans to fight for their survival.

As Hagan said, Cyrian may be brutal, but he needs them. Imatra will eradicate them.

The four teenagers I sat with at lunch yesterday—Emily, Tom, and the twins with red hair—are turned in my direction while Esther shouts. They weren't present when I was tied up this morning. The last time they saw me, my hair was black and I wore Nathaniel's golden mark across my face.

Now I am mark-free and very obviously fae with my whiter-than-bone hair falling down my back.

Emily's shoulders sink as she looks my way. I can't imagine the inner turmoil and confusion the teens must be feeling. Nathaniel, whom they love and look up to like an older brother, has made it clear he trusts me—a deadly fae with a murderous reputation—over his own people. I'm not sure how any of them can sort through that in their minds and find their way through the conflict it creates.

Esther pauses when she sees Nathaniel and me, her gaze wary as she takes in my clothing, the sling around my arm, and my bruised face, the same cautious consideration that Mathilda gave me.

But she doesn't stop speaking. "Make no mistake: The fae can be killed. They bleed, die, and hurt just like we do. *We* will hunt *them*."

I understood the reason for her instructions before she saw me, but now it feels personal. Nathaniel tenses beside me and nearby Mathilda hovers at the bottom of the steps to Christiana's hut. Mathilda's eyes widen with alarm as she glances between Nathaniel and Esther.

Nathaniel's jaw clenches and the tension increases around us.

"Don't give up on them, huh?" He growls beneath his breath.

I push hard at my own frustration, determined to keep my anger under control.

If it weren't for the Law, I could challenge Esther right now —one-handed and with no power—and demonstrate just how hard it is to kill a fae.

I would make it clear that she shouldn't be inciting any of the humans to seek a fight with a fae. But not only would I risk my own life if I hurt her, it would only make Nathaniel's people hate and fear me more.

Nathaniel could pulverize Esther and every single one of these trainees, but again, that would get us nowhere.

I grip his hand as his frustration simmers.

"Let it pass," I say. "What happens at dawn will determine the future, not this."

The muscle ticks in his jaw, but he gives me a terse nod.

Mathilda carefully makes her way up the steps, remaining in view as she steps inside.

The hut is set out similarly to Nathaniel's—a living area complete with kitchen on the right-hand side while two other rooms are situated on the left, both doors closed.

Christiana sits at the kitchen table near the far right wall. She has changed out of her armor and wears—to my surprise—a simple dress.

Her expression is blank, but it's hard to miss the red rims around her eyes.

I consider her carefully, wondering how long she was crying.

Hagan stands in the shadows behind her, leaning quietly against the far wall. He doesn't make any move other than a quick assessment of my sling and facial bruising.

A quick glance tells me that nobody else is present inside the hut.

Mathilda tiptoes into the room ahead of us before she points. "That floated in here a few minutes ago."

A glitter bulb rests in the middle of the floor.

Mathilda presses up against the wall beside the door, staying as far away from the bulb as possible.

I consider it with surprise. I didn't expect more bulbs to arrive.

"We don't know what to do," Mathilda whispers, while Christiana remains silent and still, a tense form at the table. "Even the vibrations in the floor could set it off. My magic is useless now, but you walked through the bulbs without harm—"

Nathaniel's expression is hard, his question clipped as he cuts Mathilda off. "At whose feet did it land?"

"M-Mine." Mathilda falters. "It followed me inside. Why does that matter?"

Nathaniel is suddenly a simmering tower of rage, plowing

across the room toward her. His boots thud against the floor, causing vibrations that ripple dangerously through the bulb's surface.

Mathilda screams, staring in fear at the bulb. "Stop moving!"

Nathaniel's shout cracks around her. "What did you do?"

She backs away from him, sliding along the wall, paler than pale. "What are you talking about?"

I remain where I am, surprised by Nathaniel's sudden anger, ready to step in if I need to.

"These bulbs reveal our memories," he says, pointing back at it. "They are moments of pain that we want to forget, but every single one of them leads to Aura."

He gives a harsh laugh. "That's why there were a hundred of them outside my door. But you've never had anything to do with Aura. Or so I thought. So tell me—*witch*—what did you do?"

"I..." Her eyes are wide, her lips pursed. She inhales. Exhales. Her speech becomes panicked and suddenly rapid. "It wasn't my fault. I never told her to do it. I didn't even think it was possible. It was just an idea. A stupid, silly, childish idea. I was sure she would forget all about it like she forgot about me. I wasn't sure she'd done it until yesterday!"

"What are you talking about?" Nathaniel's voice lowers. "*Who* are you talking about?"

Mathilda shakes her head, her eyes wild. "No. I can't..."

"You have to face your past, Mathilda."

"It wasn't my fault," she whispers. "I was young... She was my friend... I never dreamed..."

Nathaniel's expression remains hard. "The bulb will show us the truth. Aura can help you defuse the bulb, but only after you face your memories."

Christiana's chair slowly swishes back as she rises. Her bare feet are quiet, her steps careful as she crosses the floor to take Mathilda's hands.

"We've all done things we regret," she says, glancing at Nathaniel. "I will help you, Mathilda."

Christiana turns fully to Nathaniel. "What does Mathilda need to do?"

"She has to take Aura's hand before she touches the bulb. Aura will keep her safe so we can see whatever memory the bulb contains."

Trying to make it as easy for Mathilda as possible, I cross the floor to the bulb, stand beside it, and hold out my hand.

That way, she doesn't have to touch me longer than necessary. The last time Mathilda made contact—grabbed me around the neck, to be precise—she was trying to kill me.

Christiana leads her to me, placing Mathilda's hand in mine while Christiana supports Mathilda's other elbow.

Nathaniel moves to my side as Mathilda bends to the bulb and we all lower to the floor with her, kneeling in a circle. Hagan remains exactly where he is, leaning against the far wall.

Mathilda's hands shake.

I never imagined I would see such a proud, powerful woman as herself so broken down that she struggles to move. I can't tell if it's shame, guilt, or grief that is pulling her down like this.

A streak of light shoots across her hand as soon as she touches the bulb, the same as it did for Nathaniel.

I'm prepared for the bite of energy as it travels through her body into mine. Taking a deep breath, I calm myself and anchor the glitter bulb's power like a grounding force so it doesn't kill her.

Inside the bulb, the streak of light dissolves into tiny pinpricks that become a starry night sky filling the space above a cliff face.

A tower sits at the edge of the cliff, overlooking the crashing ocean.

It's not as tall as the towers that make up Imatra's palace in Bright, but its sides are jagged and it rises to a point at the top. Two landing pads extend out on either side of it about a third from the top. Both ledges of jutting stone stretch out into space far enough that the Vanem Dragon himself could land on either of them.

Two girls sit at the base of the tower, right on the cliff's edge. Their legs dangle over the rocky precipice while the sea water splashes high enough up the cliff to wet their bare feet.

Despite the night sky around them, the colors inside the image are overly vibrant, as if parts of the memory are stronger than others.

One girl is a younger version of Mathilda, her hair just as wildly black as it is now, her dress a faded red, patched at the side.

The other girl is slender, clothed in a glittering blue dress with bright blue delphiniums tucked into her glistening blood-red hair, highlighting her azure blue eyes and porcelain skin.

I gasp, shock running through me as I recognize the other girl.

It's Imatra.

CHAPTER 13

*N*athaniel asks the question that I'm too surprised to speak aloud. "What in all the dark stars are you doing with the Fae Queen?"

Mathilda is tense. "We were friends. That was before she became the Queen of Bright."

Nathaniel makes a harsh sound in the back of his throat. "And you think of *me* as a traitor because of my relationship with Aura?"

Christiana also appears shocked by Mathilda's revelation, casting glances at Mathilda, a new wariness settling over her face.

Against the far wall, Hagan has also become alert, but his focus shifts to Christiana.

Nathaniel's sister swallows visibly before she asks Mathilda, "What tower is that?"

"It's the Spire," Mathilda replies. "Your father would have taken you there if he'd lived. It's the only neutral territory between Bright and Fell. A place filled with old magic. It's where your father called on the Vanem Dragon before the final battle."

Inside the image, young Mathilda waves her hand across the air.

Dark light flickers around her fingertips until she opens her fist and allows the light to waft toward Imatra, who snatches it out of the air with a laugh.

Imatra promptly releases the dark light, her lips pursed in anticipation as she peers upward, watching the light float out past the cliff's edge.

Young Mathilda waves her hand again, pointing at something outside the perimeter of the bulb, but the image sputters, disintegrates, and suddenly vanishes, leaving a bright wash of white light behind.

Nathaniel leans back on his heels. "That's it?"

Mathilda doesn't answer, her fingers slowly unclenching from around the bulb.

Her shoulders relax, relief crossing her face before she replaces it with a blank expression. "That's all there is to see."

I study her as she tugs her hand from mine without looking at me.

The memory ended too quickly, was too short, and Mathilda seems far too relieved, as if she'd been expecting to see something much worse.

I wonder what could be worse than sharing dark magic with the Fae Queen?

"You taught Imatra how to use dark magic," I say.

Cold dread rises inside me. Imatra has always been the most powerful fae, controlling all of the elements of the seasons—ice, fire, water, earth.

Or... at least... *appearing* to control them.

But if she knows dark magic, then how much of her power is fae and how much is dark magic disguised as fae magic?

I close my eyes as I remember the fae children who died

because they were infected with the Ebon Rot—an illness caused by dark magic.

My adoptive father, Crispin, told me that five boys had died from the illness so far. Girls had become sick, too, but I healed them.

"What did you teach her?" I demand to know.

"Basic magic. That's all." Mathilda holds her head high, her eyes defiant. She's in control again.

"You're lying," I whisper, my mind churning. "You taught her more. In fact... you taught her something you shouldn't have, didn't you? You said it yourself, you gave her an idea. What was it? And what does it have to do with me?"

Nathaniel seems certain that the bulbs are connected to me. It worries me that Mathilda's past could have had some impact on my life.

Mathilda presses her lips together before she replies smoothly, "Imatra brought me apples—real ones. We talked about our countries and our lives. We were friends for a year and then she stopped coming to the Spire. I never saw her again."

"I don't believe you—"

"Mathilda did what you wanted." Christiana interrupts me, wrapping her arm around Mathilda's shoulders in a protective gesture.

She couldn't hide her worry before, but I guess her distrust of me runs deeper than her shock about Mathilda's past.

"You saw what we all saw: Two girls talking," Christiana says to me. "I'm as surprised as you are that they were friends at all, but it was a long time ago. It's in the past. Now, will you help us get rid of this bulb or not?"

The image was so brief—an innocent picture like Christiana said.

Two girls sitting together. And yet... Mathilda was so upset about it before she saw it; real, paralyzing fear that tells me there's more she doesn't want us to know, a connection with me that she's hiding.

Nathaniel is quiet beside me, but when I glance at him, I sense his thoughts like a compulsion.

We need to leave.

The bulb won't show us anything more—and Mathilda is close-lipped now—so I wrap my fingers around its glittering surface.

It rapidly transforms into a black petunia, its rounded petals and sunken center dusted with silver speckles that remind me of the night sky hanging behind the cliffs in the vision.

"This bulb won't hurt anyone now," I say, crushing the flower in my hand and holding it close to my side as I stand. I'll need to take it with me or the humans will continue to fear it.

Christiana draws Mathilda away from me, sitting her down in the nearest chair while Nathaniel inclines his head toward the door, confirming that I read his thoughts correctly. It's time to leave.

"We're done here," he says to his sister.

She watches him walk away as if she can't believe he's actually turning his back on her.

His big form fills the door as I follow behind, ready to step out onto the porch.

She rushes after us, veering wide when she nearly collides with me. "Nathaniel, wait!"

He only half-turns, a forbidding form.

Christiana wraps her arms around herself. I'm reminded of my first impression of her yesterday. Up close, she seems somehow smaller, more fragile than the tough facade she puts up.

She grips her own arms, turning her knuckles white with the pressure. "I fucked up. Really badly."

Nathaniel remains where he is, his expression unreadable, his hair falling across his face. "Is that your idea of an apology?"

"Hagan told me what happened during the fight," she says, her gaze flicking to me. "And what happened after it. He told me what Aura went through to save you. But... she's fae. She's bound to fight you. And I... I don't know what to think. Or do."

Nathaniel's response is a low growl. "You have two choices, Christiana. You can stay here, protected, and wait for news about the outcome of the fight. Or you can take a risk and come see the fight for yourself."

Christiana's chest rises and falls, suddenly rapid. "Those are my only two choices? I won't accept that's all I can do. If you die—"

"If I die, then you'll have much harder decisions ahead of you. To fight or to hide. But I can tell you this—it will be up to Aura whether or not she protects you from her queen. She might be your only ally among the fae. You should have considered that before you hurt her."

He reaches for my hand, drawing me outside, his boots a soft thud as he continues to walk away from his sister.

He's being hard on her—harder than I expected him to be—but I have to trust that he knows what he's doing.

I never considered the choices that would be ahead of me if I win. Without Nathaniel, his people will be vulnerable. I can see now that Nathaniel is thinking through the scenarios that could occur if he dies, just as I'm thinking through the scenarios after my own death.

Christiana stares after him, wide-eyed, stricken, and pale as she hurries after us. "How can you take the hand of the woman who could kill you?"

Nathaniel exhales, closing his eyes for a moment.

Turning back to his sister, he says, "Because Aura Lucidia is prepared to risk her own life for mine. She chose to become *my* shield. That's more than I can say for anyone else."

Christiana inhales sharply, but not with indignation. Her eyes fill with tears and she bites her trembling lip.

I know barely any of their family history, but I know that Nathaniel bargained for her safety years ago. He gave up his throne to guarantee her protection. He even bargained for Hagan's life.

He was more than Cyrian's champion. He was his people's protector too.

"I've been your shield for far too long, Christiana," he says, his demeanor finally softening. "I gave you freedom to rage against the past, to scorch whatever earth you wanted to scorch, but that meant you didn't have to make difficult choices. Now you need to choose a path. You have to decide who you are and what you stand for. I can't make those decisions for you."

He turns away from her and doesn't look back.

Christiana doesn't try to follow us, remaining quiet as Nathaniel leads me away.

A little farther along, he pauses on the path, asking that I walk beside him, as an equal.

"How long will it take Treble to fly to the western coast?" he asks once we've left the hut behind.

"About an hour," I say. "You want to go to the Spire?"

"My parents were supposed to take me there. Going without them never felt right, so I avoided it. But we need answers." He stops me on the empty path, gripping my hand while the crushed flower still rests inside my fist.

"Aura, you're the only one who can walk through the glitter field unharmed. It's connected to you somehow. The fact that glitter bulbs are suddenly floating all over Bright and Fell—right before our final fight—can't be a coincidence. These bulbs, and the memories they contain, are here for a reason. We have to piece it together."

"Nathaniel... What if you're wrong? What if it has nothing to do with me?" I ask. "The bulbs... The glitter field..."

He shakes his head vehemently, thumping his fist across the location of his heart, where he carries the stone. "The bulb reminded me to give you this stone. Even if you don't want it, it's an important part of your past."

He raises my clenched fist, the crushed petunia petals peeking from between my fingers. "*This bulb* did not arrive by chance. Mathilda's hiding something and we need to know what it is."

"You were going to show me your country," I say, a gentle reminder. "We have a choice right now too."

He lets go of my fist, running his hand through his hair. "I thought I could forget about everything else. I thought I could let it all go, all of the questions. But you need to know what really happened during the last battle between our people—and so do I. I want to push it aside, but I need to make peace with my past."

I stare at the crushed flower in my fist, the tiny pinpricks of silver like miniscule stars dusting its surface. "I want nothing more than to cling to every remaining minute with you," I say, raising my eyes to his. "But you're right. Our path has been painful and dangerous from the start. Stepping away from it feels like running away. I have no idea if going to the Spire will tell us anything."

I give him a determined smile. "Either we will find the truth or we won't, but we have to try."

CHAPTER 14

*N*athaniel pulls me into a sudden hug, excruciatingly warm and trusting, before he draws back with a sudden and determined grin. "First, we need food. This way. If anyone interrupts us again, I will end them."

Sneaking into the kitchen is far less traumatic than it could have been.

Nathaniel pauses when we come across Maggie standing at the center table kneading bread. Her hair is tied into a tight bun now, her face smeared with flour.

She doesn't look up, although a small smile crosses her face before she says, "On the end of the table. Help yourselves. Nobody's due to come in here for another hour at least, so you won't be interrupted."

A basket sits on the table and the scent of stew nearly makes my knees buckle.

I slide into the chair nearest to the door, quickly pulling out the bowls, cutlery, more fresh bread and stew, and fresh fruit.

"Thank you, Maggie," I say.

Like the bread we ate earlier, we consume the food at speed.

When we're finished, Nathaniel prowls around the kitchen gathering more food—biscuits, cheese, bread rolls, and fruit. He also fills two water flasks before he unhooks a satchel that hangs beside the door and slips the provisions inside the bag.

Maggie finishes her task, wipes her hands on her apron, and approaches me with a no-fuss expression. She checks over my face and then my sling. "Your wounds are as clean as they can be, so that's good," she says.

I take her hand before she can step away. "Thank you for speaking up for me this morning."

She sinks into the chair next to mine with a sigh. "My opinion is unpopular. You've stirred up a lot of conflict, but much of it was already bubbling beneath the surface. We've always had two enemies: Cyrian and the fae. Cyrian has been our focus because he was the immediate threat. The Law of Champions has changed that. We don't want to lose Nathaniel."

"Neither do I," I murmur.

She squeezes my hand, searching my eyes. "You are Aura Lucidia, the most feared fae champion in known history. Yet you saved my life. An old peasant woman. Why?"

I smile, attempting to deflect her question. "You're not old."

"But I certainly felt it." She continues to peer into my eyes. "You didn't use dark magic like you said. You used your fae magic on me yesterday, didn't you?"

I nod. "I've healed fae children affected by the Ebon Rot. I didn't know what the illness was until Nathaniel told me about it. I wasn't sure if I could help you, but I'm glad I could."

"Do other fae have the same powers you do?"

I shake my head. "I'm the only Twilight fae. I've always been... different."

She's quiet, her smile fading slowly. "Then... if you die at dawn, the cure dies with you."

Nathaniel returns to my side, the satchel's strap now

securely crossing his torso, and I'm grateful for the inter-ruption.

He places a gentle hand on my shoulder. "We need to keep moving."

Maggie rises with me. "Aura, please tell me one thing: If Queen Imatra gains control of Fell country, should we fight or hide?"

My stomach sinks. I spent seven years as the Queen's cham-pion cutting down any human who approached the border. I called them Fell creatures—creatures of darkness. My people consider their darkness to be contagious. The fae believe that the Fell must be destroyed at all costs.

"It won't come to that," I say.

Beside me, Nathaniel exhales carefully. "Aura speaks now as my wife, Maggie. But as Queen Imatra's champion, I believe she would tell you to hide. You have to survive for as long as you can."

Maggie gives him a firm nod. Fear lingers in the back of her eyes, but her back is straight, determined. "I will keep my son alive."

She hugs Nathaniel, squeezing her eyes closed, hiding her tears as she pulls back. "Please be safe. Both of you."

It's an impossible wish. I shove at my rising emotions as we exit the kitchen. Dealing with Christiana's anger is far easier than facing Maggie's sadness.

I rapidly swallow my tears when Hagan steps from the shadows at the side of the building.

Nothing seems to escape his attention—not the way the back of Nathaniel's hand brushes against mine or the way Nathaniel's gaze passes across my face. Not the tears I'm blinking back, either.

"Nathaniel Exalted," he says, giving Nathaniel a formal bow, the kind that a soldier would give his king.

Hagan is wearing an old black shirt and clean pants, both slightly too small. Only Nathaniel's clothing would fit him properly, but I guess Christiana did what she could.

"I want you to know that I'll travel to the border this evening to witness the fight," he says. "I'll live or die, but I won't hide."

"I didn't expect that you would," Nathaniel says. "I'll see you there, brother."

Nathaniel continues walking, urging me along the path, but Hagan's fist darts out so fast that it's a blur as he grabs Nathaniel's arm.

Nathaniel tenses, but he doesn't retaliate, even though the tension between the two men rises. Even in this place of safety, there is conflict between them.

Nathaniel once saved Hagan's life. Hagan repaid his debt by refusing to kill Nathaniel this morning, but there are years of violent history that can't be forgotten in a day.

"When you fight Aura Lucidia, remember what you're fighting for," Hagan says, his voice a deep rumble. "This is not about you or her. It's not about one death. It isn't even about honor or glory. It's about being the king you were born to be. Remember that."

Turning from Nathaniel, Hagan pins me with his tawny gaze. "How far will you go, Aura Lucidia?" he asks, the question in his eyes demanding honesty.

Yesterday, when Hagan slung me over his shoulder and carried me to the White Walls, he asked me how far I would go to save Nathaniel's life. I told him I would do whatever it took.

Since then, Nathaniel's people have screamed for my blood. They've hurt and restrained me. I could hate them. Maybe I should.

But none of that matters.

What matters to me is that Nathaniel is... *Nathaniel*. He is the only chance for a peaceful future for Bright and Fell. Even if my power is the only cure for the Ebon Rot, I have to believe that his people will recover once Cyrian is no longer draining their life energy.

I know what my path is. I just have to walk it, one step at a time.

"Whatever it takes," I say. "I promise you."

Hagan gives me a solemn nod. "Then I will also keep my promise."

I consider him carefully as he backs away from us. The only promise I remember him making was when I demanded that he decide whether to escape with me this morning.

He told me he would help me, then he would die.

I turn to find Nathaniel studying me as carefully as I scrutinized Hagan.

"What does he mean?" Nathaniel asks, a hint of worry darkening his expression.

"I'm not sure," I say. "I think he means he'll do what's right."

Putting my fingers to my lips, I give two short, sharp whistles, hoping that Treble is listening. I follow the first two whistles with a third, longer one that will tell him everything is okay; he doesn't have to hurry.

His gorgeous blue body ducks beneath the haze for a split second before rising into it again. He won't easily trust the humans after what happened this morning, but that single quick dive will have allowed him to see where I am—also to locate everyone else and decide where it's safe to land.

A moment later, he reappears on the eastern side of Null, gliding silently toward the crop fields there, the farthest point from the trainees. If we're lucky, they won't even see him. He can choose whether or not to crack his wings and he's smart enough to move with stealth right now.

Nathaniel and I hurry to meet him, making our way past Nathaniel's hut. We also pass the stables where Nathaniel's stallion, Flare, is housed safely. My heart hurts as we leave the hut and the horse behind, since this is the last time I'll see them.

Running isn't an option with my injured arm—I'm not a graceful sight even moving at a walk—but we make it to Treble's side within a few minutes. He chose a spot where Mathilda drained the environment so he doesn't crush the remaining food source.

After I pick my way through the final distance to his side, Treble lowers his head to nudge me and then Nathaniel, softly keening a welcome.

"Hello, buddy," Nathaniel says, rubbing Treble's neck. "Ready to fly us into danger?"

Treble bounces his head and rolls his eyes.

"When aren't we flying into danger?" I ask.

As we settle onto Treble's back, I prepare for the flight ahead. Treble sweeps his wings with the minimum of sound, and we rise into the air.

I take a last look across Null. In the distant courtyard, Esther is determined to teach the humans how to kill fae. Christiana will be trying to decide where her allegiance lies. A hundred glitter bulbs are safely contained in Nathaniel's hut.

And Hagan, who was once a hunter, is waiting for his death.

Treble rises beyond the height of the buildings and our view of Null is replaced with a wash of crimson plants and black vines, a magical illusion that protects everyone who lives here.

CHAPTER 15

*I*t takes us over an hour to reach the western coast.

Treble flies above the haze to avoid detection from the ground and takes a wider route so we can avoid the border where the fae squadrons will be located.

The sky is mostly clear in all directions, which allows us to check for distant thunderbirds, but toward the end of the flight, clouds have started gathering in the north closer to Bright.

It's unlikely that the fae will fly across the border into the haze, but even so, I remain on alert.

It's mid-afternoon by the time we reach the edge of the mist and can see the western coast ahead.

I inhale salt, a strange taste on my tongue after the humid air beneath the haze, while the soft sound of crashing waves fills my ears, making my senses buzz.

"It's the ocean!" I call to Nathaniel.

"Have you seen it before?" he asks, his bristly chin grazing my ear as he leans closer to plant a kiss on my cheek.

"Only from a distance," I say. "You can see the coast from the western mountains where I grew up, but I've never flown this close to it before. My border patrols were always concentrated on the central border and I couldn't stay away from Imatra for long enough to fly out here."

I never had an excuse to fly so far toward the water itself, let alone to the Spire.

"What about you?" I ask. "You said you've never visited the Spire, but what about the ocean?"

"I've never seen it before." I hear the smile in his voice as he drops another kiss, this time on my neck, light touches as he leans forward.

My own smile fades as I check our location again. The glitter field is a visible boundary on our right, miles wide and extending all of the way up to the coastline. We need to make sure we stay on the Fell side of it.

In the distance, the Spire has come into view, a majestic tower rising up from the rocky cliff's edge, the landing pads extending from both sides of it taking on the appearance of slender branches stretching out from a solid trunk.

I sense a change in the air around us—a shift in the air pressure—but I'm not sure what's causing it. Possibly the tower itself.

"We have to be careful," I say, turning again so I don't have to shout for Nathaniel to hear me. "The Border Guards patrol all along the glitter field. They shouldn't come near the Spire, but it's safer if we stay out of sight after we land."

Treble circles around the tower as we search for the spot where Mathilda and Imatra met at the base of the tower—a small ledge right at the cliff's edge.

"It's too narrow to land," I call.

"The other side is surrounded by the glitter field," Nathaniel says. "Let's land on the southern wing." He points upward to the platform on the right-hand side of the Spire—the one pointing in the direction of Fell country. "We can find a way down inside the tower."

Treble quickly rises before he coasts to a quiet stop in the middle of the platform.

Far below us, the ocean waves crash against the rocks, a lulling ebb and flow, but my senses are heightened, my instincts alert. I shiver and Nathaniel closes his arms tighter around my waist.

"This is a place of old magic," Nathaniel says as he rises with me. "If I remember correctly, blood can't be shed here. Much of the old law has been forgotten in Fell, but it's alive and strong here. My father taught me some laws before he died but certainly not all of them. We need to proceed carefully."

Descending along Treble's wing, I take cautious steps to the edge of the platform. The base of the tower is at least two hundred feet below us and the place where Mathilda and Imatra sat is a small crevice right at the cliff's edge.

Reaching my side, Nathaniel inhales deeply, a curious crease forming in his forehead. "It smells strange here."

The air contains an odd mix of salt and magic. I tilt my head to gauge the position of the sun, the sky a perfect blue above us. The clear horizon here is more beautiful than the sparkling skyscape above Bright.

"My father spoke to the Vanem Dragon on this ledge," Nathaniel says. "It was a few days before he died. He wanted to ask the dragon if there could ever be peace."

When the Vanem Dragon flew down to the coliseum to seal the Law of Champions, Nathaniel asked the dragon for answers about what really happened on the night his father was killed.

The dragon said he didn't know—on the night of the final battle, his sight became dark. As soon as the sun set, he and the other dragons and thunderbirds couldn't see or move because dark magic took hold of them. They were only released when an explosion of light split the horizon.

The dragon arrived at the border to find Queen Imatra bloodied and weeping, surrounded by the bodies of hundreds of humans and a squadron of fae.

She was holding me in her arms.

"The Vanem Dragon told my father that only great courage would bring an end to war." Nathaniel's dark gaze pins me to the spot, the way his focus on me always makes me feel like I am the center of his life.

Always the point of origin of his decisions.

"We are the ones whose courage will determine whether or not the war ends," he says.

I pull air into my chest, seeking the beat of my heart that tells me I'm alive before I press my hand to his chest.

I want to tell him that it won't be us. It will be *him*. Only if he has the courage to fight and kill me.

Instead, I say, "Yes."

My mouth is dry, my heartbeat too rapid as I step back and incline my head toward the arched opening into the tower. "We need to find whatever answers this tower can give us."

Venturing through the opening, we discover a large alcove that is wide enough for Treble to shelter inside of, so I urge him to come inside instead of flying back into the sky.

Thunderbirds can communicate silently with each other and I'm worried that a patrolling bird might sense Treble's presence. They won't be able to attack him—or us—here, but I'd prefer to avoid detection.

"It's better if you remain here," I say to Treble, stroking his neck. "The Spire is neutral territory, so nothing is allowed to hurt you, but make sure you stay out of sight at all times. Only take to the air if the situation changes and you feel it's safer. We'll be back before the moon rises."

Nathaniel waits for me at the rear of the alcove. A long, wide corridor provides a direct line of sight to the platform on the other side of the tower.

Rooms appear to lead off each side of the corridor and a set of steps is visible in the middle of it, which must go down into the tower itself.

I gasp as I pass the first room. Its walls are inlaid with gold and silver filigree while large golden spyglasses rest on stands in front of wide windows. "What are those spyglasses for?"

Nathaniel walks behind me so we don't lose sight of each other as we venture to the windows.

I brace for the wind to hit us as soon as we step inside, but it's eerily still. Not a breath of air.

After adjusting one of the spyglasses on its hinged stand, I take a look through it.

My breath stills as I make out the mountains behind which Eteri City hides, every detail of the peaks visible to me.

Turning the glass in the other direction, I can see the Misty Gallows at the edge of Fell and the misshapen trees before the mist obscures my view.

Nathaniel peers through the second spyglass, not tilting it to the earth, but up at the sky.

"You could see the stars with these," he murmurs.

I shiver. The spyglass's hinges are well-oiled, the glass itself in perfect condition despite its exposed position, open to the wind and rain.

But the lack of wind in the room indicates that the old magic protects everything from the weather.

More slowly this time, I turn the spyglass to the border, sighting along the glitter field.

As I watch, several bulbs rise up from the field, these ones floating toward Bright. Another shiver runs through me.

The bare, bulb-less stems that remain behind are sharp, pointed at the top. Weapons themselves. There are many of them, indicating that hundreds of bulbs have separated from their stems.

Is it really possible that all of those memories relate to me?

I jolt as a sudden flare of light in the distance catches my attention. Swinging the spyglass back to the crystal peaks that protect the fae city, I seek the source of the flash.

Beside me, Nathaniel has also bent to his spyglass, following the same trajectory as me. "What do you see?" he asks.

A glitter bulb floats into view, drifting toward the crystal peaks in the far distance. The spyglass allows me to see every glimmer across its surface. Another bulb glides beside it. And another...

"I count five bulbs," I whisper.

"I see two more, farther east," Nathaniel says.

The bulbs rise up, higher than the crystal peaks, as if they're going to float over the mountains.

A squadron of thunderbirds suddenly dives from the cloud cover above them.

I recognize Cadence among the birds. She is my brother, Evander's, thunderbird. She's as enormous as Treble but with deep wine-colored wings.

Evander stands up on her back, his arms outstretched. Cadence is flying higher than the bulbs, but she dips for a moment, drawing dangerously close to the cluster of bulbs as a blast of wind rushes from Evander's hands.

The gust rushes around the bulbs, pushing them even closer together.

At the same time, a second thunderbird swoops downward.

I jolt with surprise when I see its rider.

Serena, the Queen's former champion, stands on its back, wearing indigo armor, her amber hair tied back in tight braids.

The last time I saw her, I used my starlight power to defend Nathaniel against her attack. It was her black armor that I stole and wore into Fell country. I'm still wearing her boots.

At the exact moment that the bulbs gather together, her hands shoot out. Firelight rushes through her arms and pours across the cluster of glittering orbs.

The bulbs shatter.

Shards shoot in every direction, cutting through the air around Serena and flying toward Evander.

I can't hear Serena's scream, but I can see the blood spilling down her cheek as she drops to her bird's back and tries to evade the spray of glass.

Evander's wind power rages around her, lifting her bird above the deadly wash, while Cadence cracks her wings at the same time, also soaring above the explosion, taking Evander to safety.

I've stopped breathing, but I force myself to drag air into my chest as the two birds rise again.

Glitter shards crash into the ground far below them, some pieces exploding against the mountain peaks. Others kick up into the air as the thunderbirds evade the aftermath.

A quick scan of the other riders flying thunderbirds tells me that Talsa and Mia are also with them. They are both Dusk fae, with the power to communicate silently with their thunderbirds.

My forehead creases in confusion because Talsa and Mia usually work at night, not at this time of the day.

My eyes narrow when I also identify Calida—the Solstice fae who challenged me for the position of champion—riding her thunderbird close behind Mia. She is one of the Queen's Day

Guards, but she was punished after she tried to stab me in the back.

It's an unusual squadron—a mixture of Sunstream and Eventide fae who wouldn't normally fight together, but all of them are connected with me in some way or another.

My heart kicks as a final deadly shard shoots up into the air toward Cadence's stomach, large enough to cut her from the air.

Calida leans out over the side of her thunderbird and blasts the shard with a stream of fire before it can hit Evander.

All of the birds rise higher into the sky, finally flying beyond the blast radius as the remaining shards continue to explode far below them.

"I can't protect them," I whisper, my hands shaking. I press my palms together to help clamp down on my fear. "They're trying to destroy the glitter bulbs so the bulbs don't reach Bright. They don't understand they should *contain* the bulbs, not try to destroy them."

"Aura." Nathaniel reaches for me. "Your brother's strong. He'll be okay."

"For now." When we escaped from Bright, Evander ran interference between us and the Solstice fae who were attacking us, neutralizing their firelight with his Frost power while making it look like he was on their side.

Even though Imatra told Evander I was responsible for his mother's death, he said he still considered me his sister until he knew the truth.

"The glitter field is coming apart," I whisper, pain striking through my heart, as if tiny slivers of myself are separating. "The dragon said it started when Cyrian invoked the Three Chances. That was right after I—"

I freeze as the memory of Nathaniel's near-death at the White Walls hits me.

My scream. My vow. The same kind of vow I made when I invoked the Law of Champions.

Nathaniel waits for me to continue. He is suddenly very still beside me, the tension in his shoulders increasing. "It was right after you told Cyrian who you are," he says.

A hum grows in my ears, a sense of panic rising inside me. "I screamed my name. I told Cyrian that I was the Fae Queen's champion, destroyer of souls. I swore that if he hurt you, I would destroy him. No matter what price I paid."

I back away from Nathaniel. "What have I invoked now?"

CHAPTER 16

*N*athaniel grips my shoulders. "The Vow of the Avenger, Aura. The same law I invoked so that I could beat your Border Guards on our first morning. But it's not what you think."

"Not what I think? You said yourself that every one of those bulbs contains a painful memory that leads to me. They're trying to float into Bright. Whom are they intended for? Will the price I pay be my brother's life?"

"No." Nathaniel's determined eyes meet mine. "Evander will survive. Vengeance is not about taking revenge on someone, it's about breaking open the truth, revealing the past. That's why we're here. We *will* find the answers about your past and mine."

I want to believe him, but I'm struggling to maintain hope.

The sun will set in another two hours. Time is passing and I can't stop it no matter how desperately I want to. Our next step was to come here, but we don't know what we're looking for.

Nathaniel holds his hand out to me, his dark eyes compelling me to trust him. "We have to keep looking. Will you come with me?"

My answer is certain, the only certainty in my life. "Always. Wherever you go."

We leave the room containing the spyglasses and descend the stairs. The staircase is stone, but it's inlaid with glittering gems.

Torches spring to life as we pass them, lighting up the steps ahead of us. The magic in the Spire is so strong that my skin prickles.

I'm gratified that Nathaniel seems to find it as unsettling as I do. He eyes the fiery torches as we pass them, only relaxing when we reach the bottom of the steps and nothing has leaped out at us or threatened us.

"Mathilda and Imatra are bound to have come inside," I say. "We should look through each of the rooms on our way down."

The stairs let out into another corridor with a floor also inlaid with gems.

At the end of the corridor, a wide window allows the sunlight to shine through, providing natural light along with the burning torches.

One room we pass is pure white—marble walls and floor that remind me of the White Walls where Nathaniel was nearly whipped to death.

I shudder away from it, finding myself staring into a room across the corridor that holds a living flame in the middle of the floor.

The walls here are also white, but golden lettering, the same amber color as the flame, appears and disappears along them.

The writing ebbs and flows. Some sections of writing splash and fade. Some of it pulls and pushes while other sections of lettering race along the entire side of each wall.

As I step closer, a bright light above the doorway catches my eyes. Golden lettering flows across the top of the archway:

The rule of law.

Stepping inside, I try to follow the swiftly flowing lettering, catching a train of writing like catching a thought.

Once invoked, the Law of Champions must be satisfied within three days... One champion must die... The winner takes all on behalf of their queen or king...

The rules of the Law chase each other across the room.

I let them go, catching a different set of writing.

The Vow of the Avenger may only be invoked when pain is undeniable and truth will be revealed...

Daring to step closer to the hot flame in the center of the room, I take in all of the laws.

There are thousands of them. Laws of nature, life, pain, vengeance, even birth and death...

Nathaniel lightly brushes the back of my arm as he pauses beside me, taking in the entire room before he paces across to the right-hand wall, heading toward a spot where dark lettering ebbs and fades like a waning star.

I catch only parts of the message because Nathaniel's body blocks my view of it: *A king betrayed may choose the dangerous path...*

"This room holds all of the old laws," I say, shivering as I study the flame that floats in the middle of the floor.

My voice lowers to a hushed whisper as an idea occurs to me. "Maybe we could destroy it." I spin to Nathaniel. "Or rewrite it?"

He jolts away from the wall he was studying. The writing fades behind him, replaced with new lettering.

"No, Aura. The old law is life itself. To destroy it or try to change it would impact life at its most basic level. Each of these laws has been created over time, intertwining with the existing laws. Some of these laws depend on others. Some prevail over others—or are subservient to them. If we pull a single thread, the whole web could collapse."

I exhale my disappointment. "Then we need to keep moving."

Backing away from the flame, I reach for Nathaniel's hand, leading him out of the room and toward the second set of steps at the end of the corridor.

I pause before we descend into the stairwell. "Wait... What are those?"

To the left of the staircase is another archway leading into the largest room yet.

Four statues stand at intervals in a circle around the room, each facing outward and made of a different material—white stone, crimson wood, brilliant gold, and black onyx.

From where I stand just outside the door, I can only see the front of two of them, but the sunlight glints off their surfaces, a fascinating mix of white, gold, and crimson, backlit with darkness.

I shiver as the light washes over them, the memory of my dream coming back to me—as if the three powers I saw in the dream are clashing in this room.

I check for writing above the archway, but it's a strange mix of symbols that seem to make up four words. The only one I can read is *light*.

"Aura?" Nathaniel's hand is firm around mine, but I tug against his hold.

"I need to see this." I step into the room, surprised to find that the right side of the wall is nearly completely open to the outside—a wall-to-wall window with a wide ledge set at waist height.

Just like the spyglasses room, this one is whisper quiet.

Expanding my senses, I check for threats as I cross to the window and assess the view outside.

Nathaniel is quiet behind me. I turn to find him pacing around the statues, a wary crease forming on his forehead.

He stops in front of the white stone statue, which faces toward the window.

It's the smallest one—a girl wearing a soft dress that floats around her legs, her hair flying free across her shoulders and flowing to one side. Her arms are bent at the elbows, her palms up.

A book rests on her upturned hands.

Following Nathaniel's path around the room, I find that each of the statues holds a book.

The crimson statue is a woman, her head held high, but her gaze lowered. Flowers cascade from the tiara sitting around her head, down through her hair and across her long dress. She is regal, powerful.

The book she holds has blood-red binding with ivory lettering on the front, but I can't read what it says. It's not a language I've seen before.

The onyx statue is a man with a sharp nose. He wears a crown that sits, not on the top of his head, but around his eyes, concealing them. The crown's sharp peaks extend up past his head.

He's wearing a long robe, and he holds a book with black binding, golden lettering spelling out a title that I also can't read. It must be an old language.

I stop in front of the fourth statue, the golden one.

It's another woman, except that she's wearing armor and carries a curved blade strapped to her back, only partially visible.

The words on the cover of the book she holds leap out at me, the first I can read: *Light magic.*

Stepping up to it, I open the book in the middle, surprised when the images on the page leap out at me and move across the parchment.

A huge golden dragon, as large as the Vanem Dragon, breathes deadly fire across a battlefield filled with people.

At first I think the dragon's targets are humans, but the people running toward the dragon are retaliating the same way Serena shot the glitter bulbs from the sky—with fire pouring from their hands, trying to strike the dragon down.

They're fae.

I shake my head in confusion. This can't be right. The fae and dragons have always been allies. They've never fought each other. Not as far as I was told…

A fae woman with amber hair rides ahead of her people, a diamond crown glittering on her head, her sword raised.

Her horse gallops toward the dragon, zigzagging between the plumes of fire that explode across the ground.

The dragon roars again, its deadly flames narrowly missing her.

From behind the dragon, an army of humans runs toward the fae while two more dragons swoop from the sky—also golden, their scales catching the light, their fire lifting off the page and heating the air around my chest and face.

I plant my hands on either side of the pages as the scent of blood and ash fills my head, along with the shouts of a thousand humans, and the earsplitting shriek of dragon's fire colliding with fae magic.

I force myself to turn the page.

The paper is thick parchment, ragged at the edges.

The battle continues to rage across the new pages, slowly moving forward as fae and humans clash and fall, churning the ground into mud.

The Fae Queen evades the dragon's fire at every turn before she takes another run at the majestic creature.

She leaps from her horse, carving a powerful arc toward the

dragon, gaining height as the air carries her forward, her magic streaming around her agile body.

She raises her sword above her head, perfectly aimed to cut through the dragon's neck and end its life.

At the same time, a human woman runs along the dragon's back, a scream on her lips as she throws herself across the space between the dragon and the Fae Queen.

She looks just like the woman in the golden statue.

Her blade slices through the air toward the Queen.

I jolt with shock as I recognize the weapon she's holding: a halberd, its gleaming steel blade etched with the sun and the moon.

The human woman roars as the halberd cuts clean through the Fae Queen's sword, slicing the fae weapon in half before the human woman lands lithely at the dragon's feet.

The Fae Queen twists and somersaults in the air, landing a few paces away.

She retaliates without hesitation, firelight pouring from her hands as she strides toward the human woman.

At lightning speed, the woman tips her weapon, the steel flashing faster than I can see, using the blade to deflect the fiery shots and send them harmlessly into the ground before she leaps higher than a human should be able to, landing precisely in front of the Fae Queen.

Just as she drops to ground, she drives the handle of her weapon into the earth in front of her like a shield.

The Fae Queen pales, screams.

Magic blasts from the human woman's halberd, exploding across the space in front of her, the impact knocking the Queen back through the mud, deflecting her magic, and sending the flames roaring back through the Queen's own army.

"Leave this place!" the human woman shouts. "You will not steal their eggs."

Her brown eyes flash—dark eyes I would recognize anywhere.

She must be Nathaniel's ancestor.

The Fae Queen stumbles to her feet, but her people are already running, some of them racing away on horses, others sprinting on foot.

With a snarl, the Queen runs to her stallion, leaps onto its back, and rides away with them.

The human woman rises to her feet, her chest heaving, the tension around her mouth increasing as the other human warriors gather around her and the dragon.

"They won't stop," she says. "They want to control the next generation of dragons."

The golden dragon lowers its head to the woman, nudging the woman's shoulder before gently exhaling a ring of silver flames around the halberd.

"Bright Heart," the dragon whispers. "Keep the light."

I grip the edges of the book, gasping for air.

Memories, moments, wash across me.

Nathaniel's father—Tobias—told Nathaniel to keep the light.

I assumed he was telling Nathaniel to keep the faith, to stay true to his honor, but what if he meant that Nathaniel was supposed to keep the *weapon* safe?

What if *the light* is Nathaniel's blade?

Flashes return to me from my dreamed memories.

Imatra tried to kill Tobias with a stream of firelight, but he used his weapon—the same halberd that the human warrior used just now—to deflect her magic.

He not only protected himself, but he sent Imatra's power streaming back at her.

I'm taken back to the moment Imatra saw the halberd when I first took Nathaniel to her in her Inner Sanctuary. I was holding the halberd and the first rays of sunlight had shone through the windows and lit up its gleaming blade.

Imatra froze and the emblem on the steel had blazed in her eyes as if it were a living creature.

I'd never seen fear in her eyes before that moment.

The halberd isn't just a weapon. It's an object of magic—*light magic*—blessed by the dragons themselves.

Nathaniel needs the halberd when he fights me.

He'll need it to regain his throne.

The fae have it now—the worst outcome, judging from the war I just witnessed.

I have to make sure he gets it back.

Stumbling away from the book, my head shoots up at the same time that Nathaniel steps away from the book he was looking at it.

His eyes are glazed, but he shakes himself, suddenly alert as he looks at me.

"I know what you need to do," we both say at once.

I blink at him.

He stares at me.

Our twin declarations echo in the silence.

I start to speak again, but I'm suddenly aware of the change in the room.

Darkness has fallen around us, deep shadows casting across the floor. Spinning to the window, I'm shocked to see the outline of the moon in the darkening sky.

I gasp. "How much time has passed?"

Tension thrums through Nathaniel's posture. "Too much time. The sun has set."

He strides toward me but stops before he touches me.

Despite the darkness falling around us, I am his focus.

The look on his face reminds me of Cyrian when he tried to

torture me, when Cyrian had stopped, startled, and asked me how I exist.

The look in Nathaniel's eyes now... It's as if he's seeing me for the first time.

Behind his expression is fear. Raw, exposed, genuine dread.

"I think I know what happened to you," he says.

CHAPTER 17

I take a step away from him.

He keeps his voice low, cautious as he gestures to the book held by the stone girl. "You need to see this book."

The darkness inside the room suddenly presses in around me. I take another instinctive step back.

My heart squeezes inside my chest, my wary gaze flicking to the book and back to Nathaniel. "Why *that* book?"

He relaxes, his shoulders lowering. He inhales calmly, but it feels forced. "These books contain the history of the four magics. It was difficult to read their titles, but I recognize parts of the ancient languages. I should have realized we would get pulled into the pages. We've lost two hours. That was my mistake, but we can't change it now."

Pointing at the book held by the golden woman—the one I was reading—he avoids looking at its open pages as he says, "That is the history of light magic. The dark statue holds the book of dark magic. The crimson woman holds the history of fae magic. And the book I read..."

He steps to the book he was studying, pausing in front of it. "This book is about old magic."

Gripping the edges of the book without looking at the pages, he focuses on the stone girl's face.

He whispers, "I saw her in this book... Her name is *Lucidia*."

I stiffen. "That's my name."

"Imatra gave you that name. It means *brightest light*, doesn't it?" he asks.

"Yes, because of my Twilight power." My breath catches in my throat, a sense of dread filling me.

"You need to see this, but don't look at the pages for too long," he says. "We can't afford to lose more time. I'll be here to pull you out, just in case."

My feet are leaden as I force myself to move to Nathaniel's side.

He has never given me any reason to distrust him. Even right from the start, he promised to always tell me the truth.

I swallow my anxiety as I step up to the book.

The paper is pitch black, a dark abyss, an endless space that appears to have no boundaries, bleeding beyond the edges of the page and spreading across my vision.

I shiver as I recognize the *nothing* that I sink into when I sleep, the *nothing* that I remember before my first memories of waking up at the burn site.

A splash of light appears within the darkness. It's the smallest wisp, dancing across the page, growing brighter.

It expands as it comes closer before it turns and glides to the left. Tiny lights surround it, making it sparkle.

It hovers, gaining form, humanoid for a moment before it brightens again, the glow around it obscuring its silhouette.

The glow washes across the page, fading into darkness but never quite gone.

"Brightest light," I whisper, a painful hollow forming in my chest as I press my fingers to the page. "What is it?"

"It's old magic in its original form." Nathaniel's arms close around me as he pulls me gently away from the book, urging me to look up at him.

I blink as I surface into the dark room.

Unlike our descent down the stairs, torches haven't sprung to life around us, leaving us in increasing gloom brightened only by the moon outside.

Nathaniel's voice is low and soft. "Do you remember when you showed me the diamond at the heart of the Spinning Lake and I told you—"

"I was being childish."

He shakes his head, a small smile forming and then fading from his lips. "I said there was a playful heart locked up inside you. When you're happy, you're like a dancing star."

The hollow in my chest widens.

I push myself out of his arms, suddenly needing to put distance between him and me.

He doesn't try to reach for me. Instead, he steps away from the book and quietly removes his weapons, his harness, and finally his shirt.

He pauses then, a beautiful, strong man who looks at me as if he would do anything to stop the pain of the wounds he's about to cut open.

He presses his forefinger to the invisible stone he wears next to his heart. "I've carried this stone with me every day and night since I was ten years old. I wore it next to my heart. I rarely removed it. The longest I've been separated from it was the last two days. Over time—in fact, there were many days when—I felt like this stone had become a part of me. Or maybe that I had become a part of it."

He takes a step toward me.

I take a step back.

He stops. "I have been pushing away the things I see in you, denying them, because the answers seem too far beyond my reach. But the truth is that you…"

His gaze passes across my face from my dull eyes to my pale lips. "*You* are beyond my reach."

I take another step away from him, feeling like the foundations are cracking beneath my feet, but not knowing why.

"Ask yourself, Aura," he says, demanding that I answer him. "Every impossible, unique, unusual thing about yourself. Ask every question that you don't have an answer for—"

"Why am I alone?" My question sounds harsh in the deepening dark around us.

Pain flashes across Nathaniel's face, but the questions suddenly pour out of me before he can answer me.

"Why am I the only Twilight fae?" I ask. "Why do I have power over light, but I can only sleep in darkness? How can I stop breathing and remain alive? How could I heal your wound this morning when fae magic couldn't touch you?"

I press my fingers to my lips, remembering the dust that coated my body after I stopped breathing at the burn site—the same dust that I coughed up this morning. "Why do I turn to ash and dust when I begin to die?"

Holding up my hands before my face, I study the shape of my skin, desperate to find answers in them.

Flickers of starlight grow around my hand. My power is returning with the rising moon, the well inside me filling again.

Despite the power gathering in my hands, Nathaniel strides toward me, unafraid and determined.

He has never been fearful of me. Even when I unleashed my power on the first day we met, he leaped toward me, stepping right into the heart of my starlight to try to stop me from screaming the declaration that invoked the Law of Champions.

He halts three paces away from me, the exact space that a combatant would stop, his shoulders drawn back, his head slightly tilted as he looks me up and down from the top of my white hair to the tips of my borrowed boots.

"Who controls light but sleeps in darkness?" He repeats my question back to me as his dark eyes flash across me. "You do."

He prowls to my right, a movement that suddenly feels dangerous to me, as if he's about to challenge me in ways I don't want him to.

"Who turns to dust and ash when she loses hope?" He turns and prowls in the other direction, keeping me in his sights. "That would also be you."

He stops in front of me. "Who was determined to fight through agony to reach my side?"

His voice becomes low, gentle again. "Who kept me alive and breathed life into me? Who took me home despite the fact that she would be made to suffer for it?"

His dark eyes are clear, his voice compelling me to listen. "You, Aura. Always you."

He dares to close the gap between us. He always dares to challenge me, no matter how many defenses I raise.

"I know you're terrified of the truths that lie in your past," he says. "I'm here if you need to scream. I'm here if you need to cry. I can take it. All of it. But you have to face it."

He reaches slowly for the weapon harness I'm wearing. My heart pounds inside my chest, but I don't try to stop him when he undoes my harness and lays it on the ground.

He removes the sling from around my neck, deftly untying the knot as I shiver. Undoing the clasps at the left shoulder of my suit, he gently draws it down far enough to reveal the space above my heart.

The golden mark of his name becomes visible, a bright spot at the edge of my vision.

With suddenly swift movements, he reaches to his own chest, peels the stone from it, and holds it out to me. "It's yours to take."

The sliver of rock glitters against his palm.

It's so small but utterly terrifying because of the immense power I sense in it. A power that I'm sure will either destroy or heal me.

I asked him why I was alone, but I realize that I'm not.

In the final hours of my life, I won't be alone because Nathaniel will be with me.

My fingertips close over the stone, touching it for the first time.

Power shoots through my hand all of the way up my arm to my shoulder, a shot of energy reaching my heart and hitting it like a hammer.

I gasp and Nathaniel jolts, knocked away from me.

Starlight streaks through my veins, running up my shaking arm as I raise the stone, ready to position it below my scar just like he did.

Power flickers around the rock, shots of starlight so sharp that they bite my skin, suddenly burning me.

I nearly drop the stone, but the power inside it strikes out toward my torso, streaks of starlight connecting the rock to the location of my heart.

Panic floods me.

I try to pull the rock away from myself, but it continues on its path, flying out of my hand toward my heart.

Burning starlight cuts through my skin, a cut so deep and painful that I scream.

"Aura!" Nathaniel shouts as he reaches for me, but another blast of light knocks him back again.

Each stab of light from the stone tears at my skin beneath my scar, forming a new crescent—a fresh cut the precise size and shape of the stone's edge.

The rock finally adheres to my chest, plastered against me like a brand for a split second before it turns on its side and disappears inside the cut it made.

Shock seizes me, and I drop to my knees, sensing the rock burrowing deep inside my chest.

I claw at my skin, trying to stop it. The storm inside me pushes and pulls, breaking me apart and healing me at the same time.

I scream as starlight explodes inside my chest, radiating in crashing waves, the force throwing me outward and upward, just like the moment when I invoked the Law of Champions.

The force slams into Nathaniel, picking him up and hurling him across the room.

Screams tear from my throat as I stretch toward him with both of my hands, my right arm free and mobile for the first time in hours, my body pulsing with power as we fly away from each other.

Bright, white light fills the space around us.

The walls vibrate and the pages of the books flip violently open, the images inside them suddenly flying upward.

The golden dragon rages across the air between Nathaniel and me.

From the dark magic book, a herd of firehorses rises and races after the dragon, galloping through a swarm of silver humblebees that pours from the pages of the fae magic book.

As they chase each other full circle around the statues, I wait for a creature of the fourth magic—the old magic—to rise from the pages of that book, but only my starlight streaks across its surface.

Within moments, the other creatures vanish back into the pages from which they came.

As soon as they disappear, everything stops moving, even the pages, suspended in place.

Nathaniel comes to a jarring stop, his head thrown back, his arms splayed at his sides, his bare chest glistening in my light.

His lips part as his head lowers.

I can't deny the pull in his gaze as his mouth suddenly curls up into a smile that heats me all of the way to my core.

"Aura Lucidia." He says my name as if it is new to him.

I'm not sure what he sees that makes him cast me such a dangerous smile, but when I press my hands to my now-healed chest, my skin glows.

I catch sight of my luminescent hair, glittering white strands filled with light as they float around my shoulders.

The only other times my body glowed like this was when Nathaniel touched me, when he made me glow.

Across the distance, Nathaniel looks at me the same way he did when he turned me toward the mirror in Bright and showed me who I could be.

He saw the potential of my power even before I did.

Now I have no doubt that I'm glowing all over. Without seeing myself, I picture my eyes filled with emerald splashes, the dull forest green color of my pupils gone, my cheeks flushed, my lips red and full.

Only an hour ago, my energy was exhausted. Now my power feels like a limitless ocean of starlight.

A shiver of light rushes through my body all of the way from the top of my head to my toes as I meet Nathaniel's eyes.

"My power," I whisper. "You gave me back my power."

CHAPTER 18

I float to the floor, my feet coming to rest on the stone surface.

I'm conscious of the magic around me—old magic protecting the books and the room—a hundred times more aware than I was before.

Magic shimmers and ripples through the air all around us, but Nathaniel's presence is the strongest—always the strongest —overwhelming my senses with his strength.

But now... the power that ripples through his chest, his arms, every part of him, draws my attention.

Starlight—*impossible* starlight—glows through every fiber of his torso, threads that extend beyond his chest and up his neck.

Light flickers at his temples, pulsing in time to his heartbeat as it travels down his chest, stomach, and thighs, visible as a soft glow beneath his long pants.

It isn't a reflection of my power or even the wash of my starlight rippling across the room.

It's part of him.

He returns to the floor as my power releases him. His gaze

burns me, his dark eyes glinting as he crosses the distance between us.

"Aura." He sweeps me into his arms, the intensity in his eyes deepening as his hands stroke up my back, tangling in my hair.

My arm no longer hurts. Nothing hurts, not even my heart. I don't know why I was so afraid of the stone, not when it has opened my eyes to everything around me.

"Nathaniel." Tilting back my head, I press my forefinger to his lips before I trace the glimmers that travel through his skin across his jaw and neck.

He remains silent, allowing me to follow the path of my power through his body. All of the tiny paths, infinite pulses, a thousand sparks of starlight—

My power.

"Do you see this?" I ask, leaning close and looking up into his eyes.

"I see your hand glowing where you touch me. Just like usual," he says, his voice a husky whisper and his lips parting as his breathing increases.

He must not be able to see the power rippling through his body. I couldn't before, either. But now I can.

While I trace the contours of his chest with my fingertips, he follows the shape of my face with his eyes, his expression becoming wary.

"What do you see that I can't?" he asks.

I sway forward and plant a kiss above the location of his heart, right across his scar, sensing him hold his breath.

"I can see my power." Power that he should never have taken into himself. Would never have assimilated into his human body, except that his father handed Nathaniel the stone when he was ten years old and he's carried it with him ever since.

His lips part in surprise, breathing his question in a soft exhalation. "What do you mean?"

"You carried this piece of my power next to your heart. You took my power into your body—into your heart. I couldn't see it before," I say, tracing his chest. "When you touched me, I must have been connecting with my own power inside you. That's why I glowed."

When I draw away from him, the glow in my hand diminishes, but it doesn't disappear like it did before.

He pulls my hand back to his chest, placing it over his heart. "If that's true, then it was your power that protected me from Cyrian's dark magic all of these years," he says. "When everyone else was in danger, you kept me safe."

I allow myself to smile. "My power kept your heart... *bright*. It kept you alive when your heart failed this morning."

He shakes his head as if he doesn't believe it. "It's impossible. I'm human."

Still pressing my palm to his chest, I nudge a kiss against his jaw. "Look at me, Nathaniel. Look at what this tiny piece of my power has done to me now that I have it back. What would it have done to you for *fifteen years?*"

"Look at you?" he asks, his voice suddenly rough, the desire in his eyes intensifying. "Dark stars, Aura. I can't look away from you."

I meet the heat in his gaze.

I have a thousand questions, the most worrying being how my power was separated from my body—the horrifying memory of Imatra's blade ramming into my chest—but I push all of my questions away because I need this moment.

For the first time in my remembered life, I feel whole and alive. Powerful.

A smile grows on my face as I reach up to press a kiss to his lips, drawing in the scent of his skin as I explore the shape of his mouth.

With a groan, he lifts me up against him, his strength

allowing him to propel me back to the wide window ledge. The magic protecting the window presses against my back, shivers of power rippling through the opening.

My training suit already sits off my shoulder, giving Nathaniel access to the bare skin above my heart.

His lips travel the distance between my neck and shoulder, his hands firm around my waist, before I draw his mouth back to mine.

The dark outside is heavy now, the sky clear, and the moon full. The glow from my body fills the space around us, providing a soft light for us to see.

My hands follow the contours of Nathaniel's face and shoulders, explore the shape of his back and stomach, tug at his pants.

My hair lifts and falls with the movement of my shirt as I pull it up over my head and drop it to the floor.

I used to loathe my hair, the old white strands, but now it falls softly across my shoulders and breasts, each strand glowing and bright.

Nathaniel's gaze passes to my lips. "You. Are. *Mesmerizing.*"

My finger traces a single pulse of starlight across his cheek to his jaw—one of thousands—and my hand glows brighter than before, responding to the touch between us, reacting to the starlight shimmering beneath the surface of his skin.

His mouth claims mine and desire heats me, striking through me to my center. He draws back before the waves overcome me.

Shivers of pleasure make my skin tingle as he lifts me up off the ledge without breaking the contact with my mouth, to kiss me while he removes the rest of my clothing, his own joining mine on the floor.

He lifts me upward again, fitting our bodies together.

Power and pleasure rush through me at the first thrust, a heady combination so strong that it's almost too much.

I respond without inhibition as he takes two steps to position me up against the wall. Arching my back against the solid surface, I hook my legs around his hips, using gravity to draw him as far inside me as possible.

He braces, one hand against the wall, the other gripping my hip as the connection between us deepens.

Starlight ripples across my chest, glowing brighter as my breathing increases.

My body is on fire, hot as flame, cold as ice. Overwhelmed with sensations that threaten to tear me apart.

This could be the last time.

The cruel thought cuts through my desire, striking hard at the pleasure driving through me. I gasp, push the thought away, but it repeats on me.

This will be the last time.

I grip Nathaniel's shoulders, my breathing ragged, my heart shredding into smaller pieces as he draws out the moment.

It can't be the last time. I won't let it be—

Cold starlight floods my chest, my power filling me with an empty certainty, an undeniable truth.

This is the last time.

CHAPTER 19

I want to scream. Rant. Rage.

Nathaniel's hand finds my cheek. His eyes meet mine. His own breathing is out of control, even though he's holding back. "Stay with me, Aura."

But I can't. Not forever.

I tell myself I can take this moment. I can have this happiness. Even with all of the pain that will come after, with all of the heartbreak that comes with lying to myself, convincing myself for these next moments that this won't end. That this feeling can last forever.

I gasp again, trying to speak, wanting to scream, only a harsh whisper rasping against his mouth as I kiss him. "This is the last time."

"No." His eyes meet mine, shocked, then full of rage.

"It has to be."

"No!" His fist thumps the wall beside my shoulder, streaks of light shooting up through the cracks he makes.

I'm not afraid of his rage. Pushing aside my emotions, I brace my flat palms against the wall and press against the cracks he made so I can pull my hips up and away from his before crashing against him again.

Pleasure shoots through me with the movement, relief for a brief moment before my need grows worse.

He shakes his head at me, his fist forming against the wall beside my shoulder, as if he can grip this moment and never let it go, draw it out as long as he can.

I don't stop, my body rising and pushing against his, controlling the thrusts, inhaling every ragged breath he takes, accepting all of the pain in my heart.

I tell myself it's nothing compared to the pain I felt when I thought he'd died.

Sweat drips down my torso, my arms tensing with every lift and fall, but my senses spiral before I crash wildly around him.

I take him with me into the crash.

His fist hits the wall, propelling us away from it, making us seem weightless as the waves flow through us. Me to him. Him to me.

His arms wrap around me as we stop in the middle of the room, my legs wrapped around his hips.

He grips me. Hard.

His voice is an order. A command. His eyes refuse to let me go. "Stay with me."

Outside, the moon is full, a large outline hanging above the horizon. The empty space outside this room calls to me. The vast *nothing* will soon be my resting place.

I try to breathe, but instead, I tip my head back and scream.

My cry hums and vibrates through the room, making the pedestals tremble, the cracks in the wall grow.

The magic across the window ripples with starlight, sharp and biting, as my power prickles my skin.

It strikes Nathaniel, but he roars out the pain I'm causing him and refuses to let me go.

I close my eyes. The dark abyss I sensed inside the stone opens up, but now it's inside of me, a part of me, and I can't escape it.

This is why I was afraid of it.

Because the cold dark is now part of my body. Inescapable.

Opening my eyes, I grip Nathaniel's shoulders. "You gave me your word. You promised you would fight me with all of your strength."

His gaze doesn't falter. Neither does his grip. "I will fight you, Aura. With everything I have. But I will not strike you down."

Rage and fear burn through me, the coldest oblivion growing inside my chest as the stone's power—my power—expands. "You will."

He shakes his head. "No."

I push against his hold, trying to pry myself away from him, to break the connections between us, both physical and emotional.

"You will!" I shout.

"You can't believe that I would ever hurt you!" he roars.

He grips my hip when I pry his hand from my waist, grabs my shoulder when I wrench his hand from my back. Each time I try to free myself, he reaches for me somewhere else, forcing me to stay right where I am.

"You have to!" I scream.

"You can't say that!" His shout rages over me, as if he can make me believe what he believes. "You are not heart—"

He suddenly freezes, sucking air into his chest as his eyes widen. The blood drains from his face in a sickening wave.

"Heartless?" I ask.

The abyss inside me grows wider. An empty hollow filled with sudden truth. It drains my anger, leaving a rising tide of emptiness inside me.

I try to breathe as the memory of Cyrian's voice whispers inside my mind.

Where is your heart?

"My heart," I whisper, releasing Nathaniel's shoulders to grip my chest, my movement threatening to unbalance us both and topple us to the floor. "The stone wasn't just my power. It was a piece of my heart."

Nathaniel's face blurs in front of me, my vision spinning.

"But... how much of my heart is missing?" I ask.

Where is your heart?

Cyrian asked me how I can exist. Mathilda said my heart is hidden from her. She tried to see my intentions and then she backed away from me, pale and shocked.

I run cold, my ears buzz, and my power pours in streams beneath my skin. I sense starlight glowing from the top of my head to my toes, a protective shield slowly forming over my body.

My body, my... *everything*... is transforming with every new pulse of power.

Drawing air into my mouth, I sense the air slip down my throat. My chest rises in response, but I'm not sure if I'm actually breathing.

How would I know what breathing feels like when I can't tell what a heart feels like?

A thousand times I thought my heart was beating.

I felt it thud and even stop inside my chest.

I felt every emotion there is to feel—pain, love, loss, betrayal, hope.

I bled, I had a pulse, and I hurt like everyone else.

But all of the voices, all of the warnings, rage around inside my head now.

Darkest of stars.

You don't belong to them.

You were never a girl.

Aura... where is your heart?

The realization is cold but certain. "My heart was taken from me."

The glow of my magic grows between my body and Nathaniel's—a tangible force that pushes him away from me and compels him to release me.

He doesn't try to fight me this time, uncurling his arms from around me, the press and slide of his skin making me shiver as I slip to the floor and back away from him.

The ache in his eyes would tear my heart apart... if I had more than a sliver of it glowing inside my chest.

All of my life, I thought I knew who I was, where I stood in my world, the path I was supposed to walk.

Queen's champion. Nathaniel's shield. Wife. Warrior.

Even last night, I was certain that, even though my path had changed, I knew what I needed to do. I was certain that I had to die for peace to finally come to Bright and Fell.

Now... my foundations are gone.

"What sort of creature can live without a heart?" I ask. "What am I?"

The moonlight shines across Nathaniel's body through the wide window, highlighting his sculped muscles, lighting up the flickers of starlight that he shouldn't have—that he took from me.

His expression is blank now. Broken.

"You *are* old magic," he says, his voice barely a rasp. "You're a Celestial Star."

I freeze, shocked, as he raises his arm and points through the window at the starlight flickering outside.

"You're one of them," he says.

CHAPTER 20

$\mathcal{M}$y shock gives way to my need to know—to understand what I am.

I follow the line of Nathaniel's arm to the window.

Outside, the night sky is calm and clear in all directions.

I search the sky for what he pointed at, finding only the moon and a thousand stars, pinpricks of light.

I'm about to turn away when a shape flits across the air outside the window. A formless wash of bright white light appears for a second before it fades again. It reminds me of a feather, twisting and turning lightly, every angle making it appear a different shape.

I grip the window ledge as I peer into the night sky, waiting for the dancing light to appear again.

I count the flickers of light inside my chest as I wait. One... Two... Three...

Another light washes across the sky, farther to my left but closer to me than the one before. It leaves a glowing trail, a vanishing blaze, as it leaps from one spot to another, playing with the air around the tower.

Every time it vanishes, it reforms again, traveling a path like a stone skipping across the surface of a lake.

A third light joins it, this one glowing brightly in a single spot that draws closer to me.

Ripples of light radiate from its center as it grows larger before it wanes and reappears to the right, glowing brighter and closer still.

Without taking my eyes off it, I climb up onto the window ledge, still completely naked, but I'm not cold.

I extend my arm through the wash of magic protecting the room, my fingers reaching through the chill air.

The glowing form fades and brightens, drawing closer.

A ribbon of starlight glides through the air toward me.

I hold my breath, allowing my power to glow around my fingertips, waiting for the ribbon to reach me, needing the contact, desperate to know what lies at the heart of the light…

The circle of light suddenly jolts, jumping backward, a startled movement. The ribbon it was sending toward me disintegrates.

The other two light forms freeze before they dart in different directions, streaking through the air and vanishing.

"What—?"

A wash of blue lightning crackles across the space in front of the window a second before Treble drops into view.

His bright eyes are wild with fear. His wings crack, sharp lightning sizzling across my outstretched arm.

I can't hear the sound from inside the room, but I know he's trying to warn me.

I leap back to the floor. "Nathaniel! We have to go!"

Nathaniel has already pulled on his clothing, hurriedly strapping the weapon harness around his chest. I grab my clothing, dressing as fast as I can before I snatch my weapon harness off the floor.

I spin, uncertain, but Nathaniel runs toward the window, grabbing me by the hand as he passes. We leap for the ledge at the same time.

"You jump first!" I shout.

It takes Nathaniel a split second to judge the gap between the window and Treble. He leaps through the magical barrier and out into space, reaching for Treble's wing.

The light inside my chest flickers with anxiety for a moment, then Nathaniel's hand closes over Treble's wing bone.

He swings himself up and over Treble's back, crouching low.

I don't wait another moment, leaping out across the distance and somersaulting onto Treble's back, sliding down in front of Nathaniel. Treble rises up at the same time, beating his wings furiously.

As he soars to the left, I crane my neck, sensing the malevolent life forms in the sky around us.

Ten thunderbirds span out across the sky, blocking our escape in every direction—above, below, and all around us. The uniforms of their riders tell me they are Imatra's Day Guards.

My lip curls as I identify Nadina, the head of the Day Guard flying on our right-hand side. She threatened my adoptive father and then tried to kill Nathaniel when we tried to escape Bright.

Imatra rides ahead of them, directly above us.

Her crimson thunderbird's blood-red lightning crackles around her slender silhouette as she urges it to follow us. Her armor is also crimson, reminding me of the fae I saw in the book, but her hair is loose, the flying strands whipping around her face.

Her magic wraps around us, controlling the air and wind so that Treble is forced to coast on the spot, and silence falls around us.

The first time the other thunderbirds closed Treble out, he was distressed. Now, he turns his neck and casts me a rebellious look, his eyes slightly narrowed. His expression tells me he will fly us out of here the moment he has the chance.

Instinctively, I lean into Nathaniel. I can't protect his back, but I intend to remain between him and Imatra for as long as possible.

My chest hurts when he doesn't close his arms around me like he always did before.

Imatra is a picture of perfection as her thunderbird draws level with us. Her full lips are relaxed, her glittering blue eyes alive and alert, her hair swaying across her delicate shoulders and framing her narrow waist.

But her skin is a paler shade of porcelain and her ruby-red fingernails press into the armor around her thighs.

I sense her unease with every breath she takes, her inhalations slightly too rapid.

"Hello, dear," she says, her voice betraying no emotion. "You look well."

Quietly, I test my new power, taking a deep breath before I exhale, gently pushing against her power over the air around us. My starlight glows brightly, casting light in all directions.

I smile when I sense Imatra's control falter.

She grips her thighs harder.

"You will give me answers," I say, rising slowly to my feet on Treble's back.

I'm still holding my weapon harness. Drawing the sword from its holder, I crouch to drape the harness across Treble's back, before I brace, take a deep breath...

I leap across the distance between Imatra and me, landing lightly on her thunderbird's strong neck, rapidly stepping across it to drive the sword at her throat.

The tip pierces her skin before her reflexes kick in and she reacts, leaping to her feet and taking a step away from me.

Nadina and the other guards swarm inward, their thunderbirds shrieking with fury, but Imatra holds up both of her hands to stop them.

With a frustrated shout, Nadina screams at the others to stop. They don't withdraw, but they don't come any closer, either.

Blood can't be shed within the Spire, but out here, that rule doesn't seem to apply.

My sword's tip reaches within an inch of Imatra's neck.

She lowers her gaze to it, her head held high, stiff as she balances on her coasting bird.

"You don't need a blade to kill me," she says.

"I know," I answer, my starlight power building inside my chest, glimmering across the space between us.

Imatra's gaze shifts, flickering left, and a moment later, a glitter bulb rises up behind her.

It's encased in dark light, a thin thread of power twisting in the air between the bulb and Imatra. The bulb itself is a sparkling mess on the verge of shattering, as if it were about to explode, but Imatra encased it just in time.

Within the dark light, the bulb trembles and shakes, its pieces trying to come apart, an explosion needing to happen.

"I received your gift," Imatra says. "A memory of this Spire from my childhood."

The bulb is so shattered, there's no way I can see the memory inside it.

But if it's a memory of the Spire like she said, then it's probably the same one Mathilda had.

"What did Mathilda teach you?" I ask.

Imatra smiles, a spark of light returning to her eyes. "Oh, so you met my friend. It was very wicked of us. A witch and a fae meeting in secret and sharing their knowledge of magic. It was forbidden."

I edge closer to her, gritting my teeth and demanding an answer. "What did she teach you?"

CHAPTER 21

*I*matra's smile fades.

She inclines her head slightly downward, the wind from her bird's wings lifting her hair. "Mathilda and I sat on that cliff, eating apples, talking about magic, and gazing up at the Celestial Stars—the *Lucidia*—playing in the sky above us far beyond our reach."

Her eyes narrow. "The Lucidia were everywhere in the ether above Bright in those days, but you could see them most clearly out here."

Imatra leans closer, daring my sword to pierce her skin as her bright eyes meet mine and her voice lowers to a whisper. "Then one night, Mathilda pointed to the most beautiful Lucidia we had ever seen and she wondered aloud... Imagine the power we could control if we could snatch a Celestial Star from the ether and pull it down to us."

I inhale cold air, pulling it into the abyss inside my chest.

"Of course, I told her it was impossible," Imatra whispers, her voice a soft lulling sound. "It would take more than fae magic or light magic combined. In fact, it would take all of the dark magic ripped from a thousand souls to tear a Lucidia from the sky and force her to the ground."

"A thousand souls," I whisper, pressing my eyes closed for a moment.

Deep relief fills me because I wasn't the one who killed the humans during the final battle. "A thousand *human* souls. You killed them on the battlefield to give you power to pull me from the sky."

Imatra leans back a little, pride making her eyes shine. "It was easy to lure Tobias Exalted to the border. I told him to meet me on the battlefield, to bring his full force, and we would settle the war between us once and for all. He was so desperate for an end to the conflict. That part was simple."

Her smile fades, replaced by cold anger. "Ripping you from the sky was harder. But seizing your power proved *impossible*."

My voice is as cold as hers. "You cut out my heart."

"I spent years researching the old magic, the history of your species, the nature of your power. Once grounded, you would take the shape of a girl, a transformation triggered by contact with solid earth. I would have moments to cut out your heart before you woke up and defended yourself. Provided I removed your entire heart, you would die, and your power would be mine."

My memory sweeps over me.

Imatra had plunged her knife toward my chest at the same time Nathaniel's father swung his halberd at her neck.

She'd missed. She'd cut off the tiniest sliver of my heart instead.

"Nathaniel's father interrupted you," I say.

She laughs, a harsh, condescending sound. "He wasn't supposed to survive my dark magic—he should have died with the others when I pulled you from the sky—but I underestimated the power of light magic he held. That damn weapon protected him! I didn't realize he was alive until it was too late. He tried to save you, and my blade slipped."

She snarls as she leans closer. "By the time I tried again, you were waking up. I missed the stem at the top of your heart. So you lived—but with a fraction of your power. You were a shell compared to who you were before. When you woke up fully, I told you a story that gave me control over you, and you never questioned it."

Her mouth twists. "But your broken heart was useless to me. All my work, a lifetime of planning... destroyed! And now... look at you. *Glowing.*"

"Nathaniel gave me back part of my heart," I say.

She considers me with cold eyes. "I thought that first slice had been burned to ash. If I'd known Tobias stole it when he tried to save you, I would have destroyed all of Fell looking for it."

I lower my weapon, allowing it to swing to my side without harming her thunderbird. "Now I'm bound to fight for you."

She doesn't smile. "The old law binds everyone, no matter who they are. You may not be fae, but you are my champion under the Law. How sad for you to kill Nathaniel."

I don't know how much of our conversation Nathaniel can hear. Treble has remained in the same position coasting in the air behind us, a little to my right.

Imatra's voice is soft and so is mine, but the air is still and quiet, allowing the sound of our voices to travel.

"I will not kill for you," I say.

She dares to reach toward me as if she'll stroke my cheek, but she pauses before she makes contact. "Oh, my dear child. You think you love him, but consider this: His father stole a piece of your heart. You were connected to Nathaniel from the moment he held your heart in his hands. Do you really love him? Or is your love stolen, just like your heart?"

My hand clenches around my weapon.

From the moment Nathaniel stepped out of the mist, I was drawn to him.

His strength, his honor, his heart.

We formed a connection faster than I thought possible. I reasoned that it was a result of the Law of Champions—the Vanem Dragon's promise that we would walk side by side, that we would eat, sleep, and breathe together and, by the end of the third day, we would know the other better than we knew ourselves.

Every part of the Dragon's warning has come true.

We have experienced each other's lives in Bright and Fell, fought by each other's sides, battled for each other, suffered the same wounds, the same heartache, breathed air into each other, brought each other back from the brink of death.

And as for knowing the other better than ourselves... Nathaniel discovered my true power before I did.

He recognized what I was before I did, while I understand light magic—the power of his weapon—even though I suspect he doesn't.

But none of that compelled us to love each other.

From the moment Nathaniel carried my heart beside his... did either of us have a choice about whom we would love?

"You won't refuse to fight for me," Imatra says, a declaration.

My gaze flickers to the side—to Nathaniel, who waits quietly on Treble.

Nathaniel is a massive, strong, forbidding man. Broken a little now, but his expression is blank, the face of a king.

He could tear me apart if he wants to. He already has.

I breathe slowly, and when I turn back to Imatra, I wear the mask of her champion, my emotions finally hidden, my purpose all that matters.

"I will fight for you," I say. "On one condition."

"Name it."

"You will return Nathaniel's weapon to him."

Her eyes narrow. "It won't protect him from your power," she says, but she doesn't look completely certain about that. "Old magic is the highest form of magic. Your starlight can defeat light magic. Dark magic, too."

I nod slowly. When I healed Maggie's Ebon Rot, I thought I was curing her body—I even called it 'healing' in my mind—but she didn't recover until I destroyed the seed of dark magic in her heart. I didn't *heal* her. I ended the dark magic that had taken hold of her. It was the same with the girls I helped. I flooded them with my magic to make them well again.

"I can destroy fae magic too," I say, closing the gap between Imatra and me to make my point clear. I've never killed a fae. I vowed to protect the fae, not hurt them. I need her to know that right now, I *choose* not to hurt her.

"King Cyrian won't give up his kingdom easily," I continue. "He will demand that the fight is fair. If you give Nathaniel his weapon, Cyrian will have nothing to complain about."

Imatra considers me carefully. "I will grant your request, but you must do something for me first. It will be a show of faith. Well, it's not for me, really, but for your loved ones. Assuming you still care about Evander and Talsa."

I bristle at the implication that I don't. "What do you want?"

"You must stop the glitter field from sending out any more bulbs."

I arch an eyebrow at her. "The glitter field is your creation. I don't control it."

She laughs, a sudden, almost hysterical sound. "Why do you think I was stopped from cutting out your heart's stem, Aura? Why was I so far away from you when you woke up?"

She continues to laugh, the sound rising in pitch until it grates against my hearing. "*You* created the glitter field when you woke up and tried to defend yourself against me," she says. "I barely survived the blast of power you used to create the field, let alone the glitter shards that exploded around me."

She shakes her head, as if she's trying to shake off her memories. "I never imagined such a horrifying retaliation. A field of crystalline starlight to tear apart anyone who steps near you. Oh, the tears I cried."

I remember her tears. They'd turned into pearls that had scattered across the burning ground. "What did you do with the rest of my heart?"

"It crumbled to ash in my hands when I cut it out," she says, her eyes glinting in my light. "You have as much of your heart now as you will ever have."

I consider the bulb floating at Imatra's side and all of its messy, shattered edges.

My fist darts out, making her flinch as I take hold of the glittering weapon.

I yank it toward myself and snap the thread of dark magic that she's using to constrain it.

My power streaks around the shattering bulb, a bright flash, before I open my fist again.

Imatra takes a reflexive step back, stopping when she sees that the bulb has transformed into a flower resting in my palm.

It's a poppy, its petals crushed and bleeding crimson sap, just like the poppies that Imatra gripped at the coliseum when the Vanem Dragon sealed the Law of Champions.

"I will stop the glitter field," I say, even though I have no idea how. "And you will return Nathaniel's weapon to him."

She smiles again, regaining her mask of control. "Agreed."

I step away from her, my weapon raised again. "Do not try to imprison me or Nathaniel. We are caged enough as it is."

Imatra's hair floats gently around her shoulders as her gaze runs from my face to my clenched fists to my hastily pulled-on clothing. "So you are."

Turning, I leap back to Treble, but this time, I position myself with a deliberate gap between Nathaniel and me.

"Treble," I call softly to my thunderbird. "Take us to the glitter field near the burn site, please."

When Imatra's guards crowd their thunderbirds inward as if they're going to stop us from leaving, she raises her hands to halt them. "Let Aura and Nathaniel leave. We'll see them again soon enough."

Treble cracks his wings, I grip with my thighs to stay on his back, and we rise above the other birds.

As Treble banks left, we soar away from the Spire.

Nathaniel doesn't attempt to close the gap between us, but he says, "She's wrong. We always had a choice about whom we love."

My throat closes up and I can't answer. His assertion confirms that he heard everything Imatra and I said to each other, including her contention that Nathaniel and I had no say in how we feel about each other.

My emotions are in pieces.

All I hope is that Nathaniel is willing to walk through the glitter field with me one last time.

CHAPTER 22

*G*litter bulbs lift into the air ahead of us as we coast high above the field's surface.

Far to our left, explosions along the crystal peaks indicate that Evander and the others continue to protect the city from the power of the bulbs.

Nathaniel and I are quiet during the flight, sitting apart.

I ask Treble to land on the Bright side of the field so that we have a clear view around us. The Fell side is obscured by the Misty Gallows and even darker at night.

Dropping to the ground, I hug Treble's neck. "Thank you, my friend."

He keens softly as I turn to Nathaniel and draw myself upright. "You don't have to follow me into the field. I won't go so far that you can't see me."

"I'm coming with you," he says.

I give him a nod and hold out my hand, waiting for him to take it.

I'm prepared for the energy to rise between us.

He slides his hand around mine and I fight the need to tug

him closer. The last time we traveled through this deadly meadow, we were running for our lives, attempting to escape Imatra's fiery anger.

The grass never hurt me and now I know why.

As soon as I step into the field, the sharp stems soften against my legs, becoming green and flexible.

A breeze hums through the space and the bulbs sing as they bump gently against each other, making a chiming sound.

I trail the fingers of my free hand across the top of the grass, finding myself humming with the bulbs as we make our way farther into the field.

I allow my starlight to glow around my fingertips, warm and calming, the aspect of my power that I used to soothe Nathaniel's mind this morning.

Even though the bulbs transform from brittle glass to soft, living material beneath my fingertips, in the distance they continue to rise and float away from the meadow, hundreds of them.

I'm not sure what I'm supposed to do to make the glitter field stop sending out deadly memories. If vengeance and violence started this, then maybe peace and acceptance will end it.

Tipping my head back, I consider the night sky, struggling to comprehend that is where I came from.

If not for Imatra, I would still be there—somewhere in the ether—a formless blaze of light, unconcerned with the worries of humans and fae.

The moment I lower my head, my humming dies in my throat.

Three bulbs have suddenly risen up in front of us.

They spin in the air, unmoving as I consider them warily. I expect that they'll float away like the others, but it's better if I defuse them than allow them to drift toward Bright—even if I can only defuse them one by one.

The minute my fingers touch the first bulb, a flash of dark light fills it.

A shock of energy runs up my arm. The contact knocks me to the ground like a punch across the back of my head.

At the same time, my fingers clamp around the bulb, unable to let go.

With a shout, I maintain hold of Nathaniel just in time, taking him with me as I fall into the now-soft grass. I manage to turn my left shoulder, landing with my left arm outstretched, the bulb clutched in it.

Nathaniel falls half across me, punching the ground with his right fist to stop himself from crushing me and driving the air from my chest.

Alarm shoots across his features. "Aura!"

Releasing my hand, he rolls to the side but hooks his arm around my waist to maintain the contact between us.

I gasp for air, feeling like my stomach was ripped out of me.

The bulb is leaden in my hand, heavy and full.

I struggle to raise it to my eyes, shocked when the other two drop onto my chest. Each one is a crushing force that knocks into me so hard that the remaining air whooshes out of my chest.

Nathaniel reacts swiftly, hooking his leg around mine to free his arms, rearing up over me in a kneeling position, one knee between my legs as he makes a grab for the bulbs.

"No!" My voice is a bare rasp as I struggle to draw breath. *"Don't touch them."*

He hovers above me, ready to swoop. "Aura?"

I take a deep breath when the pressure on my chest eases, allowing me to inhale carefully. "The other bulbs came for you... for Mathilda... even for Imatra."

I squeeze my eyes closed before opening them again. "These must be for me."

Forcing my left hand to rise to eye-height, I focus on the bulb. The ground inside the bulb rushes toward me at sickening speed, faster than the dive of any thunderbird. I'm still high enough up to see everything below me.

The earth I fall toward is scorched to ash, blackened and covered in human bodies.

Hundreds of firehorses lie with them, latent steam rising from their silent stomachs. A squadron of thunderbirds and fae is scattered, dead, among the humans.

A fae woman with arctic blue hair the same color as Evander's rests closest to Imatra's feet.

Nearby, the outpost still stands, a tall wooden building—the place where I used to believe I lived with my fae parents, where I thought I was born.

Except that I never had parents. And I really *was* born in the ash of the burn site.

Inside the bulb, a flood of dark light washes around Imatra as she sucks the life energy from the bodies fallen around her.

The dark magic turns her porcelain skin a sickly shade of gray, but her eyes are overly bright, an expression of euphoria on her face.

The life energy of a thousand humans must make her feel more powerful than ever before.

Behind her, a single man remains on his horse. His weapon —the gleaming halberd—is clutched in his hands like a shield.

Imatra's dark light washes around him in a stream, dragging at his body. His walnut brown hair flies back from his face in the rushing wind, his muscles straining as he grits his teeth and grips his weapon, protecting himself and his horse.

"Do you see this?" I whisper to Nathaniel.

"I see it. My father's weapon is an object of power."

"It's light magic," I say, shooting Nathaniel a determined look. "But it's not your father's weapon now, Nathaniel. It's *yours*. Just like the Fell throne. *Yours*."

Before he can answer, a sensation of weightlessness fills me, flooding me from the bulb and making me feel as if I'm about to rise up off the ground.

At the same time, dread fills my stomach.

I sense the energy within the bulb about to collide with me and knock me against the ground again.

A second later, energy races through my arm, and my body thumps downward.

White light explodes across the surface of the bulb.

Inside it, the outpost disintegrates and burning shards of wood fly in every direction. Flame and ash fill the air, leaving the bones of the building behind. The sky ripples like an ocean made of white light.

I try to focus on the glowing center of the explosion inside the bulb: *me*.

My body is a gleaming silhouette, my hair spread down my chest and across the ground. My arms, legs, torso, head—all take shape, but they're too bright to make out any details.

I am the shape of a girl without being a girl.

Imatra races toward me, sliding through the ash, her dagger raised, ready to strike my chest.

She doesn't see Tobias running after her until he swings his weapon at her neck.

The bulb suddenly goes blank, becoming weightless within my fist, transforming into a thorny vine that pricks my palms and tells me the bulb has shown me everything it contained.

I reach for the next bulb—one of the ones sitting on my chest—even though I know what I'll see inside it next.

The memories from my dream are unwanted, but I have to face them.

As my fingers close around the next bulb, shock sizzles through me so sharply that I arch, the pain in my chest nearly unbearable.

I choke back a sob as Nathaniel's arms dart out, wrapping beneath my arched back and sliding beneath my head, cushioning me seconds before my back hits the ground hard enough to bruise my ribs.

Instead, his arms absorb the impact. He grits his teeth as he takes the pain.

Inside the bulb, Imatra drives her dagger into my younger self's chest. While she holds the knife in her right hand, her left hand darts toward me at the same time.

But the halberd glints at the corner of her eye at the last moment.

She jerks to the side, her blade veering too far left, as she avoids the swinging weapon.

She rips her left hand from my chest, screaming at the sliver of gleaming rock she cut off before she thrusts her hand out to defend herself, dropping the stone into the ash.

Blood sprays across the surface of the bulb like crimson jewels in the air.

Nathaniel is frozen above me, watching the bulb from its other side as his father deflects the firelight pouring from Imatra's hand.

Dark light washes across Imatra's body, protecting her from her own rebounding power, but Tobias is already following up, the butt of his weapon cracking across Imatra's cheek, knocking her down.

He rams his weapon into the harness across his torso and scoops me up, his movements so fast that I don't see him snatch up the fallen stone.

He spins with me in his arms. His horse is already racing to meet him, the animal sliding to the ground, folding its legs the same way Flare folded his so that Nathaniel and I could climb on.

Tobias and his horse move in synchrony, their timing so perfect that the horse is already rising with Tobias on its back before I can even blink.

He grips me in his arms as the horse leaps into a gallop, steam gusting from its nostrils as it speeds across the burning landscape, jumping over the bodies in its way, veering around a fallen thunderbird.

Behind Tobias, Imatra's silhouette flickers.

She disappears in a wash of dark light. Just like Mathilda does when she's transporting herself across space.

No.

Imatra reappears on the horse's back, slipping neatly into place behind Tobias, her dagger arm descending.

CHAPTER 23

*T*obias jolts and prepares to jump off the horse, but the blade sinks into his back.

Three times in rapid succession.

Nathaniel flinches above me, watching the events in the bulb with a growing storm in his eyes.

At the end of our first day, Nathaniel demanded that Imatra tell him if she was the one who struck his father in the back and killed him.

She retorted that Nathaniel was too much like his father, that he believed in truth and goodness.

His father tried to save me, so Imatra killed him.

Inside the bulb, Imatra's movements are powered with dark magic, her vicious stabs cutting Tobias down as she screams, "You can't have her magic. I won't let you steal her!"

They've reached the edge of the Misty Gallows. Tobias tips and falls, and I tumble out of his arms.

My younger form rolls across the mud and comes to a stop beneath the tree where Nathaniel and I first fought.

The dirt doesn't cling to my skin. I don't move. I still don't try to defend myself.

I'm not awake yet.

In the distance, Tobias slips off his horse, his foot caught in the stirrup as it continues to gallop away from me.

Inside the image, Imatra bends over me, grunting as she picks me up.

I must be heavy—heavier than she expected—because she nearly drops me, my arms dangling as she tries again.

Dark light flickers, the image inside the bulb flashes as if the air moved too fast to see, and Imatra reappears in the middle of the burn site again.

She rolls me onto the ground, grunting with effort as she positions me on my back.

She breathes heavily, making me think that her dark magic is all but exhausted now. There are no other living creatures around to steal energy from, and the far-off grass has already withered and died.

With a heave, she raises her dagger above her head, but with much greater care this time.

"The whole heart," she mumbles. "It has to be the whole heart."

Her dagger rams into my chest a second before she looks directly into my younger eyes.

I'm finally waking up.

She pales. Her hand dives into my chest, her movements urgent.

Just as she pulls out her hand, bright, white light blasts across her body, blowing her backward.

She tumbles through the ash, landing on her side and sliding through the dirt, collecting blood and dust along the way.

Screaming, she pulls a cocoon of dark magic around herself

just in time, yanking her arms inward, tucking herself into a protective ball.

The wash of magic continues to cascade outward from my body.

Glitter grass springs up around Imatra, rising around the fallen bodies, spearing up through them, a vast ripple of light that spreads outward and flows onward, cutting through every obstacle in its path.

It crackles and hums like lightning, a scorching blaze of old magic burning a glittering barrier north and south of our position.

The rushing sound finally recedes and silence falls.

Imatra uncurls. When she sees how close she sits to the glitter grass, she scrambles away from it, kicking her legs in panic, causing the grass to hum dangerously.

She slows, her breathing erratic, carefully unfurling her right arm from around her chest and finally revealing the object she clutches in her hand.

A glittering diamond as large as her fist catches the light of the rising moon.

In the present, I catch my breath. She told me my heart had burned to ash.

Inside the bulb, Imatra's expression is dangerously dark as she peers closely at the stone, turning it to study its misshapen, jagged side, where a small chunk is missing.

"No," she whispers, tears of rage falling down her cheeks. "It's broken. *Useless.*"

She tips her head back, but before she can scream out her anger, my whimper sounds.

Imatra quickly presses the diamond into the ground behind herself, burying it in the thick ash so she can focus on my younger self.

The glow around my young body has receded, fading to nothing.

I'm covered in ash.

Within the image, I push up on my hands, trying to sit.

My dull, white hair falls across my shoulders. My faded eyes blink slowly while I clutch my chest, the intense pain I'm feeling evident in my drawn expression.

It hurts. I still remember how much it hurt when I woke up.

My chest has healed, leaving only the small, crescent-shaped scar—disproportionately small compared to what was ripped out of me.

Imatra's eyes widen as she stares back at me. I guess she thought she'd cut out all of my heart and that, even if I *had* retaliated, I died afterward.

Tears continue to stream down her cheeks, perfect pearls spilling across the ground around her.

Her facial features quickly smooth out. She holds out her hands.

"Come to me, child," she says, her voice soft and compelling. "Come away from the fire."

Inside the image, I hesitate, but only for a moment before I crawl through the ash toward her.

Her grasping hands pull me against her side.

"I'm sorry, child," she murmurs as she strokes my hair.

A slow smile crosses her face, a smile I never saw from my position cocooned against her chest. "I couldn't stop the Fell. They took everything from you, but one day... you will take everything from them."

The bulb goes blank. I stare at the emptiness inside it, trying to process the fact that my heart wasn't destroyed.

What's more confusing is that there's one more bulb resting on my chest.

Nathaniel's jaw is tight, his muscles tensing. He knows the

full truth about how his father died now. His gaze flickers from the remaining bulb to me. "There's more."

Crushing the bulb I already hold, I stare, exhausted, at the remaining orb. "I don't know if I can take any more."

Nathaniel reaches for my closed fist, his features softening. I allow him to unfurl my fingers from around the vine that has formed and place my hand beside the final bulb.

"Truth is never easy," he says, a storm of rage lurking behind his expression that he quickly hides from me.

I rub my forehead, the back of my hand resting over my eyes. "She stabbed your father in the back. She killed your people. What more did she do to you? To me?"

I want to crush the last bulb, not look at it. But until I face my past, the glitter field won't rest.

I won't rest.

With a steady exhale, I take hold of the final bulb.

This one doesn't knock me into the ground like the others. Instead, a freezing cold chill passes through me as if I plunged into icy water.

I shiver, take a breath, and cough, a wet sound because my mouth suddenly fills with liquid.

Gasping for air, desperate to let go of the bulb as quickly as possible, I hold it up to my eyes.

Inside it, Imatra stands beside the fae palace, its white towers rising up in the background.

She teeters at the edge of the Spinning Lake, but its surface is quiet and glassy, not even a ripple.

With a heave, she pitches a glittering stone into its center—a gleaming diamond the size of her fist.

My heart drops.

The diamond falls below the surface of the lake inside the bulb.

The moment the rock hits the bottom, there is a soft *thud*

and the water begins to turn. It pulses in time with the heart's beat until the lake churns smoothly around the diamond at its center.

In the present, icy liquid fills my mouth, choking me. I've felt the water's icy clutches before—this drowning sensation—but I never imagined it was real.

Nathaniel grabs me, shifting so that he can turn me onto my side. Water spills from my mouth, whooshing out with my exhaled breath.

I crush the final bulb in my fist. It's blank now—empty of memories again—while it rapidly transforms into another sharp vine. Sharp memories.

I curl up on the soft grass beneath me, shivering violently while Nathaniel curves over me, wrapping his arms around me so that his body heat can warm me. The buckles of his weapon harness dig into my side, but I don't care.

He strokes my back, his hand running over my shoulder blades, down to my hips, but he is silent.

"My heart." I sob-laugh, cry, and try to breathe at the same time. "The diamond at the center of the Spinning Lake is my heart."

CHAPTER 24

*J*ust moments ago, Imatra told me that my heart had crumbled into dust after she cut it out.

Once again, she lied.

Darkest of stars, I can't be surprised by that. She will never stop lying.

"She hid my heart in plain sight," I say, my voice wobbling with shock. "She told everyone the Spinning Lake was a monument to the final battle—to our victory over the humans. *Dear stars*... I slept in a room overlooking the diamond for the last seven years, and I never knew what it was. I never felt like it belonged to me."

"We need to get it back." Nathaniel's eyes meet mine, his own determined, but I shake my head.

"It takes a hundred Frost fae to freeze the Lake in winter, and a hundred Solstice fae to unfreeze it in summer. Even with the power I have now, I doubt I'll be able to break through to where my heart rests on the bottom. Even if I could..."

I close my eyes, taking deep breaths. "The stone in the Lake is broken. It's what remained after the first shard was cut out. It never felt alive to me. It's not like the piece you carried with you."

The life in the shard Nathaniel kept safe all of these years was so immense that I was afraid of it.

I have never felt that way about the diamond in the Spinning Lake.

The irony doesn't escape me that the largest piece of my heart never felt like mine, but the tiniest sliver felt like it had an entire universe trapped within it.

Nathaniel continues to rub my back, my arms.

His thumb grazes my cheek, smoothing across my tears. "Do you remember the first time I kissed you?"

My body glows, sudden warmth flooding me at the memory. "I'll never forget."

He continues, his voice soft. "I thought that we'd done something wrong, because starlight speared up through the Lake. It poured through you into me. I didn't know why or what to think."

I become very still. "My heart must have been trying to connect... If you'd been wearing the sliver of my heart at that moment, then the three pieces of my heart would have been in the same place for the first time since Imatra had tried to kill me —the stem inside me, the body of my heart in the lake, and the shard you kept safe."

"I didn't kiss you because I felt compelled to." Nathaniel brushes the hair from my face and wipes the icy liquid from my lips. "I did it because I wanted to. Because you are a beautiful, complicated, loyal woman who surprises me with your strength and your mind. We always had a choice about loving each other, Aura."

I close my eyes, unable to meet his. "We have choices to make now, too."

I take a deep breath, trying to focus as his hands trail

through my hair. "Imatra lied to me at every turn. I hoped that I could trust her word, but I can't. She promised to bring your weapon to the fight, but she won't. I know that now. You need the light to kill me—"

Nathaniel's jaw clenches, suddenly furious. "That will *not* happen—"

I cut him off. "Without that weapon, you don't have a chance! Look at how much power I control!"

I allow starlight to flood my body, calming power that could just as easily turn sharp and kill him.

Nathaniel tries to disentangle himself from my arms, the rage that he's been fighting all day returning to his eyes.

Since the moment I woke up tied to the pole, he has been angry, more reckless than before.

He's fighting the future, but he can't win.

"You need your weapon," I say, my hands clamping around his forearms. "We have maybe six hours until midnight. It's hardly enough time to find the halberd, but I won't fight you without it. I *choose* to spend my last hours finding the light. You need to choose too."

He becomes still, his hair falling across his face, obscuring the darkness of his expression.

I can't follow his thoughts anymore, the rapid changes of emotion hidden behind his hair. I can't read his rage or sadness or even know if his emotions have turned to stone.

"With Treble, we can fly anywhere," I continue, not giving up. "We can fly to Bright. We can get your weapon. We can make it back to the border by midnight. We can't change what's going to happen..."

Tears burn at the back of my eyes and my voice chokes up.

"We can't change this," I repeat, this time a whisper. I hold my breath as I ask him, "Will you come with me, Nathaniel?"

He has asked me that many times—asked me to come with him, to trust him. Now I'm asking him to trust me.

His chest rises and falls. His knee still rests between my legs. His attempts to untangle himself from me have lifted me half into a sitting position while he pulls backward so that we balance against each other.

I breathe out my relief when he says, "I will."

He reaches forward instead of straining against me, sliding his arms around my waist and shoulders but staying apart from me as he draws me upright.

The light inside my chest flickers—*hurts*—as we rise to our feet.

I inhale sharply when I finally see the field around us.

The glitter stems have transformed.

In every direction, soft waist-height grass sways in the breeze.

The bulbs that were already floating away have become flowers of all kinds drifting quietly toward Bright. My pain isn't gone, but I don't need the glitter field to protect me anymore.

I slip out of Nathaniel's arms, stepping back from him and finally breaking the contact between us.

Nothing explodes.

The field is quiet for the first time in fifteen years.

The air is sweet and warm despite the chill, the scent of new growth mixing with Nathaniel's body heat and filling my head.

Treble has already risen into the sky from the edge of the field where we left him, lightning sizzling around his body as he soars toward us. His wings crack as he exercises a new freedom to fly as close to the meadow as he wants.

This place was once deadly. Now he lands on the grass beside us and extends his wing for us to climb up, his neck arched and his eyes gleaming.

I race up his wing and settle onto his back while Nathaniel follows me. Despite the distance we are starting to put between us, Nathaniel's arms close around me as we settle onto Treble's back.

All around us, night has fallen, a heavy dark while the space around me glows.

I can't dim the light that shines from my body. Maybe with practice I would be able to, but it's not the most important use of my time right now.

I only have a few hours left.

I plan on using them to do all of the things I need to do.

CHAPTER 25

"Treble, do you sense the squadron above the mountains?" I ask, pointing to the specks in the distance.

Evander, Talsa, and the others will be waiting there to protect Bright from more glitter bulbs. They won't know that the glitter field is no longer a threat.

"I need you to take me to Talsa," I say to Treble. "She knows where Nathaniel's weapon is."

The last time I saw the halberd, Talsa was walking away with it. She never told me where she put it or what became of it.

I pray to the stars that she knows, since Imatra could have hidden it somewhere—or tried to destroy it.

I regret now that I revealed to Imatra how important the weapon is to us.

Treble rises into the air, spearing a path straight for the mountains. I relax in Nathaniel's arms, stealing his warmth and nearness like a hungry thief.

Casting a glance into the grassy dark beneath us, I can't tell where the transformed glitter field ends and the flower fields begin, but as we approach the mountains, I can see where the glitter bulbs exploded.

Parts of the crystal peaks have been chipped away, the glittering gemstones they concealed now exposed in the moonlight.

Other sections have been blasted open by the bulbs, widening the pass through the peaks. Jagged edges jut dangerously on all sides.

Treble beats his wings but doesn't crack them as we speed upward.

At the same time, Cadence drops from the clouds above, soaring down to meet us.

I catch sight of Talsa's coral hair as her thunderbird follows, while Calida, Mia, and Serena span out, alert and on guard, staying focussed on the sky around us.

"Aura!" As Evander draws level with us, the wind dies down and the air quiets. He's controlling it so that we can speak without shouting.

Nearby, the quiet concentration on Talsa's face tells me she's communicating with all of the thunderbirds, asking them to continue coasting near each other while we speak.

Evander's arctic-blue hair is braided back from his face like usual, but his blue-gray eyes are dull and strained.

He never appeared angelic, but right now, the edge of rage in his drawn-down eyebrows and the stern line of his lips make him appear savagely angry.

His gaze passes across my face, my hair, and all of the changes that must be as startling to him as they are to me.

Squeezing Nathaniel's hand, I rise on Treble's back before I judge the distance to Evander's bird and leap across the space between us.

I land in a streak of light on Cadence's back, just behind her saddle but still securely on her body, bending my knees to maintain my balance, while Evander slowly rises to stand.

"Aura?" He speaks my name like a question now.

Nearby, Talsa draws closer, her pink lips parted in surprise as she studies me.

I give my brother a half-smile. "It's me. I have so much to tell you, but there's no time—"

The air rushes from my chest as Evander steps across Cadence's saddle and scoops me into a sudden hug, his big arms wrapping around me, the scent of frost and ice enveloping me. "I'm glad you're okay."

"I'm not fae," I whisper, blurting out my revelation, finding it easier to speak the truth than I thought it would be.

Evander slowly draws back, a smile tugging the corner of his stern mouth. "I can see that." A light of hope enters his eyes. "Does this mean you're released from the Law of Champions?"

I shake my head. "I'm afraid not."

His hope vanishes, his paleness returning.

"I didn't kill your mother," I say, gripping his arm urgently. "I didn't kill the humans during the final battle. I don't have time to tell you everything, but I need you to believe me."

"I do."

His response is so immediate, so certain, that my glow flickers. Warms. I'm slowly becoming acquainted with the new sensations inside my chest. The variations of warmth and light that tell me whether I'm happy, sad, afraid… or hopeful.

Now, some of the tension leaves my body. When I last saw Evander, Imatra announced that I was responsible for the death of his mother.

I didn't want to live my final hours with the weight of Evander's grief on my shoulders. "Thank you, brother."

Evander switches his attention to Nathaniel for a brief moment, giving him a firm nod, before he turns back to me. "It's not safe here. The glitter field has been sending out bulbs all day and now the field has gone dark. There's magic at play—"

I take his arm. "The glitter field is gone. It's safe now."

"What? How?"

I give him a regretful look. "It's another thing I'd explain if I had more time—I want you to know that you don't have to worry about defending Bright against the bulbs anymore—but I also need your help."

After a moment's hesitation, Evander refocuses. "What do you need?"

"Actually... I need Talsa to tell me where Nathaniel's weapon is."

Talsa's thunderbird has drawn closer to us during my conversation with Evander, its wings swishing in time with Cadence's, a synchronized movement that allows them to fly close together.

All three thunderbirds appear to be deep in silent conversation and I'm relieved for Treble. The other thunderbirds shut him out before.

Now, I'm sure he's telling them everything he saw in Fell country—everything that happened. Because Talsa is a Dusk fae who can commune with animals, Talsa's thunderbird will be able to relay everything to her after we leave.

Talsa becomes very pale as she considers my request for information about the halberd. "Aura... I don't think it's a good idea..."

I sense her reluctance to give me information, but I won't accept evasion. She's one of the few fae whom I trusted before Nathaniel entered my life—especially after I found out that she and Evander had decided to commit to each other.

I try to soften my voice, but I can't keep the hard edge from it. "Don't keep the truth from me, Talsa. I'm done accepting lies."

She presses her lips together. "Nathaniel's weapon is being stored beneath the Inner Sanctuary. I only know this because..." Her gaze flicks to Evander, who is suddenly tense beside me. "I was trying to find out what happened to Crispin."

"Crispin?" My question is sharp.

The last time I saw my adoptive father was after Nadina threatened him at his home in the western mountains. He and the Springtime fae had spoken up about the boys in the mountain community who were allowed to die from the Ebon Rot.

When the men in the mountain community spoke up, Imatra threatened their homes and their lives.

I now suspect that Imatra was draining the boys' bodies to feed her dark magic—not in small, collective amounts like Cyrian does, but in a concentrated, targeted way that quickly killed the children she drained.

"What has Imatra done to Crispin?" I ask.

"The Queen imprisoned your father beneath the Inner Sanctuary," Talsa says. "He disappeared, but nobody knew where he was. Then I overheard a conversation between Nadina and the Queen last night, and I followed Nadina into the Sanctuary. There's a hidden panel at the back, similar to the one between your room and the Queen's. The Queen doesn't dare kill Crispin before the fight in case you hear about it and retaliate. Her future rests in your hands."

Anger rises inside me. I recognize it in the sudden heat within my chest: sharp, biting flickers. "She continues to play games with me."

"Nadina caught me while I was trying to free Crispin," Talsa says, her shoulders hunching. She gestures around the group. "We've all failed or disobeyed the Queen in one way or another. So she sent us out here to die protecting the border. Now that night has fallen... Evander, Calida, and Serena will weaken. I don't think we would have survived the next batch of glitter bulbs."

I scan their faces as they glide down and draw level with us.

Serena, the former champion, is a Solstice fae who failed to kill Nathaniel on the first day. Calida, also a Solstice fae, failed to defeat me in the arena to become the new champion. That was in addition to the constant trouble her family was causing the Queen. Mia is the Captain of the Queen's Night Guard, but she spilled secrets about the Queen to me at the celebration ball after the Winter Ascending.

Finally, I turn to Evander, not certain what he might have done to anger Imatra. The last time I saw them together, Imatra had declared her intention to marry him.

"Brother?"

A small smile softens Evander's expression. "I helped heal your thunderbird. A decision I haven't regretted for a second." He shrugs. "I may also have declined Imatra's offer of marriage."

"Forcefully." Talsa gives Evander a smile that shines in her eyes, chasing away her appearance of fatigue. She and Evander are very reserved in their outward affection for each other, having concealed it for a long time, but I see their love shining in both of their smiles. "With a strong slap of ice."

Evander grins. "Imatra's Frost power is not as strong as mine."

"Because she never had it," I say, making them both startle. "She uses dark magic to make it look like she controls the other elements."

"How?" Evander asks.

"She learned dark magic when she was a girl. The boys who died—she drained them. And probably many more before them. They would have been strategically chosen from families who didn't have the power or status to speak up."

Talsa stares at me. "But how could she possibly get away with it?"

"I'm guessing a few very public demonstrations of her power when she was younger," I say. "Once she gained a reputation for controlling all of the elements, it would only take carefully staged uses of magic after that to maintain her status. I don't know which power she was really born with."

"It has to be Solstice power," Serena says, her thunderbird drawing closer. "Firelight is her strongest power, the one she calls most quickly, and I can absorb it into my body like normal."

Fae of the same class can't hurt each other. Solstice fae simply absorb the heat of their brethren's power.

Firelight was the power Imatra instinctively used against Tobias in her moment of panic at the burn site when she missed cutting out my heart the first time.

Nearby, Calida nods, confirming her agreement. She has dark rings under her marigold-colored eyes, as if she hasn't slept since the fight with me. Her mane of dark blonde hair is tied back into lank braids and her shoulders sag. She would normally be preparing for sleep at this time of the evening.

Serena clears her throat, suddenly stiff.

She bites her lip, the only betrayal of her true regret as she inclines her head to both me and Nathaniel. "I apologize, Commander Lucidia, to you and the Fell for my actions the other day."

It's impossible to say 'that's okay' to someone who tried to kill the man I love, but I give her a firm nod and respond with the same formality. "Your apology is accepted, Serena of the Solstice."

Her thunderbird coasts away from us after she gives me a grateful nod.

Nathaniel has remained silent during the interaction, but now he speaks up. "We need to free your father."

And get Nathaniel's weapon at the same time.

I nod before I turn back to Evander. "The next time I see you, our father will be free."

On impulse, I hug Evander again, but this time, he doesn't let me go so easily.

"We're coming with you, Aura," he says. "We saw Nadina and the Queen flying back to Bright before you arrived. You'll need us to run interference. Otherwise, you'll have to fight your way through Imatra's entire Night Guard to get to her Inner Sanctuary."

I glance at Nathaniel. Each time we cross the border, the tables are turned on us.

Now that we're heading toward Bright, Nathaniel's bound by the rule that he can't hurt a fae.

He won't be able to help me fight Imatra's guards if it comes to a battle between us.

Tugging out of Evander's hug, I leap back to Treble, sensing Evander assist my movement by manipulating the air around me. I arch my eyebrow at him when my landing is far more graceful than it would have been otherwise.

Giving him a smile, I say, "Okay, then. But you'll need to keep up."

Evander grins, and I sense a layer of tension break around us, as if he and the others just shrugged off a set of shackles.

"Happily," he says, his voice drowned in the sharp crackle of lightning as the six thunderbirds span out, and we soar toward Bright.

CHAPTER 26

*O*ur thunderbirds fly across the snow-covered fields at the edge of Eteri City and over the tops of glistening orchards.

The humid air of Fell country is far behind us now, and I shiver in the crisp cold.

We fly in silence but without deviating from our target: the center of Eteri City, where the palace rests on the crest of mountains that cut across Bright.

As we pass across the orchards, Evander half-turns in his seat and curls his fingers in the air, a brief look of concentration passing across his face.

I'm not sure what he's doing until two cerulean-blue apples fly up out of the trees below us and land gently in my lap, carried by the wind.

Two periwinkle-colored citrus fruits follow them, along with Evander's water flask. Now that night has fallen, his power will become weaker with every use. It worries me, but I'm grateful for the food and hydration.

I hand two pieces of fruit back to Nathaniel and we devour

the food quickly before drinking as much sugar water as we need.

Soon after, the thunderbirds arc toward the platform that is supported by the palace's highest two towers.

Evander's voice whips back to me as we spear toward the landing, his magic carrying his speech directly to me. "Mia will keep the Night Guards busy. Once we're inside, we'll have to move quickly."

I'm not sure if Mia has retained her position as the Captain of the Queen's Night Guard and whether or not the guards will take orders from her.

Mia's thunderbird soars ahead of us, the thunderbird's white feathers bright in the dark, her orange tips glowing like flames when she cracks her wings as she alights on the platform.

Four Night Guards run toward her, their indigo dresses swishing around their legs. They appear to be the only guards on duty. For now.

"Mia of the Dusk!" the first woman shouts, reaching for the concealed weapon across her left hip. "You're supposed to be at the border."

The way she and the other three take offensive stances confirms that Mia is no longer their captain.

That doesn't stop Mia.

"I bring news for the Queen," she shouts, leaping confidently from her thunderbird's back and striding toward the guards, as if her status has not changed.

I can't stop the smile spreading across my face as Treble soars onto the platform, landing with the other thunderbirds in the wide space.

Mia was always an expert at faking confidence.

The moment Treble lands, Nathaniel runs down his wing, but I somersault from Treble's back, ready to take on the guards.

Ahead of me, Mia's thunderbird spreads her beautiful

wings to create a visual shield between us. When she cracks her wings again, the bright auburn lightning makes it look like the entire platform is on fire, which masks the glow from my skin.

Even so, the guards crane their necks, trying to see around the bird's feathers.

Their distracted movement is enough for Mia to leap forward, grip the first woman around the neck, and pull her to the ground while Mia sweeps the legs out from under the next woman.

The other two guards step into the fight, swords drawn, but Evander leaps from Cadence's back, his outstretched hands pouring slippery ice beneath their feet.

It's not a snow storm like he could produce during the day, but they lose their footing and Mia's quick punches knock them both out instantly.

She stands over all four unconscious women with a cocky smile as I approach with Nathaniel and the others behind me.

"We should kill them," Serena says, pressing her boot to the chest of the nearest one. The gold highlights in her amber hair take on the fiery light that Mia's thunderbird has created.

I shake my head at her, but it's a gentle movement.

Serena was always straightforward, direct about her intentions and her feelings. She trained me for five years while she was still the Queen's champion, and I never once discovered her weakness. Beating her in the coliseum required nearly killing her.

I lean down to the fallen women, focusing on the one who is already stirring.

My power feels very different now.

Before Nathaniel gave me back part of my heart, I would call my power from the deepest part of my chest, sometimes the depth of my mind.

Now it fills my hands instantly, a well that threatens to overflow if I don't control it.

I force my power to calm, to glow softly in my hands as I press my palm to the woman's forehead. Her eyes flicker open, wide and startled before they slowly close again.

She sighs and the tension leaves her body.

I do the same for the others, moving quickly between them.

"They shouldn't wake up for hours," I say, rising to my feet.

When I turn to my friends, I find Evander staring at me with a slightly vacant expression. Serena, Calida, Talsa, and Mia also blink slowly at me, each of them seeming overly subdued.

Nathaniel is the only one who appears normal and alert. His gaze meets mine for a moment before he inclines his head toward the doorway into the third tower that leads down into the palace.

He's right: We need to keep moving.

"Brother?" I ask, reaching for Evander, not sure why he's so quiet.

As soon as my hand closes around his arm, he shakes himself as if he's waking up, triggering the same movement among the others.

He draws himself upright, taking deep, waking breaths. "Let's keep moving."

Mia clears her throat, remaining where she is. "I'll stay and stand guard over these women. Talsa, will you join me? We can keep watch while we use our power to keep the thunderbirds calm. They need to be ready to fly when Aura returns."

Talsa quickly agrees. I admire the way she gives Evander a firm nod even when he casts her a questioning glance. She doesn't need him to protect her.

We exit the platform through the stone door and proceed down the stairs. At a steady walk, it normally takes ten minutes, but we make it in five before we prowl through the quiet hallways toward the Inner Sanctuary.

The halls are a little too quiet, which sets my nerves on edge.

Nathaniel draws close to me along the way. "Your power is much stronger now. You need to be careful when you use it."

I nod. He's right. I sent my friends into a stupor when I used my power to calm the guards. If I did that at a moment when they were vulnerable, my friends might not be able to defend themselves.

We slow down before we reach the large entrance room outside the Inner Sanctuary.

The corridor ahead is well lit, but there is a shadowy alcove before the final corner that we can huddle inside.

I remain behind Evander, staying well away from the corner so my glow doesn't give us away. I reach for Nathaniel, my hand resting on his shoulder so that I can maintain contact with his body and know where he is at all times.

"Damn," Evander whispers, drawing back into the shadows of the alcove. "The entrance is full of Night Guards. The Queen must be inside the Inner Sanctuary. We'll have to get past her, as well as all of her guards, to get to my father."

The Night Guard is made up of Dusk and Dawn fae. They are all trained in combat—even more skilled in battle than the Queen's Day Guard because the Night Guard can't use the elements as weapons.

Evander sinks to a crouch, rubbing his forehead in thought before Calida creeps up to him and taps him on the shoulder.

"Serena and I can take care of this," she says. "We each have a small reservoir of firelight left. If we create a fire as a diversion, the guards will evacuate the Queen from the Inner Sanctuary."

"By setting the room on fire?" Evander shakes his head. "It's too dangerous. I don't have enough power to extinguish the flames if it gets out of control."

"It's a real risk," Serena says, her forehead creased with worry as she joins the discussion. "But so is fighting our way through the guards. Believe me, I'd love nothing more than to kill most of them. But with a fire, they will evacuate Imatra and make sure she's safe first before they return to apprehend us."

Evander's forbidding expression deepens. "How do I know you won't seek to burn the very cage where my father is being held?"

Serena jolts as if he slapped her.

"Evander of the Frost," she says sternly. "You and I have never trusted or even liked each other, but you saved my life countless times above the crystal peaks today. My queen betrayed me. She asked me to kill for her in the name of loyalty. I will never do what she wants again. Now I ask you to trust me. My allegiance lies with you. So does Calida's. We won't betray you."

Evander casts a quick glance back to me, seeking my permission. I have greater reason to distrust both Serena and Calida than he does.

This could all be a ploy to betray us.

But I also hear pain and truth in Serena's voice. Imatra asked Serena to kill Nathaniel—even though Serena would die because of the Law of Champions. When Serena failed, Imatra sent her to the border to fight off glitter bulbs and die on the crystal peaks instead.

I give Evander a nod. At the back of my mind, I consider whether I could try to use my power to get us past the guards, but it would run the risk of affecting Evander, Calida, and Serena too. It would also require Nathaniel to reveal himself with me because I can't leave his sight—he couldn't stay hiding in the alcove where it's safe. I won't take that risk.

"Okay then," Evander whispers to Serena and Calida.

As soon as they have his permission, both women draw to

their feet, preparing to step out of the shadows, but a commotion beyond us makes them pause.

I reach for Serena's hand, grabbing hold tightly before she can move. "Wait. Don't go out there…"

Beyond us, I sense a rapidly approaching squadron of thunderbirds swooping directly toward the side of the palace.

A gust of wind suddenly billows through the corridor between us and the entrance room. At the same time, the echoes of cracking wings shrieks through the hall.

Evander leans around the corner before he darts back into the shadows.

"Imatra just opened up the south wall," he says. "I can't see much through the entrance room, but there's thunderbird lightning beyond it."

The wall on the south side of the Inner Sanctuary can be opened like it was on the night of the Ball. That side of the Sanctuary leads down to the Spinning Lake and then to the city that rests beyond the palace.

"A squadron just landed," I whisper. "Imatra must have opened the room to let them in."

It's very unusual for her to do that. Normally, all thunderbirds land on the platform where we first arrived. That they've flown directly to her indicates that she was expecting them.

A shout rises up from within the entrance room and one of the guards cries, "All Night Guards to your thunderbirds! Wake the Day Guards. The Fell King approaches the border! We must defend Bright!"

My eyes widen with surprise. Beside me, the stern line of Nathaniel's lips tells me he's unsettled by this news.

We left Cyrian and his hunters at the Ditch this morning. It shouldn't surprise me that Cyrian hasn't spent the day idly waiting for the final fight, but it seems reckless for him to approach the border so soon.

Despite that, my first fears are for Talsa and Mia. The Night Guards will head directly up to the platform to summon their thunderbirds.

I grab Evander's arm. "Talsa and Mia are up on the platform. We need to warn them—"

"I'll go," Calida says, her face filling with determination. "I'm a fast runner. We can fly our thunderbirds off the platform and stay out of sight until the guards are gone."

Evander doesn't hesitate. "Go! Run as fast as you can!"

Calida disappears, a lithe form moving as quietly as a ghost as she vanishes back the way we came.

Moments later, the corridors flood with guards. They're running quickly, but even so, the glow around my body will be a problem.

My light is going to give us away.

CHAPTER 27

*N*athaniel seems to sense my fear as I sink into the back corner of the alcove, his gaze flicking instantly to mine.

"Cover Aura!" he whispers as he closes the small gap between us, bundles me into his arms, drops to a kneeling position, and covers my body with his.

I end up in a ball, my knees to my chest, and my head pressed beneath his chin.

A second later, the pressure around me increases as Evander and Serena pile onto me, wrapping their arms around Nathaniel and me, covering the gaps around us.

Suddenly, we are all hugging each other, a situation I never thought would be possible.

Fae hugging Fell, protecting each other.

Everyone holds their breath.

Running feet race along the corridor beyond us as I think dark thoughts, wishing for my light to extinguish and not betray us.

EVERLY FROST

The sound of running feet finally disappears into the distance and then there's silence.

Some of the weight lifts off me as Evander peels himself away from our hug first.

Through a gap between his body and Serena's, I can just see Evander tilt his head to check the corridor. "They're gone."

Evander tugs on his own arm, which is caught between Nathaniel's back and Serena's chest as he awkwardly attempts to extricate himself from our hug.

Serena blinks her eyes rapidly, slowly slipping away from Nathaniel and releasing Evander's arm.

Her gaze runs intently across Nathaniel's face and shoulders. "Dear stars, you smell good."

Nathaniel gives her a blank stare as he straightens, pulling me with him while he rises to his full height.

He towers over Serena with a coldly disinterested glare.

She shakes herself, a fierce blush filling her cheeks before she clears her throat and backs away.

She may have changed her allegiance, but I guess she can't fight her inner nature so easily. Fae are open about their appreciation of beautiful things and Nathaniel is more than beautiful, he is fiercely powerful.

He is also beyond me now.

I turn away before he can see the pain in my eyes. I have a job to do: Free my father and retrieve Nathaniel's weapon.

"The way is clear," Evander says with a stern glance at Serena that tells her to behave. She shrugs in response before she leads the way into the corridor.

"I'll try not to burn anything down," she whispers with a smug wink as she prowls ahead of us.

We stay on alert as we approach the entrance room and enter the Inner Sanctuary.

Nathaniel matches my careful stride, always in tune with my pace.

The Inner Sanctuary is empty. As we suspected, the south wall is open and the room is exposed to the elements. The chill night air rushes through it, whistling along the far corridors.

The fountain in the center of the room is silent and still. The flowers that normally fill the room are gone, except for a few golden roses sitting in a discarded basket on the floor.

I used to believe that the Queen filled the flowers in her Inner Sanctuary with the essence of her power, that when she gave a flower to a fae, she was sharing her power with those who needed light in their lives.

Now I believe that the flowers are receptacles of dark magic —like the poisonous violet rose she sent to Crispin—ready to use if she needs them.

She also gave flowers to Nadina and Serena to allow them to use their firelight at night.

Serena bends and picks up one of the discarded golden roses. A smile spreads across her face. She quickly pins the rose to her armor before she extends her hands.

Flames burst into life around her fingers.

But her expression quickly falls as she gestures around the room. "The Queen has harvested all of her flowers tonight. Each of her guards will receive one. They will defy the night to use their power."

Evander sighs. "I don't suppose there's Frost power in one of those roses?"

Serena shakes her head. All four discarded flowers are golden. "I'm sorry, no. But I will take one for Calida."

In the distance, a squadron of thunderbirds, including the Queen's crimson bird, soars away in the direction of the border.

As we watch, another squadron appears high above us, following closely behind the Queen. It won't be the only one. If she's called all of her guards, then hundreds of thunderbirds will soon swarm toward the border.

Cyrian may have a hundred hunters, but they will never match the ferocity and sheer numbers of the fae warriors.

"We need to move quickly," Evander says. "Imatra's orders could change at any time. We can't assume we're in the clear."

"I'll stay up here and keep watch," Serena says, taking up position in the opening leading down to the Spinning Lake.

"This way," Evander says to me, leading Nathaniel and me to the back of the Sanctuary.

Once there, my brother runs his hands across the wall, seeking the hidden door. "Talsa said it was around the middle of the wall, but I can't—"

"Here," Nathaniel says, pressing his palm to a portion of the wall with a cluster of pastel roses painted on it.

He tests a section of the wall on his right before a *click* sounds and the passage opens up.

Evander looks surprised, but I'm not. Nathaniel identified the concealed door between my room and Imatra's before I told him it existed.

It could be because of the starlight he absorbed into his body for all of those years or simply because he's perceptive.

Evander doesn't waste time asking questions. He strides along the dark corridor situated immediately in front of us while we follow closely behind until we reach a set of stairs.

A light glows below us, but it's coming from the right, as if the stairs spiral around before they reach the bottom.

Evander gestures quietly, indicating that he's going to descend.

I stay close behind him, reaching for Nathaniel's hand, checking that he remains close to me.

No matter what happens, I need to make sure he stays alive.

Our steps are light. Silent.

My skin crawls the moment I set foot on the top step behind Evander. An icy chill runs through me. A cold burn.

My eyes widen as I recognize the malice of dark magic in the steps beneath my feet. It's in the air I'm breathing.

I glance at Evander, but he keeps moving. He doesn't seem to sense it.

"Evander, stop!"

My shout is drowned in the explosion of fire that cuts across the staircase, billowing across my brother's body and knocking him down.

CHAPTER 28

My starlight bursts outward, released from its constraints, forming a shield of glowing starlight that envelops Evander, me, and Nathaniel.

Pushing back the fire, my magic hums like the glitter field, soft where it touches us but sharp at its edges.

The flames shriek away from us, leaping away from the edges of my power before the fire forms the shape of daggers—hundreds of them—that stab at my starlight.

I brace, but the flames don't pierce my shield. They sizzle and die, vanishing into the air.

With a groan, Evander slumps to the steps.

I reach for him, but Nathaniel is already at his side, catching my brother before he tumbles down the staircase.

"He's alive." Nathaniel grips Evander's shoulders. "His armor protected his body, but his face and hands are burned." Nathaniel's lips press together with worry. "He's not in good shape, Aura."

The shield of my magic fades as I kneel beside Evander. My

magic flickers hard inside my chest as I take in all of the damage to his face. "Brother, can you hear me?"

When he doesn't respond, I place my palms in the air on either side of his head, careful not to make contact with his burned skin.

Calming warmth spreads through my fingertips and glows across his temples. It will keep him pain-free for now.

Tears trickle down my cheeks, but rage rises with them. "That was a trap set for Evander, triggered by his Frost power. I felt the chill before it struck."

Angry regret fills me. I should have been using my power to shield us, starting from the moment we stepped through the door.

I'm still discovering the extent of my power, but a shield like the one I produced when the fire struck would have protected Evander.

"I can carry him down the stairs," Nathaniel says. "Crispin can heal his burns. We need to get them both out of here."

Nathaniel maneuvers Evander so that my brother rests across his shoulders before Nathaniel rises upright again.

I make sure Evander's head remains steady and that his burned skin doesn't press against Nathaniel's shoulders before I step back.

My brother is not a small person. I suddenly flash back to this morning when Hagan carried Nathaniel to Treble's back. Latent panic grips me and I clutch my thigh so hard, I'm in danger of ripping the training suit I'm wearing.

I swallow a sudden sob, trying to push away my emotions, unprepared for how strong they are. Using my power seems to increase the intensity of my feelings, making me feel raw, far less in control.

Two days ago, when I took Nathaniel to Crispin and asked him to heal Nathaniel, Crispin told me that old magic is filled with all of the nuances of the human heart: both light and dark, happiness and sadness, anger and love.

All of these things rage through me right now, heightened with every passing minute of life I have left.

I hurry down the next three steps ahead of Nathaniel so he doesn't see the flood of tears I'm holding back.

"I'll protect you both," I say, forcing my voice not to wobble as Nathaniel follows me, his steps careful now that he's carrying Evander.

Nearing the bottom of the staircase, the room opens up around us.

It's like stepping into the White Walls all over again and I shiver at the cold memories. The walls and floor here are lined with pristine white marble, except that golden chains are securely bolted at intervals along the walls.

Crispin is shackled to the opposite side of the room, fully alert but gagged.

His shirt is ripped and his ash-gray hair is singed on the ends, indicating that he was attacked with firelight. His gray eyes widen as soon as he sees us. He freezes in the act of tugging on his restraints.

His gaze quickly takes in Nathaniel carrying Evander and then stops on me.

I haven't seen what I look like now, but I know I don't look like myself anymore, not like the daughter he knew.

Crispin watches me with a startled intensity, his strong eyebrows drawing down into a perplexed expression.

I read the question in his mind, the question that broke me apart: *What is she?*

It's impossible to speak with him. Nadina prowls back and forth in front of him, dressed in full battle armor.

She is the Captain of the Queen's Day Guard, the one who

threatened Crispin in his home and attacked Nathaniel above the glitter field at the end of our first day.

She's wearing another one of those damn golden roses.

She grips Nathaniel's halberd in her right hand as she paces, but she isn't tall enough to hold the halberd easily, pointing its blade down so that the shaft extends upward parallel with her arm.

Her eyes widen when she sees me, her jaw dropping a little before she collects herself.

Her upper lip curls in disgust, as if she considers me to be disfigured now. "The Queen said you'd changed."

"Then she wasn't lying," I say. "For once."

Nadina has never been easily intimidated. Tiny flames dance along the surface of her sleeves and lick around the tips of her fingers where she grips Nathaniel's weapon. "She also said you'd come for Crispin and, if you did, I am to kill him."

I pause before I take another step. Nathaniel stops behind me, slightly to my left, but while I freeze in place, he proceeds to the side of the room.

He carefully slides Evander to the floor, propping him into a sitting position against the wall.

Nathaniel appears completely unaffected by Nadina's threat, taking his time making sure Evander will remain upright, my brother's head supported against the wall.

Nathaniel's measured movements make Nadina twitch, which only makes me relax. She won't like that he's ignoring her.

A drop of sweat rolls down the side of her face, betraying her nerves.

The shrill tone of her voice conveys her fading confidence as she takes a step toward me. "I can burn you and your family to ash, Aura. I'll give you one chance to walk away, but if you don't, I'll start with killing your beloved father."

She points the halberd at Crispin, who watches Nadina with caution. It would have taken more than a few women to restrain him and bring him here, especially if the Springtime fae tried to protect Crispin.

A faint bruise across Nadina's cheek indicates she was wounded during the capture.

I exhale and inhale a calming breath. I wait for Nathaniel to return to my side. His focus is now fixated on his weapon, the gleaming blade swinging at Nadina's side—where it doesn't belong.

His gaze follows the line of her firelight down her sleeve, across the back of her hand, but the halberd's shaft doesn't catch on fire despite being wooden.

It looks like *the light* repels fae magic, just like we saw in the glitter bulb memories.

It's time to test whether the halberd repels old magic too.

Nathaniel glances at me, his muscles tensing a second before my right arm shoots up.

My power wells inside me, an endless tide that I'm holding back.

I don't have to call it. There's no split second of waiting. It's part of my body, covering me as closely as my skin.

It follows the path I want it to travel, the perfect angle with the perfect amount of force.

Starlight streaks toward Nadina.

Her firelight sparks a second later than my power, dragging from the golden rose, filling her free hand, coursing toward me in retaliation.

My power hits exactly where I want it to: the curved, silver blade.

CHAPTER 29

The impact is so sudden and fierce that it knocks Nadina's weapon from her hand.

Her blade spins midair and lodges in the wall behind her, far enough from Crispin that it's in no danger of hurting him and close enough that Nathaniel will be able to reach it without crossing paths with Nadina.

At the same time, my starlight bounces off the blade, cutting across the air in front of Nadina's chest.

She screams but doesn't try to retrieve the weapon, focusing her attention on me.

My power floods the space in front of me as her firelight hits me, the stream of her flames boring into the surface of the shield around me.

Needing to keep her attention on me, I stride toward her, lifting my arms to pour starlight through the stream of her power, slicing through it.

She raises her other hand, firelight streaking from both her palms, pouring across my starlight like lava, but I only increase my pace.

A moment later, I reach her at a run.

My right fist snaps out, cracking across her cheek, starlight flickering through her cheekbone on impact.

At the same moment, I grab her left wrist, wrenching it upward. Starlight and firelight splash around us like droplets of water, our magic sizzling in the air.

She tries to kick me, but I spin, jolting her arm backward, forcing her to lurch forward so I don't break her limb. I leap back when she retaliates.

I could finish her, but I release her instead.

I now stand between her and Crispin, one arm outstretched, ready to let my power loose, warding her off.

Across the way, Nathaniel braces against the wall and wrenches his weapon out of it.

The moment he touches the handle, a flicker of light travels up his arm and through his chest, burning gold across his heart.

The magic he took from me sparks against the light magic in the blade, a dangerous combination that takes my breath away.

If I'd had the sliver of my heart when I first met him, I would have seen it then.

But what would I have done, if I'd known everything I know now?

Finally in control of his weapon again, Nathaniel steps toward Crispin, shouting, "Lean forward!"

Crispin immediately obeys, stretching his chains taut behind himself and closing his eyes.

It is an act of pure trust.

Nathaniel could cleave Crispin's head from his shoulders. Hundreds of years of war between the fae and the Fell should tell Crispin not to trust Nathaniel at all.

Nathaniel swings the halberd, slicing cleanly through the chain constraining Crispin's right arm and then the one holding his right foot.

The shackles around Crispin's wrist and ankle remain in place, but he is half-free from the wall.

As Nathaniel swings his weapon again, this time aiming for the remaining two chains, Nadina demands my attention, flinging firelight at Nathaniel to stop him.

My hand darts out and my starlight cuts right through her flames, deflecting the fire onto the floor at Nadina's feet.

She flinches and lurches backward, her chest heaving. "I should have been the one to challenge you at the Winter Ascending," she snarls. "I would have killed you."

I tilt my head as I consider her. She was certainly the one I'd predicted I would be fighting. I was surprised when Imatra chose Calida, but then I found out that Imatra had leverage over Calida that would ensure Calida did everything she could to kill me.

Nadina, on the other hand, has never loved anyone enough for the Queen to have any leverage over her.

Winning a fight is not only about strength and skill. It's about knowing your opponent, their weaknesses, strategizing how to use those weaknesses against them.

Nadina is proud and overly confident. She's accustomed to bullying those who are vulnerable and controlling those who are as strong as her.

If I attack her pride, she will remain focused on me and not on what's happening around us.

Behind me, Nathaniel has freed Crispin, who races to his son's side, checking Evander's wounds. He needs time to heal Evander, which I plan to give him.

"Why don't we find out?" I say to Nadina. "Just you and me. Whomever subdues the other first."

She can't kill me. I can see her working through the consequences in her mind, but I don't want her to think too hard about it.

Before she can respond, I step forward and backhand her across her cheek, right where she already has a bruise.

It's a deliberately provocative move.

She sucks in an angry breath, retaliating with force, her fist aiming squarely for my stomach.

I allow her to land the punch, grab my arm, and swing me so that my right arm is curled around her chest. Her left elbow cracks across my face before she wrenches herself around again, still gripping my arm and forcing me into a crouch.

We're now facing each other again.

A cruel smile spreads across her face. "You're not so strong."

Pulling me upright, her free fist cracks across my face before she releases me. She is not lithe and agile like Calida. Meeting Nadina's fist is like greeting a bag of rocks.

Warm liquid trickles down my cheek—blood—but Nadina takes a quick step back as she focuses on it, a suddenly startled look on her face.

I don't have time to check the liquid to see what has surprised her so much.

She quickly hides her expression, charging toward me again.

Across the way, Crispin pulls Evander into a hug. Evander's head drops to his father's shoulder. He's still unconscious, but the quick view of his skin tells me he's healed.

Nathaniel crouches and pulls one of Evander's arms across his shoulder and Crispin turns so that both men rise up with Evander between them, carrying him by supporting one of his arms across their shoulders.

I've bought them the time they needed.

My right foot snaps out in a solid kick that knocks the wind out of Nadina's chest, her own momentum adding to the force of the blow.

I follow through with two fierce punches before I leap, knocking her off her feet and onto the hard marble floor.

She screams, not expecting the full force of my fists since I went easy on her before.

My knee lands on her chest, pinning her down while my power sizzles through my hands, my palm hovering above her face and casting starlight across her startled eyes.

"It's over, Nadina," I say. "Only the fight between Nathaniel and me will determine the fate of the fae now."

She snarls up at me. "You were never worthy of Imatra's attention."

"Her games, you mean," I say. "She plays games with everyone, Nadina. You just don't know it until the rope she placed around your throat squeezes so tightly that you can't breathe anymore."

Firelight flickers in Nadina's eyes, sizzling down her chest and arms, but my starlight presses back against it. Two days ago, I told Serena that it isn't my job to kill my people, but now I'm not sure who my people are. The fae... the Fell... the Lucidia...

This close to the golden rose pinned to her chest, I can see that most of its petals have turned black. She has used up nearly all of the malice in the flower.

She might only have one solid attack of firelight left.

"We're walking out of here," I say to her. "If you value your life, you'll let us leave."

She cranes her head upward, her speech venomous. "I will kill your family. I will kill everyone who loves you. I will kill—"

My power glows across her face and her eyes turn instantly blank. Asleep. Her head drops to the floor, but I catch her before her skull splits on the hard surface.

I have to believe that there is hope for her, the same way there was hope for Serena, who tried to kill Nathaniel because she believed she was doing the right thing.

But with Nadina... I shake my head, uncertain, as I rise to my feet, leaving her where she lies.

Nathaniel and Crispin wait at the bottom of the stairs for me.

Nathaniel holds his halberd safely, blade down, on his other side. Crispin is the closest to me and I can just make out Evander's serene face where he rests between them. He's sleeping peacefully now.

Crispin reaches out his hand for me, his previous disquiet hidden. When I first arrived, he looked at me as if he didn't know me, but now he gives me a smile that softens his harsh features.

He murmurs, "Here stands before me a woman who is as bright and courageous as she was always meant to be. You are *you* now, Aura."

Sudden tears burn at the back of my eyes. Crispin was never one for speeches. He's been a steady but stoic presence in my life.

I take his hand, needing to tell him how grateful I am that he raised me, that he took me in when nobody else would.

A flash of dark light breaks across my vision.

I spin back to Nadina in time to see her rise up and throw the liquid dagger she just plucked from her hip at Crispin's heart.

CHAPTER 30

*D*esperate to stop the blade, my hands shoot out, blasting starlight across the space between Crispin and the dagger, but I'm already too late.

"No!" My scream echoes around us as the blade thuds into his shoulder.

The impact knocks Crispin back into Evander while Nathaniel tries to grab them both to stop them all from falling.

I run toward them, grasping Crispin while Nathaniel catches Evander before he hits the floor.

"Crispin!" I shout.

My father's eyes are open, his face filled with pain, but his gray eyes are also hard and fearless.

Angrier than I've ever seen him.

Nadina's gleeful laugh reaches me from where she's crouched on the floor behind us, her dagger arm still outstretched.

The petals of her golden rose are now withered and black. The last flare of dark magic must have allowed her to wake up while giving her a burst of energy.

"I warned you, Aura," she says.

I turn back to Crispin. We're all tangled up now. Crispin is caught in my arms while leaning partly on Evander, who's being held upright by Nathaniel.

Crispin grips my arm. A stronger hold than I was expecting.

My gaze shoots to the dagger.

It's lodged in the fleshy part of his shoulder. Not his heart.

I sob with relief and begin to speak. I want to tell him that I can remove the dagger, cauterize the wound, that he'll be okay. He has to be okay.

"Hush." He growls as he wipes his hand through the tears running down my cheeks. "You've protected me enough."

He lifts himself upright, putting me to the side as he maneuvers his way to his feet, the dagger still embedded in his shoulder.

Nadina's laughter fades as Crispin takes a determined step toward her, testing his balance before he takes another step until he's moving at speed toward her, faster than she would ever expect.

She screams. Pales. Begins to scoot backward. She tries to get to her feet, but Crispin reaches her, grabs her shoulders, and drags her upright.

Her hands shoot up as if she's about to draw on her power, but the flames don't appear.

She's used up all of the stored magic. The flower is dead.

Her hands form into fists instead. One after the other, her punches land on Crispin's face and chest, hard crunches that he ignores, absorbing her blows. He spent his life with Springtime fae, woodcutting, hauling timber, a life that toughens the heart as well as the skin.

"This is for the boys you killed," he says.

Holding her one-handed, he wrenches the dagger from his

shoulder. She thumps his hand where he holds her, kicks his legs, screams at him to let her go.

He drives the dagger into her throat.

Her eyes fly wide, but he shoves her away from himself, wrenching out the dagger. She lands on the white marble floor, facing away from us, finally becoming still.

Crispin's dagger arm drops to his side. He remains exactly where he stands, but his arms begins to shake.

I'm still kneeling on the floor, reaching back instinctively for Nathaniel, finding his hand in mine.

"Go," he whispers. "I've got Evander."

Rising to my feet, I take quiet steps toward Crispin. The tremble in his body tells me that shock could set in soon. He has never killed before, and he's losing blood from the wound in his shoulder.

He barely looks at me when I draw level with him.

"I never thought I'd see a day like this," he says. "When I would kill a fae while a Fell helps me escape. Trapped by my own people, freed by my enemy. And you, Aura…" He finally turns his gaze to mine. "What bright truth burns in your heart now?"

I can't even begin to answer that question. I busy myself around him, reaching up to place my hands on either side of Crispin's wounded shoulder. "I'm going to cauterize your wound now."

"No need," he says. "I can heal myself." Despite his assertion, he places his free hand over the top of mine where I pressed it across his wound.

The healing power in his palm warms through me before it reaches his shoulder. I close my eyes for a moment, soaking it up, needing it to help with the pain inside my own chest.

When he's finished, Crispin places the dagger on the floor so he can grip my shoulders with both of his hands. "Am I going to lose you today, Aura?"

I swallow my sadness, forcing myself to meet his eyes.

"I can't answer that," I whisper. "But I want you to know that I'm glad you raised me. You are my father."

Tears swim in Crispin's eyes, but I hurry on. "Come now. We don't have much time left. Evander needs you."

Across the room, Evander is beginning to stir, sitting up slowly and then more quickly. He squints across at us. "Dad?"

"I'm here, son."

Crispin hurries to Evander's side, helping him stand while Nathaniel withdraws, remaining apart from them as they ascend the stairs.

I clasp my hands together, my own shock starting to kick in before I move to Nathaniel's side.

I reach out and close my hand across the top of his where he grips his weapon.

My smaller hand doesn't reach much farther than across the backs of his fingers, but I press for a moment before I release him. "Thank you for helping my brother."

He gives me a quick nod before we follow Crispin and Evander in silence, meeting Serena in the Inner Sanctuary.

She rushes forward, but Evander waves her away. "I'm fine. I want you to take Crispin, Talsa, and Mia back to the mountains, where they'll be safe."

She nods, but Crispin scowls at his son. "Where will you be?"

"I won't let Aura fight alone. I will go to the border with her."

Crispin scowls at Evander for another moment. I read a heavy retort on his lips before he suddenly capitulates, exhaling softly. "Okay, then. We'll do what we have to do."

My father's eyes meet mine for a moment before he turns away with Serena and they disappear through the far door.

Evander spins to me. "Tell me what you need, Aura."

There's nothing he can do. The sky beyond the Inner Sanctuary is clear, the moon high. We only have two hours until midnight, one of which will have to be spent flying to the border.

Nathaniel and I have two hours left before we fight.

One of us has only hours left to live.

Before I can speak, Nathaniel steps toward Evander. "We need food. Whatever you can find. Please bring it back here and stand watch while we go upstairs to find new clothing. Aura needs her armor and a fleece to keep her warm. I won't allow my wife to freeze before she fights me."

"Wife?" Evander jolts, his eyes widening.

"Yes," Nathaniel says, a challenge entering his eyes as he returns Evander's shocked stare.

I spin to Nathaniel, cutting off their conversation. My fingers curl around his arm, sensing the undeniable tension in his body. "You don't have armor. I won't fight in mine if you don't have yours—"

"Aura." Nathaniel grips my hand. "Cyrian has come to the border. He doesn't want me to lose. He will have brought every weapon he can to ensure I win, including my father's armor. Dark stars, he would probably give me his own armor if he thought it would help."

I search Nathaniel's eyes, wondering about the likelihood of his theory. Cyrian may hate Nathaniel, but his future rests in Nathaniel's hands and the outcome of this battle.

I have to consider that Nathaniel could be right. I can always change out of my armor if he isn't.

"Very well," I murmur.

Turning back to Evander, I find him disappearing through the far door. "I'll be back with food," he calls. "As fast as I can."

Nathaniel doesn't wait for Evander to return. He sets off

immediately to the staircase on the far right-hand side of the Inner Sanctuary.

I follow him up into the Queen's Tower where my bedroom is situated. On our way, we pass the guard's barracks on the lower two levels—both empty now—and ascend onto the upper floor.

He continues along the wide, decorated corridor, passing the opulent bedroom where he stayed on our first day before he pauses outside my room.

I forgot how stark my bedroom looks—so small with nothing more than the bed, closet, chest of drawers, and a mirror, all of it gray.

I expected it to be destroyed, for Imatra to have raged through it, shredding my clothing and ripping apart my furniture, but it appears untouched.

The only difference is that the poisonous violet rose she gave me rests on top of the chest of drawers. I left it in Nathaniel's room, but I guess she wouldn't want it there in case someone touched it.

"It feels so empty," I murmur as I set foot inside my room, venturing toward the open window to look out across the sparkling lights of the city.

Nathaniel closes the door behind me, his hand resting on the door handle, his shoulders hunching before he leans his halberd against the back of the door.

He surprises me when he unhooks the mirror from the wall and brings it to me.

"You should see what you look like now," he says, stepping back and maintaining his distance once I take the mirror from him.

The mirror tilts away from me so that it reflects the light of the moon across my window ledge.

It will only take a small movement for me to look into it, but my appearance won't change anything.

I don't need to see myself to know what Nathaniel thinks of me. He thought I was beautiful when my hair was dull white, my eyes pale, my lips colorless, when I considered myself nothing more than a shield to protect my queen or a weapon for her to wield.

When every other fae and human I met thought—and sometimes expressed very publicly—that I was ugly, Nathaniel saw more.

I'm not sure how to tell him that his opinion matters more to me than what anyone else thinks.

I turn the mirror over and place it face down on the bed. Then I turn and cross the distance to him to slide my arms around his chest, ignoring the bite of his weapon harness.

I bend my head to rest my ear against his heart as the handles of his daggers press into my chest. He tenses before he relaxes within the circle of my arms.

I've kept him at arm's length for the last few hours, but I can't continue to push him away without one last touch, no matter how painful it is to expose my sadness right now. No matter how much I want to scream at the passing minutes.

His hands tangle in my hair. He presses a kiss to the top of my head before he draws away from me, turns quietly to my closet, and opens the cupboard doors.

Multiple suits of armor hang inside it, all indigo.

He pulls one out and hands it to me. I take it before I lean around him, reaching down to retrieve the pelt I rolled up and left at the bottom of my closet on our first day.

It's the pelt he was wearing when I first met him, charcoal-gray fur drawn together at the top by a golden chain. The coat of an alpha wolf.

Nathaniel accepts it but doesn't put it on.

We stand looking at each other for a moment, the silent seconds ticking past.

I close my eyes, taking every inhale like it's my last as I strip off my human clothing.

Somehow, I've never felt so naked as the beige training suit falls to the floor, followed by my underwear.

It feels like I'm removing everything that happened since I met Nathaniel and erasing all of it.

Reaching for clean undergarments, I carry them with me to the bathroom.

Nathaniel places the pelt on my bed before I can leave his sight. He shifts to stand in the bathroom doorway, staring up at the ceiling while I use the facilities and wash up.

After pulling on my clean underwear, I swap places with him, and I fixate on the floor as he also uses the bathroom and washes up.

When he returns to my side, I set about pulling on my armor and my boots. The clothing fits perfectly, designed for me. I finish doing up the final clasp, inhaling the scents of my room and my clothing. Remembering my life as the Queen's champion.

Suddenly, the act of getting dressed feels final.

The hug I gave Nathaniel and the kiss he dropped on my head were the last acts of affection between us.

He pulls my snowy-white fleece from my closet—the one I wore to my fight with Calida—and hands it to me. It settles around my shoulders, lighter than the pelt I wore in Fell.

"You're Imatra's warrior now," Nathaniel says as he pulls on his pelt.

He draws his broad shoulders back, allowing the fur to settle across his body. Strands of his hair fall across one side of his face, brushing his cheeks and the growth that shadows his jaw.

His full lips draw into a merciless line, the same determination filling his expression that did the moment I first set eyes on him.

I incline my head, as if we're meeting for the first time. "I'm not your wife anymore."

He nods. "My wife is in my heart. She's safe there."

"My husband is in my memories," I say, taking a step away from him. "For as long as I live."

I step toward the door, the air suddenly choking in my throat as I beat back the finality of our descent down the staircase.

CHAPTER 31

*W*hen we reach the Inner Sanctuary, Evander waits with a plate full of food.

Nathaniel and I take what we need and separate from each other, moving to stand as far away as we can.

Evander casts concerned glances at each of us before his expression settles into resignation.

He can't know the extent of the bond Nathaniel and I formed, but he will understand that we need to distance ourselves from each other now.

He approaches me quietly. "Aura, bringing you food seems trivial. What else can I do to help you?"

He hasn't asked me the painful question that Crispin did—whether I plan on being alive after dawn—and I'm glad.

I can't tell my brother the truth.

I glance across at Nathaniel, the way he studies the horizon beyond us, the glittering city, and the stars above it.

I wonder for a moment if he is searching for my people in the ether, the dancing Lucidia who have no reason to fear or care about what happens to the fae or the Fell.

"Nathaniel can't ride Treble with me anymore," I say. "I can't let him closer to me than he has to be. Will one of the other thunderbirds accept him as a rider?"

Evander tips his head in thought. "Thunderbirds choose their riders, Aura, you know that." He presses his hand to my shoulder. "But he can ride with me."

"Thank you." I finish my food before I take a step toward the open side of the Sanctuary, checking that Nathaniel is also finished eating before I step outside and compel him to follow me.

He immediately steps forward, his dark gaze flashing to me.

He knows where I'm going.

I can't retrieve my heart, but I want to see it, knowing for the first time what it really is.

Crossing the platform, I descend the wide marble staircase, counting the fifty steps it takes to reach the Spinning Lake at the bottom of it.

I stop at the edge, suddenly unable to step onto the frozen surface. I close my eyes, needing a moment—just one moment to try to breathe and calm the flickers inside my chest.

The city is quiet in the distance. A heavy calm rests over it. Bright moonlight shines across the Lake while the whisper willows at its side swish quietly in the breeze.

Evander stops beside me, a quiet presence. "Imatra ordered everyone to stay inside their homes tonight," he says. "Some fae are afraid, but most believe you won't fail them."

"I will do what's right for the fae," I say.

Evander gives me a thoughtful look, because my answer was ambiguous. "What do you believe is right for us, Aura?"

"Nathaniel is your only chance for peace," I say, meeting Evander's eyes.

I sense Nathaniel approach behind us, but if he heard me, he doesn't show it.

Unlike me, he doesn't stop at the edge of the Lake, proceeding straight out onto it, an immense figure, his halberd swinging gently at his side and his pelt kicking against the back of his boots.

He paces directly out to the center of the Lake before he stops and scrutinizes its surface, his expression taking on an intensity that makes me wary.

He moved with purpose, as if he has a plan, but I'm not sure what he could intend to do.

He catches my eye. His lips tug upward in a dangerous half-smile. The determined look on his face makes my heart stop flickering.

What is he about to—?

With a roar, he rises up, his halberd gripped in both fists before he crashes down onto one knee, driving the staff onto the surface of the lake.

Light magic blasts across the frozen water in every direction, knocking Evander and me off our feet and driving us back against the marble steps.

Our armor protects us from the bone-crunching impact, but it's not the danger to myself that I'm worried about.

I scramble forward in time to see a giant crack form in the ice, spreading out in both directions from Nathaniel's position.

The earsplitting shriek of breaking ice merges with the reverberating hum of light magic, causing vibrations of power to shoot through me.

In the center of the lake, the ice opens up beneath Nathaniel's feet.

He plummets from view so quietly that it stops the light within my chest.

I can't see him. I *need* to see him.

"Nathaniel!" My body and soul wrench me toward him.

I run, slipping on the frozen surface, skidding, forcing my

legs to move. My cold breath rasps in and out of my chest, grating against my throat.

I slide the last five feet, hitting the edge of the ice and leaning over it, barely keeping my grip.

A shallow flood of water rushes around the bottom of the frozen chasm, spinning like it always did, while the walls of the valley rise up, jagged on both sides, at least thirty feet deep.

Nathaniel stands in the middle of the chasm. I search for signs of injury, but his shoulders are drawn back, his head and torso upright.

His weapon is lodged in the ice wall on his right-hand side at the bottom of a long cut that descends all the way down, as if he plunged the blade into the ice to slow his fall and land safely.

He looks up at me.

His hand rises.

My diamond heart glitters inside his fist.

All sound dies in my throat. Even from this height, his dark gaze can burn right through me.

Without hesitation, he removes the daggers from the front of his harness, bends to the water at his feet, and drives the blades one after the other into the bottom of the lake. They form a circle right where I imagine my heart used to rest.

Then he unbuckles his harness underneath his pelt and repositions the straps so that they wrap around the diamond before he secures the rock to his chest.

Wrenching his halberd from the ice wall behind him, he takes a moment to consider the ice on the side on which I lie before he turns the weapon around.

He taps the dagger side of the halberd against the ice wall. Using the spike, he carves out a shallow hole before he creates another one on the right, spaced apart and higher than the first.

He draws back his arm before plunging the dagger side of the halberd as high up as he can.

Then he begins to climb, painstakingly carving out new footholds, plunging his weapon into the ice, and returning to the surface, one step at a time.

Finally, he is within reaching distance.

I grab his hands, helping him pull himself onto the surface, his body painfully close to mine as we lie on the surface, the pressure of his arms around me excruciatingly wanted.

I roll away from him before I don't have the will to separate from him.

While I rise lightly to my feet to stand a few paces away, he recovers more slowly, his chest rising and falling with exertion.

His boots are covered in a fine layer of frost—the water that splashed around his feet must have frozen over on the way up.

He takes two steps toward me before he drops to a knee and unbuckles his harness so that my heart drops into his hand.

He holds the diamond up to me.

"You deserve to have the choice," he says, holding my heart in his open palm.

I told him that my heart is broken, that I never suspected that the diamond belonged to me, that it never called to me.

I wasn't afraid of it before, but I am now.

Beneath the surface of the glittering rock, starlight flickers, beating in time with the power inside my chest. It dances within the diamond as if it's completely free, an essence that was taken away from me.

My hands form into fists before the urge to take the heart becomes too strong.

"If I take it back, will I become a Lucidia again?" I ask. "Will I lose the form of a woman?"

Nathaniel is quiet. "I don't know, Aura."

"I can't take that chance," I say.

"Life is full of chances."

"But not like this. Not one that could change me so much."

The corner of his mouth rises, the darkness in his eyes increasing. "Every choice changes us."

Pain strikes through my chest at the truth in his statement. Nathaniel made a choice to come to Bright to find me. I made a choice to challenge him, not knowing it would bind our fates.

Long ago... Imatra made a choice to pull me from the sky and Nathaniel's father made a choice to try to save me.

Every choice has led to now—to Nathaniel holding my broken heart in his hands, offering me the chance to be whole again, whatever *whole* will be.

He rises to his feet, his hand lowering, but not to his side.

He reaches for my fist, his big palm closing over mine, the contact between us making me shiver.

His hand is cold, too cold, from the ice he climbed.

On impulse, I pull his palm to my chest, trying to warm him.

At the same time, the rock presses to my heart.

Silence fills the air around us, a deep silence like waiting for a waterdrop to hit the bottom of a well.

I expected to feel sadness, fear... maybe hope. I thought my heart would burn and my emotions would rocket out of control, but... the diamond remains hard, jagged, and foreign where it presses against my armor.

Confusion is the only emotion flooding through me.

I raise my eyes to Nathaniel.

His forehead is creased, his head tilted, as if he expected more too.

When I took the shard from him, it had burned its way inside me, unstoppable, an explosive force that connected with me instantly.

But this time...

"It doesn't know me," I say.

A tear trickles down my cheek and now sadness wells inside me. "You kept the piece of my heart alive by holding it close to you. You taught my heart your humanity, your emotions, and your will to survive. In return, my heart gave you some of my light and kept you safe. This diamond is nothing more than stone with old magic trapped inside it. It doesn't know what a heart really is."

Nathaniel allows me to nurse his hand against my chest a moment longer than he should. He finally pulls away, clearing his throat as he leaves the diamond in my fist.

"You should keep it with you, where it's safe," he says.

I'm suddenly aware of Evander hovering at my side. He won't understand what's going on right now, but Nathaniel turns to him anyway.

"We need a pouch," Nathaniel says. "One that Aura can wear while she fights me. This diamond can't leave her side." He turns back to me. "Ever."

Evander gives Nathaniel a nod before he races away, leaving us in the quiet.

We back slowly away from each other again and wait while the cold air brushes our cheeks and the whisper willows continue to sway.

Finally, Evander races down the stairs again. He has barely broken a sweat when he reaches us, his strength and stamina honed by years of training.

He hands me a leather pouch attached to a narrow belt.

I try to find my voice. "Thank you, brother."

Sliding the diamond into the pouch, I secure the belt to my waist before I place my fingers to my lips and whistle for Treble.

I need to take to the air, to feel the final freedom of flight.

Evander mimics my call, but with a different sequence of sounds to draw Cadence to him.

Now that the Lake is cracked down the middle, the safest place to land is at the side near the steps.

When Nathaniel prepares to join me, I hold up my hand to stop him. He halts, but he doesn't appear surprised.

"You'll ride with me," Evander says quietly to him, inclining his head toward the clear patch of grass on the other side of the steps.

Nathaniel's gaze drops to the surface of the frozen water for a moment, but when he looks up again, he doesn't show any emotion.

Treble approaches first and I burst into a run, leaping upward to catch his wing and swing myself onto his back.

My thunderbird casts a questioning glance back at me, but I shake my head. "Nathaniel will ride with Evander now."

Treble keens, a sad sound, but I also sense him communicating silently with Cadence as she soars into view, and I'm grateful, since Treble will be able to tell Cadence that she can trust Nathaniel.

I lean across Treble's side so I can see Nathaniel as Treble banks upward and circles the lake.

Lightning pulses around Cadence's wings as she sails toward the patch of grass where Evander stands with his arm raised.

Once she lands safely, Evander removes her saddle, and she extends her wing to accept Nathaniel onto her back. He sits apart from Evander as they rise into the air.

The two birds crack their wings in unison, settling into position side by side as they soar into the air.

We will have to remain below cloud cover so that Nathaniel and I can see each other at all times, but we will need to fly quickly now to make it to the border by midnight.

I pull my fleece close to my body, lean forward over Treble's neck, and accept the rush of wind across my face, allowing it to wash away any remaining doubt about my path ahead.

CHAPTER 32

*W*e soar across Eteri City, passing over the frost-covered homes and trees before we sail between the crystal peaks, picking our path carefully through the newly jagged passes, avoiding the damage the glitter bulbs caused.

Along the way, Evander turns around on Cadence, and he and Nathaniel talk.

I can't hear what they're saying, but Evander appears to be asking questions and Nathaniel seems to be answering them.

Every now and then, my brother glances my way, sometimes with surprise, other times with sadness.

I suspect he's asking Nathaniel for all of the answers I didn't have time to give him before now.

It looks like Nathaniel is telling him everything.

I find myself filled with an unexpected sense of relief, thankful that someone will know the truth about my time with Nathaniel and the story about who I am and how I came to be.

By the time we reach the other side of the crystal peaks, Nathaniel and Evander have fallen silent.

Moments later, I sense disturbances in the air both behind and in front of us.

Up ahead, countless squadrons of thunderbirds fill the sky with a rainbow of lightning while still more have landed within the flower field on the Bright side of the border, forming a formidable force in the air as well as on the ground.

At the same time, the air behind us fills with an eerie crimson glow and the sound of enormous, beating wings.

I glance back to see the Vanem Dragon soar in our direction, surrounded by the remaining thunderbirds from the northern mountains, whose colorful lightning crackles across the sky above them.

My breath catches when I see that the thunderbirds have riders, but their riders are not dressed like the Queen's guards. These fae wear simple clothing. Many of them are male with dark brown hair shot through with forest green highlights.

They're Springtime and Harvest fae from the mountain community.

"Crispin," I whisper, picking him out where he rides with Talsa.

Serena and Mia also fly their thunderbirds close by.

The sight of them fills my chest with warm flickers. Crispin said he would do what he needed to do. I guess that meant returning home so he could bring the mountain fae back with him.

They are not aligned with Imatra and will be a supportive force for both me and Nathaniel.

The Vanem Dragon blocks the moonlight as he sails overhead, his wing beats upsetting the air around us, forcing me to grip Treble's back as hard as I can and lean low over his neck.

I inhale the dragon's fiery scent as he sails past, a reminder of the woodfire in the cabin where I grew up, and of cold winters spent shooting starlight into the night sky—never knowing that's where I came from.

As we draw closer, I can finally see Cyrian's forces on the other side of the border—a hundred hunters positioned within the remains of the glitter field.

Behind the hunters, a pack of wolves and—to my surprise— three bears are chained to poles at the edge of the Misty Gallows, all of them resting on their haunches so obediently that they can only be spelled by dark magic.

Half of Cyrian's hunters congregate around three large iron contraptions—machines of a kind I've never seen before.

They're each at least thirty feet high with a base and frame made of iron poles that support a long, metal beam attached to an axle. A metal sling hangs from the end of the beam while two large steel bins sit beside each machine.

The structures appear so heavy that they've gouged tracks into the earth leading up to their location. The machines must be some sort of weapon, but I'm not sure what they'll do.

I'm suddenly reminded of Mathilda's warning yesterday morning when she told us that Cyrian had been drawing large amounts of energy from his environment in the last day, but she didn't know why.

The Vanem Dragon soars ahead of us and lands in the wide stretch of field hundreds of feet wide that remains empty between the two armies.

Even when he folds his wings, he makes the humans and fae appear miniature as he prowls along the wide gap between them.

As Treble flies over the fae army, Imatra comes into view below me, standing at the head of her soldiers on the ground. She's dressed in her crimson armor, her hair tied back this time.

Opposite her across the field, Cyrian also stands at the head of his men, dressed in full battle gear with a double-headed axe in a holder across his back.

Crispin and Talsa, along with Serena and the fae aligned with Crispin, break off from us, their thunderbirds veering left to land at the eastern end of the gap between the two armies, staying clear of both Imatra and Cyrian's people.

I'm not sure what Imatra will make of Crispin's appearance —or Serena and the others—since Imatra wanted them all dead, but she won't be able to retaliate as long as the Vanem Dragon is in control.

I lean over Treble's neck and ask him to land as close to the Vanem Dragon as he can. It's best if Nathaniel and I avoid our monarchs as much as possible.

When Treble lands lightly, coming to a stop near the dragon, I leap from his back, somersault to the ground, and then rise to my feet, clinging to the sensation of the rushing wind against my cheeks.

Turning back to Treble, I wrap my arms around his neck. "I love you, Treble. I need you to take to the sky now and fly clear of this battle. Don't fly back to me, no matter what happens. Even if I call you. Okay?"

He shakes his head at me, butting his forehead against my torso, refusing to leave, but I stroke his neck, my voice lowering. "Remember when you were angry with me two nights ago for leaving you behind? Nathaniel told you that I would take risks, that you would spend your life worrying about me, but you'd love me anyway…"

I swallow the lump in my throat. "I need to know that you'll be alive at the end of this. Please, Treble. Do this for me."

Treble closes his eyes. He nudges his head against my shoulder for a moment before he keens softly in agreement.

"Fly clear of Imatra's birds," I say. "Seek shelter in the crystal peaks. Don't come down from the northern mountains until Nathaniel is king. He will protect you. Now, go!"

Treble beats his wings, making a cracking sound that thuds through me as he rises off the ground and soars into the sky.

I follow his careful flight along the clear gap between the armies, out past Crispin's birds, and then east as he flies wide of Imatra's army and safely away.

I let out my breath, relieved that none of the other birds attempt to intercept him, grateful that Treble will be safe now.

I'm grateful that he won't be here to see my end.

Cadence landed while I was speaking with Treble. As Nathaniel steps carefully down her wing, he removes his sword from the harness at his back and hands the weapon to Evander.

I'm not sure what he's doing until he slides his halberd into the empty slot where the sword used to be.

He had to carry his weapon before, but now his hands are free.

Evander remains behind with Cadence as Nathaniel strides toward me. I'm already as close to the Vanem Dragon as I need to be.

Nathaniel stands taller than all of the fae and humans on either side of us, his broad shoulders held back, moving with the same stealth with which he attacked me on the morning he walked out of the mist.

His expression is shadowed, his hair falling across his face adding to the darkness in his eyes.

He is as merciless now as he was in the moments I first set eyes on him.

CHAPTER 33

I pull myself upright, setting my own emotions in place.

Only three days ago, I wore a careful mask over my emotions, teaching myself not to feel anything.

Since then, Nathaniel has brought every emotion out in me, but now I need to bury my feelings again.

My arms and hands are relaxed, but I'm poised to react at any moment, my senses heightened and the glow around me increasing. I am stern and unreachable.

Nathaniel's dark gaze rakes across my face and lips as he draws level with me.

We turn in unison and take a knee in front of the dragon.

The Vanem Dragon's growl thrums through me. "Rise, Aura of the Lucidia, who has discovered her true self. You are old magic. Far older than me. You will not bow to me again."

I lift myself, meeting the dragon's deep brown eyes. Fire burns inside the beast's mouth as he lowers his head to mine.

He inhales, and his eyes close for a moment. "It is an honor to meet a Lucidia. I only wish I had sensed your true nature sooner, but it was hidden from me, the same way my sight went dark on the night you were born."

"Many truths have been hidden until now," I say.

"Indeed." The dragon draws back his head, his eyes brightening as he addresses Nathaniel. "Rise Nathaniel Exalted, the true Fell King."

When Nathaniel draws upright, the beast casts his gaze across Nathaniel's weapon with growing reverence.

"Bright Heart," the dragon says, dipping his head and lowering his shoulders in a deep bow. "You kept the light."

"I will protect it for as long as I live," Nathaniel says. "I ask only that you give it to someone worthy if I die today. Whether that person is fae, human, or..." He glances at me. "Someone precious to me."

The dragon's smile fades. Deep sadness settles in his eyes. "I will honor your request, Nathaniel Exalted."

The dragon swings his mighty head toward Imatra and then to Cyrian, his voice rising in a fiery roar. "The monarchs will approach!"

Imatra strides through the flower field with two of her guards beside her. I know them only vaguely—one is a Solstice fae, the other is a Dawn fae. It's a wise combination. The Solstice fae can protect her while the Dawn fae can heal her if she's injured.

Cyrian approaches on our left, his black hair slicked back and his upper lip shadowed by growth.

Snake and another hunter stride beside him, both of them carrying an arsenal of weapons. Neither of the hunters is as intimidating as Hagan, but I remind myself that Nathaniel's mother trained them. Esther was correct when she taught the human trainees that fae take a second to harness their powers.

These hunters could strike down any number of fae before the fae could retaliate.

Imatra throws her head back, a disinterested expression on her face as she returns Cyrian's hard stare.

"You have both brought your armies to this battle," the dragon growls at them. "Do you intend to break the Law?"

Imatra blinks at the dragon. "Never," she says. "I will honor the outcome reached today."

Cyrian smirks. "I'm here only to support my champion." His smile fades as he casts a glare at me. "It appears that the fae champion has already been given the advantage of armor."

Cyrian raises his hand, the merest twitch of his fingers, and one of the hunters steps forward carrying a suit of armor. I recognize it as the armor Nathaniel's father was wearing when he died.

Nathaniel stiffens beside me as the hunter hands it to him. It's mahogany, the same color as Christiana's armor, but a golden emblem is emblazoned on the front depicting Nathaniel's family name—the same curve of the moon and rays of the sun as the marks that remain on my left shoulder and above my heart.

"You will find that the three unfortunate cuts in the back of this armor have been repaired," Cyrian says, a cruel twist on his lips. He tips his head at Imatra, as if to acknowledge her part in his path to becoming the King of the Fell.

Imatra's jaw clenches before her expression becomes deadpan.

Nathaniel is quiet as he holds the suit, pressing his palm over the emblem on the front. "I accept this armor and vow to honor the warriors who wore it before me."

"Very well," the Vanem Dragon says. "The monarchs will both—"

He pauses, his head swinging toward the western end of the Misty Gallows beyond the location of Cyrian's hunters.

A commotion builds as figures emerge from the mist—a

hundred humans wearing beige clothing and carrying a multitude of weapons.

It's Nathaniel's people.

I recognize Esther's golden hair as the human army takes up position in the gap at the western end of the two armies.

There are two riders on horseback with them—both of whom I recognize immediately.

Nathaniel tenses beside me as Christiana and Hagan ride toward us despite the threat of the armies on either side of them.

They slow their horses as they draw nearer, stopping clear of the Vanem Dragon's position before they dismount. The horses are skittish, but Christiana hands her horse's reins to Hagan, who calms both animals while Christiana strides toward us.

She's dressed in her armor, her hair braided. She looks tired and drawn, but her expression is open, the press of her lips hopeful as she pauses to bow to the Vanem Dragon before she walks directly toward Nathaniel.

"Brother." She takes a knee, bowing her head to him.

Farther behind her, Hagan also looks tired, making me doubt he slept after we left the Bitter Patch this morning. He won't have had any rest since yesterday. He's wearing the same slightly too small clothes, but he's carrying more weapons than when we last saw him.

His lips are drawn into the same unforgiving line, the look of a warrior that Nathaniel wears. His perceptive gaze passes across me, pauses, then takes in my glow, my bright eyes, before he moves on to the armies around us.

Finally, his attention returns to Christiana, watching over her.

Nathaniel's forehead creases, wary as he considers first Hagan and then his sister, waiting for her to speak.

She takes a deep breath without raising her eyes, her head

still bowed. "Nathaniel, you honored our father by carrying out his wishes. You lived your life as he taught you. But I was afraid and lost. And so... *so* angry."

She swallows. Pauses. Takes another deep breath. "You asked me to decide who I am and what I stand for," she says, raising her eyes to his. "I've come here to tell you that I stand for you, for my brother who was meant to be King."

Cyrian takes a threatening step forward as she speaks, but Christiana casts him a sharp glance.

He is bound never to touch her again and the frustration on his face is fierce. Dark light increases around his fingertips, but he doesn't release it.

Christiana rises to her feet. "We have come here to fight beside you," she says to Nathaniel. "All of us. If you need us." She gestures to the human army behind her before she turns to me. "We want to fight beside you *and* Aura. If you'll let us."

Pain strikes through my chest. Christiana is a proud and stubborn woman. I understood her motivations when she acted to protect her people this morning. I hated the pain it caused me —and the conflict between her and Nathaniel—but before I met Nathaniel, I would not have treated a human any better than she treated me.

Now she has offered to support Nathaniel *and* me.

It's... too late for me, but Nathaniel will need her help to defeat Cyrian once the Law of Champions is decided. He will need to act quickly, a challenge for the throne that must be swift and precise.

Nathaniel considers her carefully, his astute gaze passing across her open expression before he leans forward to grip her shoulders. "I'm glad you're here."

"I can't ask you to forgive me, but—"

"I do," Nathaniel says, the merciless line of his mouth softening.

She blinks rapidly. Bites her lip. "Then we'll be waiting and ready when you need us."

Behind her, Hagan gives me a nod and I return it with a small smile, grateful that he will be there for Nathaniel when I'm gone.

Gratitude is the strangest emotion to feel for a hunter who imprisoned me, but Hagan and I understand what we each need to do.

He knows that the fight for the Fell throne will be furious once I'm dead.

CHAPTER 34

*H*agan's lips hitch up into a wonky half-smile, a
rare and unexpected sight before he tips his head
at me and turns away, choosing to walk between Christiana and
the hunters until she reaches her horse and they ride back to the
human army.

I sense Nathaniel's worry as he glances between me and his
departing sister, but his expression hardens when I turn fully in
his direction.

He looks at me now the way I want him to—as a warrior.

The Vanem Dragon remained silent throughout the whole
exchange.

Now, he lowers his head to us again. "Before the fight begins,
the champions have the right to walk with me and ask anything
they need to know. They may not be separated from each
other's sight, but their conversation with me will be private."

He looks to each of us. "Do you wish to walk with me?"

"Yes." Nathaniel's response is so immediate, his glance at me
so fierce, that I shiver.

He clearly has something he wants to ask the dragon in private but I'm not sure what it could be.

"Aura?" the dragon asks me.

"Yes," I say, feeling more uncertain than I have for hours. "I want to walk with you."

"Very well," the dragon says. "The monarchs will now step back. The fight will begin once the champions have spoken with me. Aura will walk with me first."

Despite the dragon's order to step back, Imatra gives me a hard glare, her mask of control slipping. She has played so many games with my life that I wonder if she even has the capacity to see that she created her own worst enemy.

"Remember who you fight for, Aura," she snarls. "You are bound to me in duty and honor. You *will* kill the Fell creature for me."

I step up to her, unafraid. I see through all of her faces now —the benevolent leader, the conspiring fae, the cruel weaver of dark magic—to the frightened and desperate woman she is beneath.

Lowering my voice to a careful murmur, I say, "I will do *nothing* for you, Imatra of the Solstice. I will do only what is right for the people of Bright and Fell."

Her hand snakes out to grab my arm, her fingernails biting against my armor, her ruby-red lips pressed together so tightly that they become bloodless. "You *will* kill him."

My voice is a mere breath of sound. "If you believe that I could ever kill the man I love, then *you're* the one without a heart."

With a sharp breath, she lets me go. Her glare fills with loathing and resentment before she smooths out her features, pasting over her stormy emotions with an expression of supreme control before she glides away with her guards.

Cyrian takes several backward steps, still facing forward, dark light glimmering around his form, sparking in the moonlight. Unlike Imatra, he remains silent before he turns on his heel and stalks away.

With a final glance at Nathaniel, I move to the dragon's side, feeling very small beside the giant beast.

Nathaniel remains behind, a solitary figure in the middle of the field as I hurry to keep up with the dragon's large steps.

The Vanem Dragon exhales a sigh into the night air, the warmth of his breath comforting me. The armies are quiet on either side of us and the humans are silent ahead of us, but it will only take a spark to light up the tension around us.

"Nobody can hear us now, Aura," the dragon says. "The Law of Champions gives me a very small amount of control over what happens between now and your fight with Nathaniel. The old magic came alive when you and Nathaniel were sealed, and it has rested inside my heart since then. I can use it now to give you peace, comfort, or advice. This is your chance to speak your heart, to voice your final words. If you wish, you can give me permission to repeat what you say in the instance of your death."

I don't need to think about my final words. The light inside my chest is never as bright as when I'm near Nathaniel and right now, my light glows dull without him.

"I love him," I whisper. "Will you tell Nathaniel that?"

"I will." The dragon takes another measured step. "Do you have a message for anyone else?"

I've already said the closest to a goodbye to my brother and father that I can manage. I hugged Treble and made sure he was safe. All that remains is the fate of the fae and humans. If I weren't controlling my emotions so tightly, I might cry at this moment.

The fate of the humans and the fae rests on the outcome of this fight.

"If the fae will listen, tell them that Nathaniel will treat them fairly," I say. "Tell them that he carries old magic inside his heart —*my magic*—even if he can't use it. He will be a good king. And if the humans will listen... tell them that Nathaniel never betrayed them. He was just the first person to see that I was not their enemy."

The dragon is quiet. "You don't plan to survive the fight?"

I hope my silence is enough to answer his question. I step carefully through the grass, picking my way between the trailing flowers.

Tugging my fleece closer around my shoulders, I glance back to see Nathaniel standing beside Cadence. She holds her wing up, giving him a small amount of privacy while he pulls on his father's armor.

"What will happen if Nathaniel refuses to fight me?" I ask, turning back to the dragon.

Fire smolders in the dragon's mouth as he speaks, suddenly fierce. "You must make him fight you."

"What if he refuses?"

"Then he will die at dawn." The dragon pauses. "If you don't kill him first."

My jaw is tight, the light inside my chest a flickering mess as I grasp at a final way out. "I'm old magic. The Law of Champions is old law. Can I unbind us? Can I use my magic to change it all somehow?"

"The old law binds everyone," the dragon says, shaking his head sadly. "Even a Lucidia."

Nathaniel told me that the old law doesn't only govern humans, but the environment as well. He said it was part of everything: every living creature, every change of season, even every heartbeat.

To try to stop it is to try to stop life itself.

We are still a long way from reaching the human army gathered at the end of the field, but the dragon draws to a stop, considering me quietly.

"Aura?"

I nearly can't speak.

Soon, I will have run out of words and there will be nothing left but the fight.

"I know what I am," I say. "I know *who* I am, and I know what I need to do." I tip my head back to see the stars, imagining for a moment that I can see the Lucidia dancing in the cloudless ether. "But I have one last question: What will happen to my magic when I die?"

The dragon lowers his head to mine, pinning me with his big, brown eyes. I once thought his eyes contained endless pools of fire. Now I see endless space, the vast cold of a starry night.

"Your magic will return to its source in the ether," he says.

I try to smile but fail. I press my palms to my cheeks, tracing the shape of my face, marking the form my magic chose to take. "Then I won't really be dead."

The dragon nudges my shoulder with the tip of his nose before he turns and we walk in silence back to Nathaniel.

Nathaniel has returned to the place where we left him, except that now he is dressed in armor. Evander has stepped back with Cadence, keeping their distance, although they're much closer to Nathaniel than anyone else.

I step aside as the dragon lowers his head to Nathaniel. It's my turn to wait now.

"Nathaniel Exalted," the dragon says to him. "You may walk with me now."

I try to read Nathaniel's expression before his back is turned to me. It's the first time in three days that I haven't been part of his conversations or been able to read his emotions.

It's like being cast adrift with no anchor, nothing to keep me tethered.

All I can tell is that Nathaniel is asking a lot of questions. The dragon frequently nods or shakes his head, speaking quickly before pausing to hear what Nathaniel asks next.

Finally, they stop much farther along than I did, but Nathaniel's posture changes.

Even from this distance, I can read the tension in his shoulders as he turns to face the dragon.

I gasp when the dragon suddenly jolts, rearing back, his wings spreading.

Nathaniel steps right up to him, an angry intensity in his expression that I wasn't expecting. He shouts something that looks like a demand, or an order.

The dragon trembles and lowers his head as if he's fighting an invisible force while Nathaniel stands his ground, fists clenched, compelling the dragon… to do *what*, I'm not sure.

Fire rushes from the dragon's mouth directly at Nathaniel, making the distant humans shout and the fae and hunters reach for their weapons.

But the flames split before they reach Nathaniel's body, rushing around him, scorching the earth on either side but not touching him.

The dragon drops into a crouch as if he's suddenly exhausted before he finally speaks again. He keeps speaking for a long moment while Nathaniel listens, unmoving.

When the dragon falls silent, Nathaniel casts his gaze upward at the sky, then toward me.

He steps back from the dragon with a curt bow before he breaks away from the majestic beast and strides back to me.

A shiver runs through me as Nathaniel draws nearer.

His steps are full of purpose, his focus on me unbreakable.

The dragon suddenly raises his head, his voice roaring across the distance. "Nathaniel Exalted! *Do not do this!*"

Nathaniel ignores him, reaching for his weapon as he strides through the field toward me.

His muscles bunch as he slides the halberd free and swings it across the air in front of himself, then lowers it, blade to the ground.

The way he handles the weapon, his grip and perfect balance, tells me how comfortable he is with it.

I brace, my hand on my left shoulder, ready to draw my sword if Nathaniel intends to begin our fight immediately. I'm prepared and ready for whatever's coming my way.

Nathaniel stops four paces away from me.

His lips are pressed together in the same forbidding expression with which he first greeted me.

"Answer my question, Aura Lucidia, and speak only the truth," he commands me. "Who killed my father?"

I fight my confusion. He knows who killed his father. He saw it in the glitter bulbs.

I stop myself before I ask him what's going on. A deathly silence has fallen around us that makes me pause.

I sense a tug of magic, as if his words have triggered the change in our environment.

The silence extends up into the sky and out on either side of me. Thunderbirds crack their wings but don't make a sound.

The Vanem Dragon rises into the air behind us and I can see that he's shouting, but I can't hear what he's saying.

As soon as the dragon stops speaking, Imatra suddenly launches into action, shouting orders at her guards.

To my left, Cyrian is also agitated, dark light flashing around his torso while the wolves and bears snap, snarl, and pull against their chains. He is also shouting orders, yelling at his hunters, but I can't hear a thing.

I don't understand what's going on. Nathaniel asked me to answer his question and to speak only the truth. My lips part, my chest glows, and I meet Nathaniel's merciless eyes.

He once promised to always tell me the truth.

I can only do the same.

"Imatra of the Solstice, the Fae Queen, killed your father," I say.

A muscle clenches in Nathaniel's jaw. "Tell me also, Aura of the Lucidia, star of old magic: Who stole my throne?"

I don't know why Nathaniel is asking me these questions when he already knows the answers. I don't know why the entire field around me is silent, even though every fae, hunter, and human is shouting and running into position as if they're about to go to war.

I also don't know Cyrian's full name and it suddenly feels very important that I get it right, but then I remember what the Vanem Dragon called him last night.

"Cyrian Deceiver stole your throne," I say.

Nathaniel draws in a deep breath. The hard line of his lips softens as his gaze passes across my face in a way that could make me forget where we are and why we're here.

"You are my Witness, Aura Lucidia," he says. "You have named my Betrayers. The Vanem Dragon must protect you now."

I reach for Nathaniel as he steps away from me. "Wait… Nathaniel, what is this? What have you done?"

Nathaniel casts me a dangerous smile, as if he's about to step off a cliff.

He raises his voice to a swelling roar that cuts through the silence, breaking it like shattering glass, a storm of magic suddenly gathering around him and carrying his voice across the fields.

"As Aura Lucidia is my Witness, I am the King Betrayed!" He

raises his weapon from the ground, catching the moonlight and casting it around us in impossibly bright rays.

The force of old magic sweeps across me like wildfire.

Nathaniel's voice lowers to a determined rumble that echoes in my ears.

"I choose the dangerous path," he says.

CHAPTER 35

*V*iolent sounds break across me.

In the distance, the Vanem Dragon sweeps his wings so abruptly that the stormy wind his wings creates knocks the fae warriors and the hunters on either side of the field to the ground.

He shoots across the air toward me, flying low to the ground.

"Aura Lucidia!" he roars. "Catch my wing!"

Nathaniel drops himself flat to the ground to avoid the dragon's claws as the enormous beast flies so low, he nearly gouges Nathaniel's back.

I don't understand what's happening, but my instincts fire, giving me speed as I leap and catch hold of the dragon's wing bone. He is far bigger than Treble, and I nearly miss the mark as I swing myself toward his back, reaching out with all of my strength.

I slip, cling, and finally heave my legs into position. His back is so wide, I have to kneel instead of sliding my legs to the side.

Just as I lean low over his neck, a bolt of firelight explodes into the ground where I was standing a moment ago, kicking up dirt and grass.

Nathaniel rolls to the side to avoid the attack, but I'm sure the blast was intended for me.

I stare in shock as the Vanem Dragon rises and banks, tilting his wings as another bolt of firelight narrowly misses us.

What in all the dark stars...?

The fae have never risked hurting the Vanem Dragon before.

Trying to see my attackers without upsetting my position, I discover two squadrons of thunderbirds soaring after us.

Their riders are all Solstice fae, the women's blonde hair gleaming in the moonlight.

The dragon's speed has taken us high into the sky within seconds.

Far below me, Nathaniel leaps to his feet, darting along the quickly closing gap between the armies. Sliding his weapon into the harness on his back, he races toward his people, his arms pumping, running as fast as when we escaped through the glitter field together.

I crane my neck to follow his movements, but several attacking thunderbirds block my view.

For the first time in days, my body doesn't tug toward him.

The anchorless sensation within my chest expands, the empty breadth of a night sky opening up inside me.

I was always afraid of my *nothing*—the vast expanse from which I came and within which I could become lost. It is the place where I am nothing more than another glittering light that glows and fades, a spark of magic without a heart.

Firelight explodes on both sides of us as the Vanem Dragon evades the rapid-fire attacks.

I scream. "Why are the fae trying to kill you?"

"Not me!" the dragon shouts. "You!"

"But if they kill me, Nathaniel wins under the Law of Champions!"

"Nathaniel invoked the Path of the King Betrayed," the dragon cries, tilting again as I cling to his back. "It is one of the oldest laws, forged from countless betrayals of human kings and queens over millennia. The Law of Champions is suspended until Nathaniel has walked the Path."

"A king betrayed may choose the dangerous path…" My heart sinks as I remember the room at the Spire that is filled with old laws.

Nathaniel had stopped at one side of the room, fixated on one particular law, but his body blocked me from reading it.

I don't know whether or not Nathaniel knew about that law until he stood in that room. Either way, he's chosen to invoke it now.

"What is the Path?" I scream, anxiety burning inside me. "What does Nathaniel have to do?"

"He must kill his Betrayers."

My eyes widen as the wind shrieks around me. "He has to kill both Imatra *and* Cyrian?"

"You are his Witness under the law. You named his Betrayers," the dragon roars. "Nathaniel has to kill his Betrayers before his Betrayers kill his Witness. We are now in a race to the death."

Starlight pumps inside my chest, flooding my arms and legs, filling my head. "Did Imatra and Cyrian know this was a possibility?"

"Neither of them knew about this law! Even Nathaniel didn't know about it until today—he said he read it at the Spire. It was my duty to explain it to him. Just as it was my duty to explain it to Imatra and Cyrian while Nathaniel questioned you."

I remember the way the dragon rose up behind me, shouting to Imatra and Cyrian while everything went quiet around me.

"What about the Law of Champions?" I scream. "What does 'suspended' mean?"

"Do not concern yourself with that right now. Cyrian and Imatra both want you dead, Aura. If you die, Nathaniel will be denied the Path back to his throne."

"What should I do?" I'm just about ready to blast every one of the attacking Solstice fae out of the air, but every action has consequences.

I could break a rule if I kill someone—with disastrous consequences.

The dragon turns his head, slowing for the first time despite the fact that we are now counting down the seconds to who will die first.

His lips curl into a smile that carries the threat of violence. "You must run, Aura. You are the Witness. It is up to Nathaniel to kill them. But it is up to *me* to protect you. Because you are the witness to the truth, you are afforded greater protection than they are."

A cloud of thunderbirds rises up ahead of us and I tense before I recognize Crispin, Serena, and the Springtime and Harvest fae.

They must be the reason that the dragon slowed down. From the corner of my eye, Evander soars parallel with us, darting and evading the firelight attacks from the Solstice fae, who target him as well as me. He had leaped onto Cadence's back and taken to the air seconds after I did.

"Protect Aura with your lives!" the dragon shouts, diving beneath the force of friendly thunderbirds.

We soar beneath Crispin, who flies ahead of the others with Serena and Calida in the air beside him while Mia and Talsa coast well back, their faces filled with concentration.

They will use their communication skills to help the thunderbirds that the Springtime and Harvest fae are riding, since many of them will be new to aerial combat.

Evander soars toward Talsa, joining her. His Frost power is nearly exhausted, but he is physically strong and will do his best to protect her and Mia while they work.

The Vanem Dragon soars into position behind my new defenders, safe for now, giving me the chance to take a breath and allowing us to see the entire battle.

The fight in the air is violent. Serena and Calida are vastly outnumbered, but they are agile, darting between their attackers.

Serena's firelight hits the first attacking Solstice fae, her thunderbird darting between them while several thunderbirds ridden by Harvest fae cut to the right and disrupt the attacking fae's formation.

The Harvest men are used to felling trees. They are all muscular, strong from years of physical labor, and they carry makeshift wooden spears. Evading the firebolts aimed at them, they use their spears to full effect to defend my position.

I search the battle on the ground for Nathaniel, the light inside me pulsing with anxiety until I find him in the center of the field.

The human army protects his back, facing Imatra's army, while Nathaniel faces Cyrian and his hunters.

Nathaniel isn't alone. Hagan fights on one side of him while Christiana battles on the other.

I wasn't sure if he would seek to fight Imatra or Cyrian first, but it appears that he's going for Cyrian.

The Fell King isn't making it easy. Cyrian stands well back at the edge of the Misty Gallows beside the bears while his hunters charge at Nathaniel.

The fight is fierce and bloody. The hunters are brutal and it's clear that Cyrian has given them orders to kill Nathaniel by whatever means necessary.

Even so, Nathaniel, Hagan, and Christiana are making ground, bodies piling up around them as they cleave and hew their way through the hunters.

At Nathaniel's back, Esther leads the humans, trying to hold back the immense tide of fae warriors converging on Nathaniel's position.

Imatra herself has taken to the sky—a safe place for now—but she made a critical strategic mistake when she mixed the powers of her troops.

Fae of the same class can't hurt each other, but fae of different classes can. Her women on the frontline should have annihilated the humans already, but they're pulling their power, trying not to hurt each other, only taking clean shots when they can.

The women's hesitation gives the humans time to move swiftly through the fae, cutting them down with skillful sweeps while making inroads into Imatra's defenses.

Imatra was never a good strategist. She had me for that.

I can see her thunderbird's agitated wing beats as it reacts to her tension and her screams of rage.

The battlefield is too densely populated for her to use her own magic, but she appears to be rallying her riders in the sky, screaming orders at them.

I'm not sure what she plans to do next.

I'm suddenly drawn to movement on the field closer to my location. Several hunters push against the iron weapons that Cyrian brought with him, swiveling the machines in my direction.

The top portion moves on some sort of axle so that the beam is in line with the thunderbirds protecting me. A group of hunters works around each of the metal slings, filling them with what appear to be jagged iron shards, pouring oil over them before setting the shards alight.

Fear shoots through me as the beam releases from its anchor.

The sling flies upward and the burning projectiles arc through the air toward us.

"Look out!" I scream, twisting to see Talsa and Mia.

Their arms are outstretched, their eyes glazed, but they adjust just in time. Every friendly thunderbird suddenly soars upward, avoiding the arc of the burning shards.

Some of the attacking fae aren't so lucky, their birds' wings catching fire as the shards fly through their feathers.

One of the riders—a Frost fae—screams as she tries to put out the flames, but the fire keeps burning, tearing through her bird's body.

My stomach turns. "It's dark magic!"

I thought the hunters were pouring oil over the shards, but it must be a substance powered by dark light so that it continues burning.

The Frost fae's thunderbird screams in agony as it dies, plummeting to the ground while the Frost fae leaps from its back onto another bird.

Tears fill my eyes. No thunderbird deserves to die that way.

On the ground, the hunters adjust the beams on all three weapons and prepare to fire again.

They want to cut me from the sky.

Every thunderbird and rider around me is now in danger.

As the Vanem Dragon soars higher, not making it easy for the men on the ground, I shout above the wind. "You told me to run, but I want the truth: Can I fight?"

The dragon's breath leaves his torso in a gusty sigh. "I was afraid you might ask me that."

He beats his wings carefully, turning his head to consider me with his bright eyes. "Nathaniel's conversation with me is private. I can only break that confidence where he has given me permission, but I can tell you this: He knows you are willing to die for him. But he will not allow that to happen. He would rather die trying to defeat Imatra and Cyrian, than be forced to fight you to the death. *I*... however... see the future that you see, Aura."

The dragon exhales heavily. "Nathaniel is the only chance for peace."

My chest squeezes. "That's why you were angry with him when he spoke with you. By invoking the Path, he's risking his life because of me."

I choke back the grief rising inside me, forcing myself to focus. "You haven't answered my question: Can I fight?"

The dragon exhales. "You may fight, but you must not kill Imatra or Cyrian. Nathaniel must do that himself. But know this, Aura: If you die before Nathaniel completes his path, he will die too. His life is connected to yours even more closely than it was before. It is your duty to stay alive so he can reclaim his throne."

I squeeze my eyes shut. Nathaniel knew that I didn't plan to be alive by dawn. Now he's forcing me to stay alive because he knows I won't risk *his* life.

I tip my head back and scream. "He's forcing me to live!"

If Nathaniel and I both survive this, I might just kill him for putting me in this position.

"He wants to protect you," the dragon says. "Just as you are willing to lay down your life for him."

My voice quiets and so does the light inside my chest. "But he knows I won't sit and idly watch while others die."

The dragon sighs. "He gave me a message for you, Aura. He said to tell you, and I quote: *'Beautiful woman, the choice will always be yours.'*"

My chest burns, my light striking sharply through me. Nathaniel said that to me when I asked him if we were still married. He accepted my trust and gave me his faith. He told me he wanted to fight beside me, not against me.

"Then I choose to fight," I whisper. Giving a final exhale, I lean forward. "Vanem Dragon, fly me to the iron machines!"

A gleam enters the dragon's eyes. "As you command, Aura Lucidia."

CHAPTER 36

*T*he Vanem Dragon banks to the left, steering a course toward the Misty Gallows while maintaining our height.

On the ground, the hunters halt in the process of preparing to release the slings, rushing to swivel the weapons toward my expected trajectory.

Behind us, Imatra's squadrons haven't given up, but now I'm like a magnet drawing them away from my friends in the air.

The Vanem Dragon plows a course to the far left, deliberately turning himself into a target as he aims for the haze above the Gallows, attracting the fae behind us and the iron machines in front of us.

The slings fly high and the burning shards arc toward us.

Just a little closer…

My hands shoot out. My power explodes through my arms.

White, hot light bursts across the burning shrapnel, blasting through the projectiles and spreading across the space in front of the Vanem Dragon as the dragon flies directly toward the machines.

My power keeps pouring from me, widening and rippling, blasting down across the weapons themselves, burning through the hunters and racing outward into the Misty Gallows.

The dragon pulls up before we would crash into the burning remains. He soars up into the night sky as the ripples of my starlight flow around the misshapen trees at this end of the Gallows, lighting up their strange silhouettes.

The mist clears where my power spreads, revealing the barren plain that lies beneath the thick haze.

The muddy earth suddenly glistens and the dying trees sparkle white. In the distance, a cloud of mold moths rises up from the crooked branches, the creatures' wings glowing silver.

The breath catches in my throat. I'm aware of the warriors across the battlefield as they flinch and duck because of the explosion of my power, while the fae in the air steer their thunderbirds wildly away from me.

I've deterred the fae who were following me, but it's only a few seconds before the fight on the ground resumes.

Up ahead, Nathaniel has nearly made it to Cyrian. A single line of hunters, along with the wolves and bears, remains between them while Cyrian stays well back, his arms raised, dark light seeping from his hands.

One of the hunters facing Nathaniel is Snake, the long scar down his arm visible when he swings his axe. I've seen Nathaniel cut hunters down in seconds, but Snake's silhouette flickers with dark light.

I can only guess that Cyrian is giving his men strength, speed, and invincibility.

Imatra has finally taken control of the air above Nathaniel's position. The fae are now attacking from the sky while Cyrian's hunters attack from the ground.

I don't have to tell the Vanem Dragon what we need to do.

He rockets across the sky toward the Solstice fae circling Nathaniel's location.

The roar of the battle below us sweeps across me. I'm trained to block it out, to focus. If I hadn't been, I'd curl up in fear right now. The ground is already covered with the dead and dying, the fallen lying on the crushed flowers.

On the ground, Nathaniel swings his halberd, intercepting the cut of Snake's axe before he spins to deflect a rapid stream of firelight thrown by the four fae circling above him on their thunderbirds.

Each bolt hits Nathaniel's weapon and bounces back at the fae in the air, forcing them to scatter.

It won't take them long to regroup and try again.

Nathaniel's gaze rises to me as the dragon flies toward him. Any distraction could get him killed, but I don't miss the fierce smile that touches his lips when he sees me.

He knew I wouldn't stay out of the fight.

My power demands to be released into the regrouping fae flying above Nathaniel, but I have to control it, concentrate it, and target my enemies carefully.

Any reckless action on my part could get Nathaniel's people killed.

Just as I prepare to take aim, the Vanem Dragon rapidly ascends. I glance back to see that the fae who followed us have also regrouped, now blasting alternating streams of fire and ice at me.

The Vanem Dragon quickly plummets again, right above the fae attacking Nathaniel.

I lean over the dragon's side, barely holding on as I extend my left arm beneath his wing and target the Solstice fae soaring directly toward Nathaniel, her power building around her torso.

She's approaching from his back this time, timing her attack to the moment when Snake lashes out so that Nathaniel will be most vulnerable.

Starlight shoots from my hand, more than I intended, straight into her chest. It washes away her power before it cuts through her body. She doesn't even scream. Her body folds up before she falls off her bird.

She's dead before she hits the ground, landing at one of the remaining hunters' feet.

I squeeze my eyes shut, suddenly afraid of the power inside me, afraid of its destruction—how quickly it cut down a woman I would have once protected.

A blast of wind around us forces me to focus.

The fae who are following us are coordinating their attacks, the Frost fae combining their power over the wind to upset the Vanem Dragon's flight, forcing him into the path of the Solstice fae's firelight.

Flames sizzle past my torso, far too close for comfort.

"You must stay alive!" the Vanem Dragon roars, as if he hears my internal doubts. "They are not your people anymore. You must fight with everything you have. Even if your power makes you afraid."

Every time I fought to keep Nathaniel alive, I told myself it would lead to the best outcome for my people—the fae. But the Vanem Dragon is right.

I have no people.

I only have family. I have Crispin and Evander. Talsa. Possibly Serena in her own way.

But more than anyone else in my life, I have Nathaniel.

Imatra tried to make me believe that I had no choice about loving him, but when he held my heart for all of those years... it just meant that we knew each other before we met.

Rising to my feet, I balance on the Vanem Dragon's back, face the oncoming fae, and let my power loose.

Opening up the vast chasm inside my chest, I allow the old magic to flow through me.

Blasting starlight through the hearts of the fae chasing after us, I cut through their bodies one by one, knocking them off their birds, filling the sky with starlight and blood as if I'm blasting snowflakes with Evander again.

Except that this game is deadly.

I spin, turning in every direction, my power streaming from me in fatal bolts, clearing the sky above Nathaniel.

His roar draws my attention to the hunters on the ground. Nathaniel shouts for Hagan and Christiana as he clashes with Snake.

Nathaniel's halberd pushes against Snake's upraised sword. The light in the halberd drives away the darkness around Snake's body, making him vulnerable—but only for a moment.

On Nathaniel's left, Hagan's dagger is a blur, his muscles bunching as he drives his weapon into Snake's exposed side. At the same time, Christiana's sword tears through Snake's throat.

The hunter falls, crushing flowers beneath his big body.

My breath catches in my throat as Nathaniel's weapon meets the next hunter while Hagan and Christiana fight beside him, the three coordinating their attacks now, as if they'd practiced them many times before.

Together, they plow through the remaining hunters with swift, brutal cuts.

Cyrian roars in anger, but he still has his wolves and bears to protect himself—as well as his dark magic.

I'm wary of Imatra as she drops to her thunderbird's back in the distance. It looks like she's preparing to fly toward us now, and I have to keep Nathaniel alive.

"Dragon!" I scream.

He responds immediately, spearing a path toward the wolves and the bears.

I may not be able to kill Imatra or Cyrian, but I can protect Nathaniel the same way I protected him from the wolves on our second day.

Just as my arms extend, a heavy blast knocks me off the dragon's back.

CHAPTER 37

The impact is like a hook, wrenching me toward the ground.

I tumble, trying to get my feet under myself before I hit the ground, but the force dragging me down yanks me off-balance, pulling my shoulders faster than my legs.

I thud into the earth, hitting it on my side just as I identify the source of the power: *Cyrian.*

Pain explodes through me. My power releases but sputters beneath the overwhelming dark light washing over me in waves.

It reeks of death. Sickening. Turning my stomach.

The ground shifts beneath me and thick ropes rise out of the earth, pushing up from beneath the mud to coil around my feet and torso. They slide around me like snakes, hissing and pulling tight.

My power recovers enough to explode through my arms and legs, but it splits around the ropes holding me.

Strands of my power flow beyond me, reaching the edge of the Misty Gallows and passing through it like glowing ribbons.

For a second, forms light up inside the mist.

Human forms. All of them bound and gagged.

Many of them are dead, sprawled in the mud, their glassy eyes turned in my direction.

I'm shocked to see Ethel, and the other lords and ladies, among the dead. Ethel's arm twitches, as if her life energy was just consumed to create the ropes that now bind me.

Cyrian has been using their life energy to power his dark magic, killing the humans one by one.

Even his allies aren't safe.

Inside the Misty Gallows, a female figure runs between the dead, stopping beside a girl who still lives.

As the woman enters the wash of my light, I recognize Mathilda. She carries a knife that she uses to swiftly cut through the girl's bindings, releasing her, urging her to run.

The moment the child is free, Mathilda turns to the next person, but she's too close to Cyrian now.

Her eyes widen as she sees me across the distance. Dark light flickers around her body, a protective shield. Even so, Cyrian's dark magic is strong enough to bind me. Mathilda won't be able to fight it.

I scream at her to run, but the next wave of Cyrian's dark light builds, breaking through her shield and sucking the life energy from her body before she can move.

She drops to the ground, her eyes vacant.

Her power gives Cyrian more strength than the humans' energy did.

The ropes around me tighten, squeezing the breath out of my chest while I struggle against them.

"Aura!" the dragon shouts above me. "Get up!"

Fire builds inside the dragon's mouth as he prepares to pour flames across the ground between me and Cyrian, but a new blast of magic hits his side, flames exploding across his entire body.

His wings fold up and his eyes glaze over.

He tumbles from the air and crashes into the mud, his big body plowing into the trees, breaking them apart as he comes to a stop and lies still.

Imatra soars toward me, standing upright on her thunder-bird, her arms lowering.

Far behind her, four fae women suddenly fall from their birds, dead. Just like Cyrian, it seems she is now using her people to make herself stronger.

She leaps from her bird, landing gracefully on the ground, striding toward me at the same rapid pace as Cyrian, both of their arms outstretched, dark light streaming at me from both sides.

My power pulses, pushing back, forcing the ropes to loosen, but the sickening stench of death fills my head, flowing in on me.

Another three women fall in the distance.

I can't see the remaining humans hidden in the mist, but I sense their quiet screams before they fall silent.

"I pulled you from the sky, Aura," Imatra screams at me, her once-beautiful features twisted and cruel. "I will bury you in the ground."

Across the clearing, the bears and wolves I was trying to subdue are now free, running at Nathaniel, their teeth slashing at the air, claws slicing as they leap at him.

Impossibly, his focus is on me.

If I die, he dies.

But the fear in his eyes is not for himself.

"Aura!" he shouts, a second before the first wolf reaches him and he's forced to switch his focus.

Hagan punches one of the wolves from the air while Christiana steps in front of another, spearing it through its belly. The wolves' attacks are unnatural, fearless, fueled by dark magic that makes them mindless as their teeth and claws slash at everything around them.

The bears are close behind them. One of them leaps onto Hagan's back, mauling at him as he tries to fight a wolf, while a second bear crashes into Nathaniel, its claws cutting across his chest as it knocks him to the ground.

Christiana screams, wildly stabbing at the back of the bear attacking Nathaniel before another wolf leaps at her, forcing her to defend herself.

The bear that knocked into Nathaniel rears up, preparing to rip out his throat.

The flickers in my chest stop.

This time, I can't stop it from happening. I can't be his shield.

Light bursts from Nathaniel's chest, tearing through the bear's body. The spike of his halberd rams into its throat. With a roar of effort, he pushes the animal off himself and rolls to his feet.

He's covered in blood now and I don't know how much of it is his.

In a glowing burst of light, he spins, cutting through the bear that is tearing at Hagan before Nathaniel whirls and slices the head off the wolf attacking Christiana.

As the last animal dies, Christiana and Hagan both drop to the ground, wounded. They drag themselves across the dirt when Nathaniel shouts, "Stay behind me!"

The moment that Hagan and Christiana are clear, Nathaniel drops to one knee, knocking his halberd into the ground. The explosion of light magic streams across the clearing toward me, blasting Cyrian off his feet, hitting Imatra so hard that she flies backward.

The explosion burns through the ropes around me, and the scent of death lifts.

My head clears, filled with Nathaniel's light.

The old magic inside me responds, raising me to my feet. The sensation of freedom inside me makes me feel weightless.

On either side of me, Cyrian and Imatra recover, dark light building around them again, their faces gray and sallow, their eyes lit up with malice, as they storm back to me.

My magic swells as I extend my arms out at them, but Nathaniel also runs toward me, his arms pumping, legs stretching, racing to reach me before they do.

Every muscle in his body tenses, his dark eyes burning through me, more scorching than any magic I've ever felt.

He swings his weapon as he shouts, "Aura, get down!"

Dropping back into a crouch, I duck as his weapon's gleaming blade slices across the air above my body.

It thuds into Cyrian's chest, cutting right through him. Cyrian's chest separates in a spray of blood as the light magic slices through the dark magic building around him.

The darkness shrieks like a living thing, mingling with Cyrian's dying roar.

In a spray of blood, Nathaniel wrenches the weapon upward, spinning in the other direction and swinging the blade again.

The gleaming steel carves a path through the dark light building around Imatra.

Her scream shrieks around me, her magic pushing back, but my starlight glows. Not toward her.

My power streams into Nathaniel, filling the space between us, uniting with the flickers of my starlight that already exist inside his body.

Our power—his and mine combined—gleams as sharp as his blade.

Imatra attempts to harness the fae powers she always

claimed she had but the wind is a feeble breeze around her now. The vines she attempts to conjure from the ground shrivel before they can twine around us.

Her sputtering power cuts off as abruptly as her scream.

Nathaniel's weapon sails through her neck, separating her head from her body.

Her magic vanishes.

My chest heaves. My breaths are short and sharp as I look up at Nathaniel.

Silence falls around the battlefield. Every human and fae stops mid-swing, mid-flight, pulling away from each other.

Before I can stand, Nathaniel kneels to me, brushing his palm across my cheek.

"Imatra and Cyrian are dead," he says, his speech formal, as if he's speaking what he's required to say. "My Betrayers have fallen. The Fell throne is mine. The Path of the King Betrayed... has ended."

In the distance, Hagan and Christiana huddle on the bloody ground. Hagan pulls her close, stroking her hair, rubbing her back while she curls up against him, sobbing against his chest. She tilts her head back to see him. I can't hear what she says to him, but it's not for me to know regardless.

In the distance, the battle between the humans and fae has stopped.

The fae who were loyal to Imatra are retreating beyond the battle lines, a sign that they don't intend to resume fighting. At least for now.

Serena and the others haven't landed, soaring cautiously to the side. They fought for the humans, but Nathaniel's people won't trust them easily and they must avoid any actions that could be interpreted as aggressive right now.

In the distance, the Vanem Dragon stirs, signs that he's recovering.

"It's over," I whisper.

Nathaniel slides his arms around me, pulling me close while we remain kneeling, but his jaw is tense, his breathing too fast, his heart thudding too rapidly in my ears.

I tell myself it's from the battle, that my own chest is flickering because of exertion. It has nothing to do with the growing dread building inside me.

"Nathaniel?" I tilt my head back to find him looking up at the sky, the same way he looked up before he invoked the Path.

The sky is lighter. The sun will rise soon.

"It's not over," he says, a truth I dread.

He crushes me close, but I refuse to release him from my gaze. I start speaking slowly, then more quickly. "The Vanem Dragon said… the Law of Champions was suspended."

"Suspended. Not finished." Nathaniel brushes my cheeks as if he could hold me forever. He drops his forehead to mine, a light press, but I sense the urgency in his movement.

He whispers what I'm afraid to hear. "I don't want to fight you, Aura."

CHAPTER 38

A shiver rocks my body.

If we refuse to fight, we die at dawn. I don't know who I'm fighting for now that Imatra is dead, but it doesn't matter, because I'm prepared to face my fate.

Nathaniel doesn't want to fight me, but I won't accept that. I won't allow him to die.

I shove him away from me, taking hold of my power and containing it within me, even though I want to release it with a scream of anger.

Nathaniel remains kneeling on the ground, his hair clinging to his blood-splattered cheeks, his lips drawn but not without mercy.

My chest heaves as I look down at him, at the halberd that he placed carefully on the ground beside him. I glance behind me toward the east—to the horizon where the sky is brightening with every passing second.

Spinning back to him, my voice is harsh with desperation. "Pick up your weapon."

He shakes his head, a slow, determined movement, denying me the only thing I need from him.

"Pick up your weapon!"

My scream echoes around us, startling Christiana and Hagan, even the fae and humans who are still recovering in the distance.

The hum of my magic courses through the mist and up into the air.

A cloud of silver mold moths flutters, disturbed, out of the haze and flies east along the edge of the Gallows, coasting in the air above the dragon before disappearing toward the brightening horizon.

"Nathaniel!" My fist shoots out, thumping his cheek, but he takes the blow, leaning back on his hands instead of retaliating. "You fought for your throne. If you kill me, you can be King of All. How can you throw that away?"

"The throne is safe. Christiana will be a good queen. Hagan will help her. They won't make the mistakes of the past."

"But you'll die!"

He looks up at me, his gaze passing across my face. "I'd rather die than live a hundred years with an empty heart because I killed you."

The light inside my chest burns, ripping me apart.

I shake my head *no*.

"You promised me!" I shout, landing a vicious blow against his shoulder, trying to provoke him, needing him to hit back. My fist crashes across his cheek again. "You promised to fight me!"

My blows rain down on his body and head, wild and desperate, but there's only one thing I can do that might make him move against me.

I lurch for his weapon.

My left hand barely closes around the handle before Nathaniel's fist whips out and grabs it, pulling the halberd to a halt midair as I try to lift it.

A wary look enters his eyes.

This weapon—*the light*—is important for the human's future. He may be prepared to die, but Christiana will need this blade after he's gone.

My lips twist. Cruel threats spill from my mouth. "I will take the light from you. I will break it. Rip off its blades. Destroy its magic. Burn and melt it. Unless you stop me."

I wrench the blade upward while he grips it. At the same time, I reach for the liquid sword at my shoulder.

He leaps to his feet, agile and smooth despite how tired he must be.

I strike.

My sword cuts toward his chest. I'm ready to veer to the side if I have to, but his arms shoot up, wrenching the halberd into a defensive position.

His weapon's blade grates against my sword's wickedly sharp edge, stopping my strike just in time.

The blades spark against each other before I leap back into the only clear patch of ground behind me—away from the bodies.

I grip my sword, testing its balance as Nathaniel prowls toward me.

His voice is a low rumble, conveying the danger I want from him. "Don't do this, Aura."

I shake my head at him, slowly. "We were always headed here, Nathaniel. From the moment we met."

He draws himself up to his full height, shoulders back, his weapon held in his strong grip.

His lips draw down, truly angry with me. "No."

"I'm your enemy, Nathaniel," I say. "You asked me what I

would choose if there was no fae and no Fell. Well, I'm neither. I don't have a choice because I don't belong here. I never did."

He steps into the clear ground and that's all I need. I've already put away the light inside my chest—the fire that burns for him.

Striding toward him, I raise my weapon, sweeping it toward his throat.

He blocks the blow, but my left hand shoots out, starlight streaking between us, biting his face and hands.

He reacts on instinct, provoked by the pain, his halberd flashing as he cuts the air, blocking my power and forcing me onto my back foot.

He strikes back.

Our weapons clash, colliding against each other so hard that his light magic and my starlight explode around us, two immense forces bursting across the field and far into the sky.

Every fae and human who was standing near us turns and runs, escaping the deadly energy pouring around us.

I break the connection before my starlight would cut through his weapon, deftly angling my blade so he will be forced to retaliate.

We trade blows at lightning speed, every deadly attempt more brutal than the last as we fight with everything we have.

My muscles scream as I take the force of Nathaniel's blows, his strength. The light magic in his weapon streams through me every time our blades connect, a strange agony of pain and weightlessness while I fight back with my starlight, every sharp bite making his instincts fire, not giving him time to think or question.

I'm facing west, away from the sun, waiting for the moment just before the first rays strike across the air, fighting Nathaniel with every muscle in my body, every ragged breath until then.

Above us, the sky brightens.

The moon's outline becomes pale and the stars fade.

My time is up.

"Where is your power, Nathaniel?" I scream at him, pouring my starlight across his face, filling his vision with bright, white light as our blades clash so savagely that the metal shrieks.

For a moment, he can't see me.

My final moment.

My sword clashes against his halberd's blade and slides upward.

I was holding my weapon with both of my hands, but now I let it go, my right hand flying wide.

At the same time, I grab his halberd with my left hand and add my strength to its momentum, pulling the blade toward me in a single brutal blow.

Light magic floods his weapon, giving it the power to cleave my armor.

His blade carves a space through my chest.

My power beats outward, raw magic pouring across Nathaniel and the field as the pieces of my heart are exposed. Dying shards cut in half.

My knees can't hold me.

I slip to the ground, but Nathaniel's hands shoot out, his muscles tense, a reflex as he catches me, his arms circling my back, tracing my body by feel alone.

Finally, his vision clears, my starlight fading from his face, his wide eyes focusing on me. On the blade. On my open chest and my silver blood flowing to the muddy earth.

"Aura!" His roar is faint in my ears, even though he's shouting at me. "What did you do? *Aura!*" He grips me, trying to support my head, trying to keep me upright.

His voice is far away and fading, screaming at me as he collapses to the ground with me, rocking me in his arms. "*No... Please... Aura!*"

The sun's first rays wash across the battlefield as my head tips back and my vision finally fails.

Death is mine.

Now he will live.

CHAPTER 39

*T*here is no waiting.

Within a single beat, everything changes around me.

I stand in a vast, empty space.

Darkness spreads in every direction. It doesn't have any corners or edges, no beginning or end.

It is my *nothing*, the place I feared my heart would take me.

I'm wearing my indigo armor. My chest is whole, not cut apart, but silver blood slides down my left arm from my shoulder, trickling across my palm.

The color of my blood is what must have startled Nadina when I fought her.

Slow drips of silver liquid fall from my forefinger and disappear silently into the nothing at my feet, a reminder of my death.

I am dead.

There is no sound or breeze, but forms take shape in the distance, four figures striding toward me from my left, right, front, and back, as if they each occupy the four corners of the world and are now converging on each other.

I recognize them, even though I've never met them before. Not really.

Crimson light surrounds the woman on my left, flowers cascading from her tiara down her long, amber hair, falling to the hem of her long dress. She draws to a stop at a safe distance, considering me with sharp eyes, her head held high.

The human woman on the other side of me tilts her head cautiously as she stops a little closer to me, golden light glinting off the armor that hugs her muscular body, while her halberd sits comfortably across her back.

Behind me, I sense the approach of the man whose crown sits around his eyes, concealing his sight.

Half-turning to see him, my gaze passes from the points at the top of his black crown down his gray face to the bottom of the long, black robe that swishes across the floor.

His silhouette flickers with dark light, making him appear wraith-like as he slides to a stop, standing the farthest away.

The final figure is the girl with the white hair that flies at her side as if she walks in a breeze I can't feel. The light dances around her as she moves, making her appear as if she's never in one spot for longer than a second.

Her pearly dress ripples gently, but her bright, ivory gaze passes warily across the others before coming to rest on me.

They each stare at each other, their arms slightly extended at their sides, their power flickering around their fingers. Golden, crimson, white, and dark.

The tension rises around me, a charge in the air.

I break the silence. "Why am I here?"

My voice sounds faint. As far away as Nathaniel's shouts of pain when he called my name as I died.

It's like I'm listening to myself through water, like my heart has sunk to the bottom of the Spinning Lake again.

I don't like it. Somehow, my soul has brought me to this place, but I won't accept that I have no control over what happens here.

As soon as I speak, the newcomers look startled, glancing at each other.

The human woman's eyes are wide as she picks up her jaw. She gives a shocked hiss, speaking about me as if I'm not here. "She should not have a voice!"

On my other side, the fae woman arches an eyebrow, attempting to mask her own surprise with a haughty declaration. "Clearly, her magic has not separated from her soul yet. Perhaps we are too early."

I spin to the girl, whose glowing silhouette flickers and vibrates as she takes a step closer to me.

She peers into my eyes, the first to speak directly with me. "Do you know who we are?"

"You're the keepers of magic," I say.

Because of their positions around me, it's impossible to keep all of them within my sight at the same time, but I sense the darkness growing behind me from the sightless man.

"Correct," he whispers, his voice much closer than I would like, sending a chill down my spine. "*You*, on the other hand, are a problem."

"A problem?" I turn to him while I stand my ground. "Why?"

He doesn't answer. Instead, the fae sweeps her amber hair behind her ear as she begins to circle around me. "For starters, you still have a voice. And second... your magic has called *all* of us."

"Why is that a problem?" I demand to know.

The girl in the white dress flickers closer, her form brightening and fading as she floats around me, tracing a path that avoids the fae.

"When magic dies, it must be claimed," she says. "We are charged with ensuring that all magic returns to its rightful keeper. All magic must be... *controlled*." She glances at the others. "Unfortunately, it appears that we all have a claim on you."

As she moves, the human woman—the keeper of light magic —also begins a slow prowl around me, pacing a wider arc than the other two women and walking in the opposite direction.

Now all three are circling me like moons around a sun.

"Your heart was held by a Bright Heart who carried *the light*," the woman says, reaching back to tap the handle of her weapon. "Your magic belongs to me."

The fae woman scoffs. "Hardly. She lived the life of a fae. She willfully molded her magic to their customs and beliefs. She took on their traits. Her magic belongs to *me*."

"But it was dark magic that created her," the man snarls, his still form a dark spot in my vision. "Dark magic pulled her from the sky and broke her heart into pieces. She has scars that burn with darkness beneath her light. I see the darkness in her. She can't hide it from me. Her magic is mine!"

The girl raises her voice, a cry that vibrates in the air the same way a piece of glass hums before it shatters. "She is Lucidia! A Celestial Star. The oldest magic. Her essence never changed. She is *mine*."

"Stop!" I shout. Anger rises inside me, hot and boiling.

They're talking about me as if I no longer exist, as if I am a *thing* to be owned, my heart a possession. A trophy.

I take a threatening step toward the fae woman, who has moved the closest to me. My eyes narrow to sharp slits as I reach for the dagger that should rest against my hip, but it's not there.

It seems my armor doesn't work like normal in this place. I have no weapons except my body and my mind.

The fae stops in her tracks and blinks at me. Her lips are parted in surprise again.

My silver blood drips into the nothing beneath me as I continue to close the gap. "Why," I ask, "do you think I would accept that I belong to any of you?"

"It's the law," the fae woman says. "Your magic must return to one of us." She gives a laugh, but her amusement fades as I continue to glare at her. "Those are the rules," she repeats. "It's only a question of who has the right to claim you."

"The law?" I snarl. "The *rules*? I'm sick of the fucking rules. I *died* because of the rules. I will not be controlled by rules or laws anymore. Not for one. More. Second."

My outburst makes the keepers freeze again. They all stare at me, appearing as wary of me as they were of each other when they first arrived.

The girl finds her voice first. "You refuse to comply?"

I cast my gaze across each of them. "I'll make you a promise. Whoever can beat me is the one who has the right to claim me."

The girl arches an eyebrow at me and then the others. "Well, that sounds sensible. Whoever can dominate her obviously has the greatest claim to her magic." She spins to the fae. "Fae, why don't you try first?"

The fae hisses at the girl. "Just because you think my claim is the weakest…"

She thinks I'm not paying attention. While she speaks, her power gathers in her chest and pools in her palms. Firelight… Frost… Springtime… Harvest… Dawn… Dusk… Each power controlled separately and completely.

I sense the approach of thunderbirds behind and above me— illusions she must be controlling with her thoughts. I sense the ground beneath my feet coming alive with plants and her preparedness to heal herself if she's hurt. A faint breeze picks up around me, chilling my face while the heat at my back builds like a furnace.

She calls all of her powers within the space of a single breath —a breath I exhale, frosting in the air while sweat pours down my back.

She blinks. Just once.

The thunderbirds take shape and rage toward me, crackling with lightning, their talons extended and ready to rip off my head.

Vines spring up under my feet, whipping around my legs, preparing to yank what remains of my body in the opposite direction.

Ice freezes across my chest, coating my armor and making it brittle.

Burning fire blisters my back, screaming agony raging through me.

My chest glows. A single *thud* pulses out from the location of my heart.

The dangers pause around me, suspended. Deadly talons glint, thorny vines gouge my calves, my skin burns with ice and flames. The fae woman's arms are outstretched, all of her powers streaming toward me.

I take my own breath, dragging air into my body.

Sweet, fresh air.

Thud.

Starlight explodes through the birds, the vines, the ice, and the flames and knocks the fae woman backward. Shards of ice impale in her chest and thorns hit her arms. Her tiara flies off her head and drops into the *nothing*, disappearing into the darkness.

She screams, trying to stop her descent, reaching out desperately as the emptiness sucks her down.

I spin to the human woman, my left arm flying up to block the downward cut of her weapon, my right palm pressing to her chest.

Her light magic ripples across me, her halberd thrumming with power.

Thud.

My power bursts through my palm directly into her heart, throwing her away from me.

Her eyes widen, her mouth opens. She screams, trying to hold on to her weapon, but it spins, over and over, whooshing wildly into the *nothing*, taking her with it.

Dark magic falls across me like a heavy blanket, suffocating my thoughts and my instincts, pressing down on me as the man whispers inside my mind. "I do not need sight to see the darkness in your heart. You will succumb to me."

"We all have darkness," I say, rising upright.

Thud.

Starlight streaks through his body, burning holes in his cloak and knocking the crown from his head.

His eyes are hollow. He shouts and throws his arm across his eyes, his dark light disintegrating like burning paper.

His crown bounces against the nothing, clangs, and then disappears while his body seeps into it, his shout fading.

I spin to the girl, but she stands back, the light in her eyes sharp with fear.

"What are you?" she asks.

I exhale and allow the silence to stretch. "You're not the first to ask me that."

Her white eyes narrow, sparkling with discontent. "That isn't an answer."

I tip my head to the side. "Maybe you'll never know what I am."

Slowly folding my arms across my chest, I curl the fingers of my left hand around my right arm.

My body doesn't feel like it did before.

I used to have a phantom heart, regular beats I was sure I could feel.

When Nathaniel gave me back the piece he'd kept, my heart-beats became flickers, glowing hot or cold depending on my emotions.

Now I wait for the next solid beat.

The next thud.

A calculating light enters the girl's eyes, a determined crease forming in her forehead, a confident smile twitching her lips.

"Well," she says. "It won't matter in the end. What matters is whether or not you can beat me—"

Her starlight crashes toward me, an explosive force so immense that it will destroy me, body and mind.

Air slips through my lips.

Breathe, Aura.

I sense the tingle in my torso, the most basic impulse…

The *thud* kicks my chest. At the same time, I flick my forefinger.

The thinnest sliver of starlight, not much bigger than a needle, spears across the distance, cutting through the girl's power. It hits her directly in her forehead before it shoots out the other side.

Her attack diminishes in front of me, her power washing harmlessly into the *nothing*.

She blinks twice. Then slower.

A pinprick of silver blood slides between her eyes from the spot where my power struck her.

She reaches up to touch it, then stares at her fingertip.

Her lips part, her breathing increasing. "You don't belong here," she whispers, looking up at me. "You must not stay."

Her head tips back a second before she collapses, slipping through the surface and disappearing into the dark void.

I am alone and unclaimed.

My chest aches, but not with pain.

I press the heel of my palm against my heart, waiting for the next thud, not knowing what it means or where it will take me.

I control my breathing as I wait. One breath. Two—

Thud.

CHAPTER 40

I open my eyes to pain and blood.

The sky fills with white, hot light, an ocean of power rippling across my vision.

My back presses into the ground.

A thudding beat crashes through me, every kick like the world opening up beneath me and then closing again.

Nathaniel's roar fills my ears.

He leans over me, pressing both of his palms on my chest right where I cut myself open. Bright light spears up over his body and face, flames coursing up his arms and along his armor.

I don't know what's happening, what he's doing, until my hand jolts against my side and I realize…

My diamond heart isn't in its pouch anymore.

My eyes widen and a scream rips from me as I realize what he's trying to do, as I realize where the thudding was coming from.

He's pressing my diamond heart into my chest and holding it there.

His bare hands hold my power, but he's screaming with agony every time my heart beats.

The diamond doesn't want me.

I don't want it.

My heart's power saved me from the keepers but it's fighting Nathaniel too, burning his hands, burning his arms. *Burning him...*

Behind him, Christiana's screaming and Evander's sprinting toward us with a dozen Frost fae, but nothing will put out the fire while Nathaniel's holding on to me.

I grab Nathaniel's arm. "I'm killing you!"

Thud.

My power kicks through him, a raw force that threatens to tear him apart, but still he holds on to me.

His gaze shoots to mine. He heard me. Sees that I'm awake.

A savage smile crosses his lips. "You did it, Aura. I'm the King of All. But *you* will never do what I command. And I love you for it. So choose! Live or die?"

My response is instinctive, my choice instant.

I slam my left hand over my chest and wrench his arm away from me at the same time, using all of my strength to shove him as far from my power as I can.

As he falls back, the Frost fae converge on him, pouring their ice over him, extinguishing the flames and covering his skin in glittering frost.

They're screaming at each other to "save the King"!

Their king.

Behind them, the Vanem Dragon rises above us into the ripple of my magic, buffeted by the storm.

I hear the echo of his roaring as he tries to fight the force around him.

A hundred thunderbirds also rise into the air as if they're being drawn skyward by my exposed power.

More running forms appear—Crispin and a group of Dawn fae—while in the distance every other fae and human has dropped to the ground, clinging to each other.

The healers converge and block Nathaniel from view. All of them fight the growing storm as they try to save him.

My left arm presses against the heart that doesn't want me, but I meant what I told the keepers. I will not be controlled by rules or laws anymore. Not even the laws of nature. I will not fear the vast expanse that I came from, or the heart that was taken from me, or the war between light and dark inside me.

I accept this broken heart with all of its flaws.

Closing my eyes and pressing the diamond deep inside my chest, I receive the burning pain that comes with connecting, the icy cold water that once surrounded my submerged heart, the dusty ash that coated my skin from the fire I was born in, and the dancing light that gives me freedom, the glow that makes me shine.

I am pieces of it all.

I wait for the next *thud*, but it is soft, quiet, not fighting me this time.

Carefully, I slide my hand away from my chest as the sky above me clears, the thunderbirds lower, and the wind dies.

A final burst of power glitters around my fingertips, compelling me to remove my hand as my chest seals and my silver blood stops flowing.

I draw to my feet, sensing my power settle inside me, calming with the new beat of my full heart.

I inhale. Real breaths.

My footing is certain as I step toward the fae converged around Nathaniel.

They part to let me through.

He lies with his burned arm outstretched while Crispin and the other Dawn fae work over his right side.

I kneel in the gap on his left.

Nathaniel opens his eyes, still dark, still piercing, but lighter in my glow. Despite the pain the burns must be causing him, the tension leaves his shoulders when he sees me.

He takes my outstretched hand without speaking, closing his eyes as I curl over him and press my cheek to his.

His strength, his body, and his heart anchor me.

We have walked our path and now the future opens up ahead of us. It won't be easy. The history between the fae and humans can't be erased in a single battle, but together, we'll try.

The keeper of old magic asked me what I am.

I finally know.

I am enough.

EPILOGUE – THREE MONTHS LATER

a soft breeze brushes my face as I step carefully through the silver flowers carpeting the floor of the forest, the place we used to call the Misty Gallows.

High above me, lush tree branches stretch across the sky, swaying gently, their bright emerald leaves whispering as they swish against each other.

The dawn's light filters through the branches, soft on my face and arms. It has taken me months to stop counting the minutes and the hours in each day, counting them down until dawn.

Even now, I sense every passing moment. Especially the quiet moments when I sense the shifting of all living things beneath and above the ground.

I bend to scoop up a handful of flowers, the sleeves of my dress pulling up to my elbows.

I pause when a silver humblebee rises up from the flower I was reaching for, buzzing as it relocates to another patch of foliage.

The air is peaceful, disturbed only by the occasional fluttering of a butterfly's wings. Or maybe it's a silver moth. It's hard to tell them apart these days.

My lips hitch into a smile when the familiar scent of steam and woodfire fills my senses seconds after I detect the distant thudding of hooves.

Flare bursts into view, black as coal, snorting steam while his stomach glows red with flames.

His arrival disturbs the fluttering creature—a butterfly, as it turns out—which follows the bee to the branches of a spreading oak.

The trees here are slowly recovering from the dark magic that shrouded them for years. Some of them have transformed completely, but many still retain their misshapen boughs.

The one I stand beside is the tree where I first met Nathaniel, its branches reaching to one side, even though it's no longer fighting whatever force caused it to grow that way.

I press my hand against its trunk, sensing the spirit inside it, allowing my power to glow through my fingertips, feeding the new life around me.

The transformation started the day that Nathaniel became the King—the day I died. Every spark of my power since then has helped the environment heal. Even the burn site has become green again.

Nathaniel slides from Flare's back, but, despite his dramatic approach, he seems content to take his time approaching me, casting his gaze from my head to my booted feet.

He's wearing a simple beige shirt, short sleeves hugging his biceps, dark pants covering his legs, but a golden fleece is thrown across one shoulder, tied with a golden chain like the one that was attached to his pelt when we first met.

His brown hair is cut short now, sitting close to his head, no longer falling across his eyes.

My heart kicks in my chest at the heat in his eyes. My *whole* heart. A real beat that sends a wash of starlight all of the way to my toes.

The moments we spend together at the beginning and end of each day are some of the few we have to ourselves.

I am awake at night and Nathaniel is awake during the day. Given how early it is, he must have woken up and come straight here.

The quiet space in the forest is ours alone. It's not a law, but the fae and humans don't come here. They call it my garden. Some fae are even afraid of it because of the magic that thrums through every leaf, flower, and especially the bees.

Nathaniel leans against the nearest tree as he allows Flare to graze in the clearing.

I hide my smile, bending again to the flower, but another bee stops me. They like visiting the flowers each morning. They *don't* like me disturbing them.

"Curse the stars," I whisper, attempting to reach around the creature—which doesn't budge—before I rise and plant my hands on my hips in defeat.

Nathaniel grins at me. "I can help you," he says, an echo of his offer to help when we first met and I was trying to carry Evander to his thunderbird.

I smile. "I want to give one to Talsa and Evander as a Spring Pairing gift tonight. So they can grow them around their home in the Grove."

The silver flowers are unique to this forest, a result of my explosive power on the night of the battle.

The silver vines trail between the trees and beyond the forest to cover the flower fields. They quietly twine over the graves that rest there.

Every human, hunter, and fae who died in the battle is buried at the western end of the field with a stone to mark their final resting places. Even Imatra and Cyrian. It was Nathaniel's first act as King to treat all of the dead equally.

Nathaniel prowls toward me, apparently abandoning his intention to give me space—or to help me—but I don't mind at all. Every moment we snatch together is precious.

With a smile on my lips, I wait for him to reach me.

His arms slide around me, his golden fleece soft against my skin as he draws it around my shoulders and wraps me inside it with him.

It's still cold in the mornings, but I never notice until I feel the contrast of his warmth.

That's when I remember my human side—the parts of Nathaniel that my heart stole from him. When he first gave me back the sliver of my heart that he carried for all of those years, I thought he was the only one to benefit from my heart.

But my encounter with the keepers made me realize how much light magic I control because of Nathaniel.

Also how human my heart is.

A month after the battle, I sought out the Vanem Dragon to ask him what would have happened if Nathaniel had died instead of me.

The dragon told me that there was nothing already written in the Law of Champions to govern that situation because Imatra had no living family and no clear heir. I would have had to choose the outcome and write that part of the Law myself.

The idea horrified me—that I could dictate someone's life, maybe even their death. Nathaniel once told me that pulling a single thread of the old law could cause the whole web to collapse.

As far as I'm concerned, creating a new thread is just as dangerous.

I shake off the memories as I enjoy Nathaniel's warmth.

His dark eyes were always shadowed, but now my light reveals every inky fleck in his irises.

I reach up to plant a kiss on his lips, inhaling his scent. Comforting. Irritating because I want more of it.

"How was your night?" he asks, capturing me so that his lips brush mine. He asks me the same question every morning. He wants to know how I am, but I focus on what's happened first.

"Peaceful," I murmur. "Talsa's gown is ready for tonight. The feast is going to be huge. No intrigues to report. Oh! Evander gave me a message for you."

"Hmm?" Nathaniel casts me a questioning look, but the kisses he plants on my cheek and chin tell me he's more interested in me.

"He says it's time for you to choose a thunderbird."

Nathaniel pauses.

I grin as his startled gaze meets mine.

Nathaniel has been riding Flare within Fell country—which we now call New Bright—but flying Treble when he needs to travel long distances, including within Bright itself. He asked me about choosing his own bird, but it was a cautious idea.

"Do the other fae support Evander's suggestion?" Nathaniel asks.

His second act as the King was to form an advisory council made up of elected representatives from each fae class plus an equal number of elected human representatives.

He made it very clear that their role is advisory only—he doesn't always follow their suggestions—but he treads very carefully when it comes to fae traditions and beliefs.

"They support it."

"Even the Solstice fae?"

"Especially the Solstice fae," I say. "They value strength, Nathaniel. Imatra manipulated and dominated them. You are forthright, clear about your expectations, and you don't play favorites."

My smile grows. "You could also kill all of them—even without *the light*. They respect that."

I rest my chin against his chest as I look up at him.

He casts me the look of a warrior king. "I'll climb the peaks tomorrow."

"Good," I whisper, pressing a kiss to the underside of his chin.

He groans, his arms tightening around me and his voice lowering like a growling wolf. "I missed you in our bed this morning."

I give him a sultry smile. "There's plenty of soft ground here."

He casts a glance askew at the flower I was trying to pick and the congregation of bees hovering around it. "If we want bee stings in nasty places."

I laugh, tugging myself out of his arms, but I catch hold of his hand. His right palm still carries the burn marks from my death, the shape of my heart imprinted forever on his hand.

"How about over here, then?" I wrap my fingers around his and draw him toward the nearest tree—and then around it.

On the other side, the canopy above us descends like the fronds of whisper willows, creating a much smaller, shadowed clearing that is fully carpeted across the bottom with gleaming silver flowers. Despite the dawn, it could be twilight in this enclosed space.

Nathaniel pauses in the opening, his voice hushed. "When did you do this?"

"In between taking messages for you from Evander and having a long conversation with your sister—"

"Christiana?"

"Unless you have another sister, yes."

He gives me a quizzical look. He knows I'm deflecting, but what Christiana and I spoke about is between us.

Abandoning his questions, Nathaniel draws me into his arms, the heat in his eyes increasing. "Here is perfect."

His lips nudge mine briefly before trailing across my jaw and down my neck, exploring the curve at the top of my breasts.

An hour later, even the thick canopy above us can't stop the increasing brightness of the sun.

All of New Bright will wake up soon and there's no escaping all of the responsibilities Nathaniel has now.

I watch over his kingdom at night, but the hardest work is done during the day and also at twilight when both the Sunstream and Eventide fae are awake.

Even so, I pull Nathaniel's fleece over both of us as we lie on the bed of flowers, tugging the wool up over our heads to block out the growing light.

My glow builds, casting across Nathaniel's broad shoulders and muscled arms.

My magic still pulses through him from the time he carried my heart.

In time, it might fade, but I don't think so. Every time I touch him, I give him a little more of my light—and at the same time, he gives me a little of his light too.

"You're everything to me," he murmurs, dropping kisses on my forehead, cheeks, and lips.

"You have my heart," I whisper back. "Now and always."

By the time we're dressed and we emerge from the enclosure, the sun has risen fully and my glow is hidden in the golden daylight.

I'm ready to sleep—but first I'll go with Nathaniel to hear the morning reports.

He whistles to Flare, who canters between the trees toward us.

Flare carries us beyond the clearing and along the edge of the forest toward our new home. Well, *one* of our new homes.

This one on the border is still under construction, being built by both the humans and the fae working together. It's a simple design that melds with the forest.

Nathaniel and I divide our time between the Fell castle, the fae palace, and here—the place I feel most at home.

On our left as we approach, training grounds have been constructed for Nathaniel's new army.

Hagan is already out there, standing at the head of a hundred new trainees—both fae and human. Emily and the other teens are among them. Serena stands at Hagan's side. They are relentless trainers, but not a single trainee has quit so far.

Instead, the group is growing, which tells me Hagan and Serena must be doing something right.

Nathaniel and I thought Christiana might want to be involved in the new army, but she chose a different calling—one that is much truer to her heart.

We stop at the edge of the courtyard that has been constructed at the front of the new castle.

Two thrones sit side by side on a smooth stone slab embedded in the earth in the center of the clearing.

The back of one throne is carved with Nathaniel's family name. The other is carved with a symbol of a star, a longer line at the bottom of five shorter ones. It's the symbol I chose for myself.

A group of humans and fae wait around the throne at a respectful distance, but Christiana stands closer to the front.

Her eyes look blurry from lack of sleep. She came to see me after I got back from Bright after midnight last night. She was the first human—or fae, for that matter—to dare set foot in my forest, but she needed my help and she wasn't afraid to ask for it.

She and I have walked a very jagged road to understanding each other, but we've both worked hard to build trust between us.

Gehrig, the Springtime fae who is a good friend of my father's, stands directly behind Christiana with other Springtime and Harvest fae, along with Esther. She also stepped away from training others to fight.

Instead, she took it upon herself to clean up the human castle, including the White Walls, which has been restored to a place of quiet contemplation.

Despite her sleeplessness, Christiana wears a smile. She steps away from the others to give her brother a hug, and then me too. The open displays of genuine affection still make some of the fae shuffle, but they're slowly getting used to human culture.

"We've had a breakthrough," Christiana says, stepping to the side to allow Gehrig to move forward.

While Nathaniel and I take up position in front of the thrones, Gehrig hands Nathaniel a sheaf of wheat he was holding.

For years, the humans have struggled to grow crops because of the dark magic in the soil. Even with my help, it's been impossible to dispel all of the damage done to the environment. But the bundle of wheat Gehrig gives Nathaniel is a healthy golden color.

Christiana launches into an explanation, the passion in her voice telling me how much it means to her to grow food for her people again. "Gehrig discovered that if we burn off the old wheat, instead of cutting it, and then replant with seeds from fae crops, the soil revives. This wheat was cut this morning from a test site in the western fields near the old Bitter Patch."

Behind Christiana, the fae and humans lean forward, waiting on Nathaniel's verdict as he studies the wheat.

"This is excellent progress," he says.

Everyone breaks into smiles.

"How soon can you burn and replant the fields throughout New Bright?" Nathaniel asks, handing the bundle of wheat back to Gehrig.

"Right away," he says with a respectful bow. "We'll ask the Frost fae to help us control the winds so we can contain the burn and make sure nothing gets out of hand. We should have the replanting finished before summer ends. We can use winter seeds so that the crops grow even if frosts settle."

Nathaniel nods. "Thank you, all of you. Let me know if you encounter any problems. We'll solve them together."

The group bows and heads away, but Christiana remains behind, quietly moving to the side of the courtyard to stand under the shade of a tree. She will be able to see the training ground from there and her focus shifts to Hagan. She has something she needs to do this morning, but she'll wait until Nathaniel has met with the other people waiting in the courtyard.

At the front of the line is the little human girl Mathilda saved during the battle. The girl turns four years old this week.

She clings to the hand of a female Dusk fae—Mia's sister. I didn't see Mia fall during the battle, but I've visited her grave many times. She wasn't my friend while I was Imatra's champion, but she fought for me in the end.

The little girl stares up at Nathaniel, her eyes wide.

He bends and says something to her that's too quiet for me to hear before he carefully produces a silver flower—one I didn't see him pick when we were in the forest.

He tucks it into her hair and picks her up, still speaking with her.

She drops her head onto his shoulder, listening and sometimes nodding, her little face very serious before he places her back on the ground.

The traumas of the past can't be erased.

All we can do is focus on the future.

I slip onto my throne as Nathaniel meets with the other fae and humans. My eyes slowly lower. I don't stay up all day anymore, accepting the limits of my body and the need to rejuvenate the power inside my heart.

But despite my resting eyes, I remain alert, sensing when everyone leaves.

Raising my gaze to Nathaniel, I find him giving me a smile. "You stayed."

Normally, I slip away and he doesn't see me again until twilight.

"Your sister needs your support."

Nathaniel's eyebrows rise in surprise, but I catch his hand.

"Come with me," I say.

Christiana rises from her lean against the tree as we approach. She's wearing simple pants and a long-sleeved shirt, a flattering cut.

She quickly reaches into a pouch at her waist and retrieves a small bottle.

"Brother," she says with a more formal bow than the hug she gave him before. She opens her palm to reveal the small pot of golden wedding ink. "I want your blessing to make my match."

Nathaniel's focus shifts quickly to the training ground beyond us—to Hagan—and then back to Christiana.

"With whom?" he asks, even though he knows the answer.

She bites her lip. "With Hagan Shield, the man who claimed me and then pushed me away."

I didn't see what happened between Hagan and Christiana right after the battle, but she eventually told me that after she opened up her heart to him on the battlefield, he pushed her away—literally lifting her out of his arms and placing her on her feet away from himself.

He made sure she was safe and then he walked away.

I saw firsthand the quiet battle Nathaniel fought with him, trying to convince Hagan to stay and train the new army.

For a while, we thought Hagan might disappear into bear territory, but he eventually told Nathaniel that he would stay for a week, maybe a month. *Then* he would leave.

Nathaniel exhales, shaking his head as he considers his sister, but it's a gentle motion. "Hagan may be my champion now, but he can't atone for the past. He knows that. You need to accept it too. You're free to make a match with anyone else you choose."

Christiana listens quietly, pressing her palms together before she says, "You're trying to protect me. *He's* trying to protect me. But, Nathaniel… who else is going to challenge me when I make the wrong decisions? Who else is going to stand firm and deal with all of my fears? My flaws?"

She points to the field. "That man is the only person who truly knows me."

She grabs Nathaniel's hand, the one with the scars. "You took hold of your future, fought for love, when everyone— including me—fought against you. I'm ready to fight for my future too."

He covers her hand with his. He's quiet for a long moment as she looks up at him.

She will never beg him, but she won't stop fighting for what her heart wants.

"Then what are you waiting for?" he asks.

She stares at him, surprised, hope filling her face. "I have your blessing?"

He inclines his head toward Hagan. "You don't need it."

She steps back from Nathaniel, flashes me a smile brighter than the sun, and then spins on her heel and strides onto the field.

Nathaniel slips his arm around me as we watch her go.

In the distance, Hagan's focus shifts toward Christiana the moment that she appears.

He takes a step away from the trainees he was working with, his head raised, the sunlight catching the silhouette of his broad shoulders and back.

He has never lost his dangerous intelligence. For a moment, he freezes, his chest rising and falling as if his breathing increased just from seeing her.

His gaze locks on her and doesn't let go.

He won't be able to push her away this time.

I lean into Nathaniel, warmth filling my heart, catching the smile in Nathaniel's eyes as his forefinger traces the shape of his family name across my face.

With each stroke, he murmurs, "The sun, the moon. And you —the starlight in between."

I turn in his arms, reaching up to his face, tracing my own symbol across his forehead and cheeks, stroking the last line down his lips and chin. "All of the stars. And you—my anchor."

He returns the kiss I press against his smiling lips.

Very soon, I will sleep.

But when night falls and the world is dark, I will wake up and shine.

THE END

A SKY LIKE BLOOD

(KINGDOM OF BETRAYAL #1)

The Vandawolf owns me.

My heart and my power are his to control.

I am a Blacksmith, a wielder of the arcane magic that once scorched our land and brought blood-storms to our skies. Now, I live at the mercy of the Vandawolf, the dark king whose power forced the Blacksmiths to their knees.

But the price for my life is high.

When his enemies scheme against him, I cut them down.

And when the dark storms rage, I'm sent to fight the monsters that rise from our damaged land.

To fail is to betray the Vandawolf, and my family will pay the price.

Then a breathtakingly beautiful man steps from the blood-rain, and I'm faced with a terrible choice.

Do I end him or save him?

Is he a man or a beast?

Betrayal is only a step away.

Content information: A Sky Like Blood is fantasy romance, enemies to lovers, the first in the Kingdom of Betrayal series. Recommended reading age is 17+ for sex scenes, mature themes, violence, and language. Ends on a cliffhanger.

This series is part of The Ever Realms. A seven-series world by Everly Frost.

STORM PRINCESS

A COMPLETE FANTASY ROMANCE

"Will you wait for me?" he asks.
I whisper, "I would wait a lifetime for you."

The last warrior in the House of Rath...

I thought he died. I watched him bleed out on a cold
mountainside while thunder and lightning formed a cage
around me, trapping me in a power I never wanted.

The Storm...

It chose me. A furious force unleashed in vengeance, the Storm's
destruction would rage across the kingdom if not for me.

Day after day, I survive its wrath, taking the lightnings strikes,
the icy needles of rain, and absorbing its deadly force, stopping
its fury.

Through it all, I bury my memories, and force myself to forget the promise I made, denying what I want most.

My heart...

Now, Baelen Rath has returned, wearing the scars of battle, and vowing to fight for me.

He burns through the walls I've built around my heart, drawing me in, body and soul.

But the closer he gets to me, the clearer it becomes that he has secrets he didn't have before.

So do I.

Because the Storm is changing and its power is growing.

Like the fire Baelen ignites within me, soon it will be beyond my control.

Content information: Storm Princess: Book 1 is the first in a complete romantasy trilogy.

Recommended reading age is 17+ for sex scenes, mature themes, violence, and language. Ends on a cliffhanger.

Tropes for the series include:

Touch her and…, second chance romance, forbidden love, high fantasy, elves, gargoyles, and magical creatures.

*This is a revised edition. Now including alternate point of view chapters previously only available in the complete collection.

HUNT THE NIGHT (SUPERNATURAL LEGACY BOOK 1)

The angels only let me out to hunt.

But it's not demons I'm sent to destroy—it's dragons.

I'm corrupted. My soul was impure at birth. I'm an angel born with an insatiable need for vengeance so intense that they caged me, branded me, and kept me in the dark.

I've been promised purity and redemption, freedom from my cage. Failure is not an option. My soul depends on it.

I must hunt the Dread—a merciless clan of dragon shifters whose true nature reveals itself in the dead of night. For once my killer instincts might set me free.

But one mistake is all it takes.

One moment that costs me my freedom once more.

Now, my life rests in the hands of Callan Steele, a Dread dragon whose touch sears my corrupted soul.

He claims my strength and my vengeance for his own and tells me that the fire in my angelic heart belongs to him.

That *I* belong to him.

Some angels fall, but I won't crash and burn.

Content information: Hunt the Night is dark paranormal romance, the first in the Supernatural Legacy series. Recommended reading age is 17+ for sex scenes, mature themes, violence, and language. Ends on a cliffhanger.

This series is part of The Ever Realms. A seven-series world by Everly Frost.

ALSO BY EVERLY FROST

ASSASSIN'S MAGIC

(Dark Urban Fantasy Romance)

1. Assassin's Magic

2. Assassin's Mask

3. Assassin's Menace

4. Assassin's Maze

5. Rebels

6. Revenge

7. Rogue

8. Assassin's Match

SOUL BITTEN SHIFTER - COMPLETE

(Dark Urban Fantasy Romance)

1. This Dark Wolf

2. This Broken Wolf

3. This Caged Wolf

4. This Cruel Blood

DEMON PACK - COMPLETE

(Dark Paranormal Romance)

1. Demon Pack

2. Demon Pack: Elimination

3. Demon Pack: Eternal

SUPERNATURAL LEGACY - COMPLETE

(Angels and Dragon Shifters)

1. Hunt the Night

2. Chase the Shadows

3. Slay the Dawn

4. Claim the Light

DARK MAGIC SHIFTERS

(Dark Urban Fantasy Romance)

1. Wolf of Ashes

2. Bond of Flames

3. Crown of Fate

KINGDOM OF BETRAYAL

(Fantasy Romance)

1. A Sky Like Blood

2. A Sin Like Fire

3. A Storm Like Iron

4. A Soul Like Glass

BRIGHT WICKED - COMPLETE

(Fantasy Romance)

1. Bright Wicked

2. Radiant Fierce

3. Infernal Dark

STORM PRINCESS - COMPLETE

(Fantasy Romance)

1. Book 1

2. Book 2

3. Book 3

MORTALITY - COMPLETE

(Science-Fantasy Romance)

Mortality Complete Set: Books 1 to 4

1. Beyond the Ever Reach

2. Beneath the Guarding Stars

3. By the Icy Wild

4. Before the Raging Lion

Stand-alone fiction - dark romance

Corrupt Me: Immortal Vices and Virtues

ABOUT THE AUTHOR

Everly Frost is the USA Today Bestselling author of fantasy romance, urban fantasy and paranormal romance novels. She spent her childhood dreaming of other worlds and scribbling stories on the leftover blank pages at the back of school notebooks. She lives in Brisbane, Australia with her husband and two children.

- **a** amazon.com/author/everlyfrost
- **f** facebook.com/everlyfrost
- **O** instagram.com/everlyfrost
- **BB** bookbub.com/authors/everly-frost
- **g** goodreads.com/everlyfrost

www.ingramcontent.com/pod-product-compliance
Lightning Source LLC
Chambersburg PA
CBHW030527120726
47904CB00005B/1658